D0124229

Flint Memorial Library
147 Park St.
North Reading, MA 01864

Don't Ask Me Where I'm From

Jennifer De Leon

A
atheneum

NEW YORK LONDON TORONTO
SYDNEY NEW DELHI

A Caitlyn Dlouhy Book

$\mathcal{A}$
atheneum

An imprint of Simon & Schuster Children's Publishing Division • 1230 Avenue of the
Americas, New York, New York 10020 • This book is a work of fiction. Any references to
historical events, real people, or real places are used fictitiously. Other names, characters,
places, and events are products of the author's imagination, and any resemblance to actual
events or places or persons, living or dead, is entirely coincidental. • Text copyright
© 2020 by Jennifer De Leon • Jacket illustration copyright © 2020 by Elena Garnu •
All rights reserved, including the right of reproduction in whole or in part in any form. •
Atheneum logo is a trademark of Simon & Schuster, Inc. • For information about
special discounts for bulk purchases, please contact Simon & Schuster Special Sales at
1-866-506-1949 or business@simonandschuster.com. • The Simon & Schuster Speakers
Bureau can bring authors to your live event. For more information or to book an event,
contact the Simon & Schuster Speakers Bureau at 1-866-248-3049 or visit our website at
www.simonspeakers.com. • The text for this book was set in Minion. • Manufactured
in the United States of America • First Edition • 10 9 8 7 6 5 4 3 2 1 • Library of
Congress Cataloging-in-Publication Data • Names: De Leon, Jennifer, 1979- author. •
Title: Don't ask me where I'm from / Jennifer De Leon. • Other titles: Do not ask me
where I am from • Description: First edition. | New York : Atheneum Books for Young
Readers, [2020] | Audience: Ages 14 up. | Audience: Grades 10-12. | Summary: "Liliana
Cruz does what it takes to fit in at her new nearly all-white school, but when family
secrets come out and racism at school gets worse than ever, she must decide what she
believes in and take a stand"— Provided by publisher. • Identifiers: LCCN 2019040448 |
ISBN 9781534438248 (hardback) | ISBN 9781534438262 (eBook) • Subjects: CYAC:
Racism—Fiction. | Hispanic Americans—Fiction. | High schools—Fiction. | Schools—
Fiction. | Secrets—Fiction. | Family life—Fiction. • Classification: LCC PZ7.1.D39814
Don 2020 | DDC [Fic]—dc23 • LC record available at https://lccn.loc.gov/2019040448

For my mother, for believing

1

Picture it: me in the middle of Making Proud Choices class—that's SEX ED for anyone not born in this century. You know, when you have to get a parent or guardian to sign a yellow paper that says it's okay for you to be learning about all this stuff—like we didn't already know about sex, but whatever. The guest speaker, Miss Deborah, had JUST passed out condoms. No big deal. I mean, I hadn't had sex yet. But still, condoms = ain't no thing but a chicken wing. My best friend, Jade, had a bunch of them hidden in her room. But what Miss Deborah was showing us that day were *female condoms*.

I know.

Have you ever even seen a freakin' female condom? Don't lie. Did you even know they existed? Don't lie!

If my mom heard me talking about female condoms, she would say that's some straight-up Americana gringa shit. For real.

I joined the rest of my class, including Jade, and hollered "Whaaaaat?" and "Noooooo" and "Huh?" until our real teacher, Mrs. Marano, who was sitting in the corner and like twenty months pregnant herself, told us to calm down or else.

Miss Deborah passed around a few of the (female) condoms. Jade got a pink one. I got one that was mint colored. It felt rubbery, kind of like the gloves Mom uses to wash dishes. It had zigzagged edges, like someone had actually gone to the trouble to make a nice design along the perimeter. I swear. So I was holding this rubbery thing in my hand when this cute boy, Alex, stopped in the hall and stared at me through the doorway. Of course. I froze. But then the Making Proud Choices lady, Miss Deborah, was packing up her things in a big black duffel bag and I had to, you know, return the female condom. Then Mrs. Marano waddled over to the front of the room. "All right, everyone. Take out your independent reading books."

The class groaned.

"Yo, girl. Got anything to eat?" Jade whispered over to me.

"Nah," I said.

Jade had grown up right next door to me. Our apartment bedroom windows faced one another, so we'd knock on our own window, real loud, three times when we needed to talk. Because one of us was always having our phone taken away, the knocking came in handy. Jade's family was from Honduras (her favorite T-shirt had the word "Afro-Latina" printed across the front). She was a total sneakerhead—I swear she had about seventeen pairs, and she wore her hair different every day (a top bun, straightened, braided, or crazy curly). Jade and me, we were real cool, even though she was spending waaaay too much time with her boy, Ernesto, but whatever. She was family.

"Any gum or anything?" Jade pleaded.

"No, girl. I—"

"Girls," Mrs. Marano said.

"Girls," Jade mimicked under her breath. I couldn't help it. I laughed.

"Liliana," Mrs. Marano said.

I sat up straight and took out my independent reading book. "Sorry, Mrs. Marano."

"I expect better from you, Liliana." She reached for an Expo marker and wrote my name on the whiteboard.

I must have turned red, because Jade leaned in and said, "She's whatever, Liliana. Don't sweat it." Then she pulled her backpack up onto her lap, where she texted without Mrs. Marano seeing.

"Ernesto?" I don't know why I bothered to ask.

"Yeah. He wants to go to this thing at the Urbano Project on Saturday. You wanna come?" Ernesto liked attending rallies and marches and poetry slams. I think he just did it to get girls. I mean, it had worked with Jade. True, the Urbano Project led art workshops too, and Jade liked drawing, but still.

"Nah. I'm straight," I said.

"Come on, Liliana. Why don't you bring your poems or something to read?"

"Like, in the microphone? In front of strangers? Yeah . . . no."

I could barely hear Jade's answer even though she was seated right next to me. Mrs. Marano could not control the class. No one was reading. Jade did take out a book, but she just left it on her desk. Aaron was playing with the paper cups that were supposed to stay in a neat pile by the water bubbler. He had one in his mouth like a megaphone, and he didn't take it out even when Mrs. Marano wrote his name on the board. Chris R. was making a pyramid out of cups on his desk. Marisa asked if she could draw designs for a new bathroom pass that her dad, a carpenter, was going to help her build for our room. Mrs. Marano said no and started writing more names on the board. Chris R., Aaron, Marisa . . . Marisa took out a piece of paper anyway.

Finally, hand resting on her gigantic stomach, Mrs. Marano gave the Done With This countdown. "Five . . . four . . . three . . ."

I took out my journal. Started writing stuff down. Maybe I'd set a story in this crazy classroom. Maybe Mrs. Marano would go into labor right in front of the class, which was so loud that I didn't notice that the vice principal, Mr. Seaver, was all of a sudden standing right by my desk.

"Liliana," he said.

Oh snap. Was I in trouble? If anyone should be in trouble, it should be Yulian, who was crunching his water bottle over and over; or Johnnie, who was shooting an invisible basketball into an invisible net.

"Miss Cruz?" Mr. Seaver said, louder. His voice was all deep, and somehow that made everyone quiet down.

"Why she in trouble?" Jade asked, her eyes narrowing.

"Get back to your reading, young lady," Mr. Seaver said. "Miss Cruz, I need to talk to you for a moment. In the hall."

My face burned. I never got in trouble. I was an A . . . okay A- . . . okay B+ . . . fine, sometimes B- student, so I didn't know why I would be called out of class.

I stood up and followed him. From the corner of my eye I could see Chris R. wagging his finger in the air. Oh, please. He was so aggy. And his hair looked like Justin Bieber's.

The hallway was much quieter. I was surprised Mr. Seaver hadn't brought up the fifty-five rules being broken in the class, but that just made me sure that whatever he was about to tell me was important, or worse: really bad. At the end of the hall he opened the door to what we students called the bat cave—a small office that used to be a janitor closet—and asked me to step inside. It was where students went when they were really disruptive, like when Joshua called the substitute teacher an old-ass bitch.

Look, I don't want to give the wrong idea. Not every class was crazy, and not every day. Just down the hall was Mrs. Palmer, who ran her class like a corporation. Every kid knew what to do and when and how, and it was peaceful and smelled like a cinnamon apple air freshener. Or even my nasty-breath math teacher—in his class we sat in rows and the volunteers from Simmons College helped us when we had questions. So, Mrs. Marano's wasn't totally the norm, is what I'm saying.

As Mr. Seaver and I sat down at two student desks because (a) his office was being treated for something called asbestos, and (b) a real desk couldn't fit in the bat cave, he took out an envelope from the inside of his suit jacket with a flourish. "Well, Miss Cruz, you were accepted to the METCO program. A spot has opened up for you off the waiting list, and you start on Monday." He raised his eyebrows and leaned back, clearly expecting me to leap into the air cheering.

I opened my mouth but no sound came out.

"Yes," Mr. Seaver continued, "I realize it's already a few weeks into the school year, but nonetheless, it's a great opportunity. And it's in Westburg." He adjusted his glasses, still looking for that cheer.

I was still trying to understand *You were accepted to the METCO program.* Um . . . what?

Inside my brain a dozen questions were zapping around, but the first that bubbled out was, "Where's that at?"

"About twenty miles west. Listen—"

"Does this have to do with the essay thingy I just won? Because I told Mrs. Marano I wasn't reading that at any assembly or whatever."

"Well, that certainly would have helped your application all the more. Liliana—"

"Mr. Seaver, I don't even know what METCO is."

"Here." He handed me a glossy pamphlet. "It stands for 'Metropolitan Council for Educational Opportunity.'"

"Huh?"

He began again. "It's a desegregation program."

I ran my finger across the pamphlet. Oh wait! I *had* heard of this. A girl from the church we go to was in METCO. She talked like she was white. But she did get into college, so. Oh yeah, and another kid from down the street was in METCO too, I think. I saw him once, waiting for the bus when it was mad early and Mom was taking me to a doctor's appointment before school. But *me*, really? *I* was accepted? I sat up straighter. Cool. But I had plenty of other stuff going on and didn't need to add a new bougie school on top of it all. So yeah, no.

"Mr. Seaver, thank you," I said in my most polite talking-to-the-vice-principal voice. "But I'm not interested in that program. I'm good here."

Now he lowered his glasses. "Excuse me?"

"I'm not interested in switching schools," I said, opening the pamphlet up. Yep, total bougie vibe! "Besides, my parents would never let me go."

He adjusted his glasses once more, then said, "Your parents are the ones who signed you up, in fact."

"They did?" *My* parents?

"Yes."

"When?"

"Years ago, in fact."

Why did he keep saying "in fact"? We weren't in court.

And all of a sudden we heard shouting. And the sound of feet pounding. "Mr. Seaver! Mr. Seaver! Mrs. Marano's having her baby!" It was Jade.

Whoa! It was like my story idea had come to life! Mr. Seaver bolted out of the bat cave, and I bolted after him. When we reached the classroom, Mrs. Marano was gripping her stomach with both hands, and her jaw was mad tight.

Jasmine was bringing her a paper cup of water while Aaron held a little battery-operated fan up to her face. The rest of the kids were going wild, standing on chairs to get a better look. Other teachers stormed in and instantly got on their cell phones. Somehow that gave kids permission to do the same, only they weren't calling 911. They were taking pictures and going on Snapchat.

I ran over to Jade. What. The. Hell. No way I was going to some other school in some other whack town called Westburg. I would miss this world way too much. Besides, I was the best writer in my class here. I had a winning essay to prove it.

I stuffed the METCO pamphlet into my backpack and reached for my phone. **What is METCO??** I texted Mom. She didn't reply.

Jade was hitting me with questions. "Liliana? Hello? Do you not see that our teacher is gonna have a baby? And what did Mr. Seaver want?"

"Nothing." I shooed her away.

"Dang. What's good with you?"

"*Nothing.*"

Mr. Seaver and another teacher helped Mrs. Marano out the door and down the hall toward the elevator. I could hear sirens outside. Then another teacher came in and took control of our class. She passed out worksheets, but I couldn't concentrate. I couldn't stop thinking about METCO and Mr. Seaver and how he'd said my parents had signed me up in the first place. Parents—as in Mom and Dad. Did my *dad* really know about it? Sometimes one of them signed me up for something without telling the other. Plus, right now things were . . . complicated with him, as in, he'd taken off—again. Truth, he had to know. He was the one who got me all into reading, which got me into writing, in the first place.

And now I couldn't even ask him. I had to find out more about this METCO program.

METCO was nagging my brain for the rest of the day. What if the kids were all whack? What if Jade and I stopped talking on the regular? What if the schoolwork was too hard? What if I threw up on the bus? So finally, during last period, I asked for a pass to see my guidance counselor. I was hoping Miss Jackson could give me some backup for NOT going to METCO. I sat on a metal folding chair in the main office while I waited to be called in. The place smelled like muffins. There was a box of them sitting on Miss Patricia's desk—she was the school secretary. She gave out pencils and granola bars and sometimes, if you were lucky, muffins. I was lucky, muffin day. I took a blueberry one and mouthed *Thank you*, and she went back to reading the *Boston Globe*. I don't get why old people love reading the paper so much. I started reading the METCO pamphlet, a whole lotta blah, blah, blah:

- The mission of METCO is twofold:
  (1) to give students from Boston's
  underperforming school districts the

opportunity to attend a high-performing school and increase their educational opportunities, and (2) to decrease racial isolation and increase diversity in the suburban schools.

- In order to qualify for the program, a student must be a resident of Boston and be nonwhite. Eligibility does not take into account a student's record (including academics and behavior), English language proficiency, socioeconomic status, attendance record, or immigration status.

- METCO host families are designed to bring the communities together and provide support for students within the program in the town in which they attend school. Students are also assigned "METCO buddies."

"Liliana?" Miss Jackson asked from the doorway. She sounded surprised to see me.

Most of the counselors here were old and white, except for mine. Miss Jackson was young and Black. So young actually that she kind of looked like she could be a student herself. She had dozens of long thin braids, and she liked to wear skirts with cool patterns like zebra prints.

"Oh, hi, miss. I had a question. It's about this program."
I waved the pamphlet at her.

She led me to her office in Guidance Row. Her phone
rang, and she held a finger in the air. "Excuse me, baby." So
I looked at the pictures pinned on the corkboard beside her
desk. They were new since the last time I'd been in there. In
one she wore a cap and gown. In another she was screaming, wind in her face, as she jumped out of a plane. I had
no idea Miss Jackson liked to do stuff like that, skydiving or
whatever. I would NEVER do that; you'd have to kill me first.
I don't even like roller coasters. Miss Jackson finished her
phone call and hung up. She was like one of three adults in
the whole school who could get away with calling students
"baby."

"Now, what can I help you with, Liliana?"

"Well, I got into this thing called METCO. It's a program
that buses kids from the city to the suburbs."

Miss Jackson leaned forward, her eyes all kinds of bright.
"I'm real familiar with the METCO program, Liliana." She
smiled big. "I did METCO."

Whaaaat? "For real?"

Miss Jackson put her hands together so that they formed
a little tent. "For real."

"Well . . . what I was hoping was, maybe you could help
convince my mom that I shouldn't do it. It's too far away,
and um, I need to help out more at home."

"Help out more at home? Why? Is something going on?"

"No . . ." No way was I getting into the whole Dad-stepping-out-again thing.

"Liliana. Change can be tough. I get it. But this program—it's worth it. These opportunities don't come up very often. What's the worst that can happen? You absolutely hate it, and then you transfer back to a Boston school."

Huh. Okay. Good point. But, uh-uh. "No, Miss Jackson. Sorry, but I really don't feel like switching schools. Sophomore year already started. Plus, I don't know anyone over there."

"Listen, baby. Try to hear me. I know it might seem like high school is forever, and your friends are your life. I get that. But what you do now—or don't do now—can really affect your future, and the choices you have in the future."

"But what's wrong with this school? *You* work here." I added a smile so she wouldn't think I was throwing attitude or anything.

"That's true. And I love my job."

"But . . . ?"

"But, nothing."

"Okay. Fine. I kinda get what you're saying. Why not at least *try* it?"

She grinned.

I spent the rest of the period listening to her explain more about the program, about the opportunities I would have access to, about the honors classes and the cultural capital, and other terms I didn't totally get, like "stereotype threat." She even told me she believed she got into a great college because of METCO. "And—this could be great for your writing," she added. I still wasn't 100 percent convinced, but I did feel a little better about it.

Maybe it was the muffin.

After school I picked up Christopher and Benjamin from the bus stop.

"Liliana?" Christopher asked in his trying-to-be-so-innocent voice as the school bus wheezed away. I could tell my brothers were still heated. Last night they had been wrestling in the living room and had knocked over a lamp, so Mom had forbidden them to play video games until further notice. Benjamin had wailed like he was on fire, and Christopher had stopped breathing for like, a whole minute. Video games were their LIFE. Anyway, Mom had told them, *No más*, and she'd had that nostril flare that meant business. Don't let her sparkly headbands fool you; Mom can be fierce.

I knew exactly where Christopher was going with this sweetie-sweet voice. "Don't even ask," I said, shutting him down.

"Come on!" he cried out.

"Please, Liliana!" Benjamin joined in. He's the twin with a freckle on his chin just like Dad. When they were babies, it had helped me tell them apart.

"Look, Mom hid your stupid games, so I couldn't help you even if I wanted to."

At the apartment they moped around, then totally ignored me when I told them to get working on their homework, like *I* had hidden the games. Mom had left a note saying that she'd gone to the store. Maybe it was the Super 88, the Vietnamese supermarket! Not because I am obsessed with Vietnamese food, but because Mom is. See, even though my mother grew up in El Salvador, she is capital *O* Obsessed with Vietnamese food. And if she's cooking Vietnamese food, that means she's happy. She tried it when she first came to Boston, and then, when she was pregnant with me, she only wanted to eat Vietnamese. Same when she had my brothers six years later.

So while Mom was at the store hopefully picking out lemongrass and nuoc mam, I sat in the apartment practically sweating to death (yes, it was hot for the middle of September, and no, we don't have air-conditioning) and trying to write in my journal. I say "trying" because Benjamin and Christopher were tearing the place apart, searching for their video games. I mean, they moved the couch, dug under cushions, inside Mom's pillowcase, behind the toilet. They were like cops hunting for drugs. Finally, after like forty-five minutes, Benjamin found the video game box. He almost cried. He really did. So he plugged it in and got all settled on the living room floor—which was so stupid, because by the time he heard Mom coming home, he wouldn't have time to put the box back where Mom had hidden it, which was inside a cardboard shoe box labeled *fotos* at the bottom of her closet. But he was an idiot, so.

Turns out Christopher and Benjamin still weren't able to play video games because Mom had hidden the controllers separately, not in the box. Sneaky! So round two of the search began. Now they were flat-out pissed.

Finally Christopher said, "Get off your fat butt, Liliana, and help us look for them!"

I was like, "Whaaaat? Who you think you talking to, little boy?" and stayed put on the couch and kept working on my short story, the one about the girl who gets a new boyfriend and forgets about her best friend and then one day the boyfriend dumps her. The story was inspired by the Greek myth of Daedalus and Icarus. You know, flying too close to the sun melts your wings, or whatever. We had just read it in English and it wasn't *that* boring. We were supposed to hand back the photocopies of it, but I kept mine.

Christopher and Benjamin finally gave up the controller hunt and put the video games back in the closet, just in time, because Mom came home not two minutes later. But with only one white plastic bag instead of the usual ten pink plastic ones from Super 88. Shoot. The Vietnamese food she cooked was mad good, even though the windows got all steamed up whenever she made pho. We usually had it with beef or chicken, depending on how much money Mom had earned that week. She cleaned houses, and people were always going on vacation or something and then didn't need her at the last minute. So, all right, her Vietnamese food was bomb. Well, almost. Except for those spring rolls. Hers tasted like soap. Truth? I would've eaten those soapy spring rolls if it meant Mom was actually cooking that night. But a white plastic bag meant no dice. No pho. I peeked inside: five boxes of mac and cheese, a carton of milk, and two sticks of butter. Dang. This meant Mom was in a deep, dark state.

While I took out a pot to boil water, Mom washed her hands, then winked at me as she pulled the controllers out from her black purse. She's super smart like that. Despite that small victory, though, she looked utterly defeated. Every day Dad was gone, the look grew worse. But here's when her mood changed—when I brought up METCO.

"So, Mom, a crazy thing happened today—"

Her eyes immediately fixed on me.

"Yeah, so the vice principal said I got into this METCO program—said he left you a couple voice mails."

"¿Cuando?" I swear, her hands started shaking. She dropped one of the controllers.

I gave her the pamphlet. "Today. He said I got in, but I told him I'm straight. It's in some town like an *hour* from here."

"You got in? ¿De verdad?" She began digging in her bag.

"Yeah . . . but—" I folded up the plastic bag so we could use it later.

"But nada. You're going." She tucked one of her dark curls behind her ear in a that-settles-that sort of way, and checked her voice mail.

We stood there having a little stare-off while she listened. A huge smile spread across her face. *Huge.* "You got into METCO!" she exclaimed, as if I hadn't told her this thirty seconds before.

"No!"

Now she was hand-talking. "Liliana." Hands sweeping toward me. "Do you know how many kids are on that waiting list?" Hands in the air. "It's one of the few programs that doesn't have requirements like certain grades, income, or . . . other things." Hands on her hips. "Listen, you're going. Besides, your father and I—"

And there it was. Dad *did* know. I looked at my mother's beaming face and imagined him having the same reaction.

Truth. My dad has been MIA since the end of the summer. All Mom would say about it was, *Your papi went on a trip.* There's really nothing worse than being lied to by your own parent. Why couldn't she just tell me the truth? I could handle whatever it was. What? Dad left to go live with another woman and her dumb-ass kids? Dad left on a bender and Mom didn't know when he'd be back? Dad took some shady job in some other part of the country? He'd left before on those sorts of jobs, but he'd always come back. Then he and Mom would spend the whole day in their bedroom (ew), and that night we'd all go out to dinner at someplace like Old Country Buffet or Olive Garden.

But he'd only ever been gone for a week, tops, before. Never *this* long.

"Bueno," she finally said, giving the pamphlet a *kiss*, I kid you not. "You're going. Punto."

I slammed the door to my bedroom, put on my headphones, and played music so loud I swear my hair was vibrating. Why did I need to go to some school an hour's drive away? Where I didn't know a single person? I pictured myself eating chips all alone at a table in a sea of strangers.

I planned to protest in my room all night—except I got crazy hungry. I needed to get me some Honey Buns from the corner store, is what I needed to do. But they had six hundred calories in each one, and two come in a package, and once you ate one, it was virtually impossible not to eat the other. So—not. I knocked on my window for Jade, trying to distract myself from my growling stomach. No answer. So I took out my notebook. Something that always made me feel better: writing. I have always capital L Loved writing. Even more than sleep. I'd stay up late and I'd wake up early to write, even on the weekends. Like, I *had* to. I'm not talking about some five-paragraph bull they always be giving us at school to practice for the state tests.

I'm practically the same way about reading. Right now I was totally into books by Sandra Cisneros. From her website she seemed cool, but in that way where the person wasn't *trying* to be cool, you know? She didn't have a dozen piercings or anything, but she had a tattoo of a Badalupe on her left bicep. She wore BRIGHT red lipstick and lots of mascara. And sometimes she had really short bangs. If I even tried to have bangs, then my whole head would just frizz. *Not* cute.

Something *else* I capital L Loved—and this is kinda weird, but whatever—I capital L Loved building miniatures. Houses and buildings. Like, out of cardboard, or cereal boxes or receipts, scraps of paper, shopping bags, stuff like that. *That* obsession started way back when I wanted the Barbie Dreamhouse soooo bad. Mom said it was too expensive, but then one day she came home with a big cardboard box—a lady she was cleaning house for had just gotten a new TV—and helped me make my own. Like I said, Mom = smart. Then, when I was in fourth grade, Dad took my brothers and me to the Children's Museum, and a lady was offering a free art class in one of the studios. She showed us this one artist, Ana Serrano, who made little hotels, stores, and apartment buildings. But this was like, next level. She *only* used cardboard! I'm talking teeny tiny air conditioners, teeny tiny potted plants, and even teeny tiny satellite dishes on teeny tiny rooftops. All. Made. Out. Of. Cardboard. So crazy! So cool. And boom, I was obsessed. Under my bed is like half a city's worth of teeny tiny buildings. I was building a bakery now—Yoli's Pasteles y Panadería—but that night I didn't have the patience to focus on it. My stomach was mad growly.

So I gave up and left my room. Mom was in the living room, whisper-yelling into her phone. All of a sudden, she began crying like someone had died! I couldn't tell if I was hallucinating from how hungry I was. Wait, maybe someone *had* died, someone in Guatemala or El Salvador or Arizona (about one hundred relatives I'd never met lived in these places), or *hello*, my *dad*. It was hard to hear exactly what she was saying between the wails, but I caught phrases: *too dangerous, too expensive, I just don't know.*

What was too dangerous? What was too expensive?

JENNIFER DE LEON

METCO was a free program. She couldn't have been talking about that, and besides, who was she talking *to*?

Afraid she would hear me snooping, I speed-walked to the kitchen, grabbed two granola bars (what? the cheap kind are small), and hightailed it back to my room, thinking, thinking. No. She wasn't talking about METCO. *That* news had made her happier than she'd looked all week. When had they signed me up, anyway?

As I thought about it, it started making sense. See, every February when I was in elementary school, my dad had dragged me to a charter school lottery. The last time we went, I think I was ten. I remember because Dad got us a blue raspberry Coolatta from Dunkins, even though it was snowing. The school basement was packed. I even recognized a girl from my grade. She was with her grandmother, who clutched a rosary as she prayed. I was kind of scared at first, but Dad explained that we were there to put in our application for a spot at the charter school. I didn't know what a charter school was, and to be honest, I still don't really understand how it's different (besides the fact that they make you go to school longer, sometimes even in the summer). But Dad was all psyched about it.

Like the other parents, Dad filled out a form and received a poker chip with a number on it. Then we sat and waited on benches for, like, ever, passing the Coolatta back and forth until finally a lady at the front of the room said it was time to start the lottery. Inside one of those big round bingo cages were poker chips that matched the ones that had been handed out. That cage was *packed* with chips!

"Let me tell you how this is gonna work," the lady announced. "I'm gonna call the numbers, and if your number is called, your child gets a spot. At the end, we'll put the rest of the names on the waiting list."

"How many spots are there?" a man with red cheeks asked.

"Twenty-eight."

"How many poker chips have you given out?"

"Two hundred and twelve."

The audience gasped. I looked at Dad, who rubbed at his knuckles. No lie, I was ready to be done with it. My butt hurt from sitting so long. And I had to pee. As the lady called the numbers and the spots filled up, some parents cried tears of joy. The sleeping babies woke up in a daze. The old people clapped. But as we got to the twenty-third and twenty-fourth slots, other families—most families—began to weep into crumpled tissues. *This must be one special school,* I remember thinking. And when she called the number for the twenty-eighth slot, a man screamed, "¡Así es!" as around him the weeping grew louder.

The lady at the front looked around—I gotta admit, she looked really sad—and said, "Thank you all for coming. If your number hasn't been called, you'll be added to the waiting list."

Dad's nostrils opened and closed like a bull's in a bull-fight. In a low, calm voice he said, "Let's go."

I grasped his hand, glad we were leaving. But he was heading for the lady. "Thank you for organizing this lottery," he said to her, dipping his head. "I know you have lots of kids on the waiting list. My daughter Liliana would love to attend this school. Is there something I could do? Work as a janitor at night or on the weekends? Or maybe—"

"Sir, please," she interrupted. "There is a waiting list, as I explained. Fair is fair."

"But I want her to have a chance. I couldn't finish school. Please at least hear me out."

The woman looked at my Coolatta-blue lips.

"I'm sorry, sir. You have to go." She pointed to the door where families were inching their way out of the hot basement.

I thought maybe Dad was going to jump over the table and tell this lady off. But he didn't. He nodded. "Thank you anyway," he said, so, so politely. And we walked away.

"Dad? Can't you talk to her boss or something?"

He shook his head.

"Dad? Why can't I go to this school? That's not fair."

"Life isn't always fair, mija," he said.

"But, Dad—"

"Listen to me. This is not a problem. Oye, there are worse things in life. At least you have a public school you can go to. I didn't even have that." He looked up. Outside, the snow had almost covered the basement windows.

"Dad?"

"You want something, Liliana, you go after it. No matter what. You'll get an education, whether it's at a charter school or not. Okay?"

"Dad?"

"You have a goal? Stick with it. ¿Entiendes?"

I nodded. "But, Dad?"

"What is it?"

"I really have to pee."

I must have fallen asleep, because the next thing I heard was my morning alarm.

At lunch, Jade and I sat together like we always did, except she spent most of the time texting with Ernesto. Jade was the only friend I spoke Spanish with—okay, Spanglish. Unlike me, Jade wasn't born here. She was three when her parents moved to Boston from Honduras. I knew she didn't have her papers. It was something that just *was*, something we never really talked about. When it came time for city-subsidized summer programs or the opportunity to get stipends from the YMCA, Jade never bothered applying because she knew she wouldn't qualify. That, and she didn't want to get sent back to Honduras. Jade's phone buzzed for, like, the sixth time in three minutes. Her boy, Ernesto, was cool. I mean, I liked that he made Jade happy (even though he was mad old, like seventeen, I think). I reached for the bag in front of her. "You gonna eat the rest of those chips?"

"Um, YES." She snatched the bag back. "But you can have *one*." She smiled.

As I licked the salt off the chip then nibbled the edges, Jade stared.

"What?" I asked.

"Liliana, please. Don't *what* me. What's good with you lately?"

"Nothing," I said. "I just got in a fight with my mom last night."

"'Bout what?" Jade asked, looking down at her phone.

She was obviously more interested in Ernesto than in me. So why bother? "I don't want to talk about it. Can I have another chip?"

She handed me the bag, laughed at one of Ernesto's texts, and began typing away while I sat there crunching. I might as well have been sitting alone. METCO wasn't looking so bad all of a sudden.

"Oh look! Mrs. Marano is on Insta. Oh shoot!"

"What? Let me see." I grabbed the phone. There was Mrs. Marano, holding a baby in a pink blanket, waving into the camera. Aw, she'd had a girl. Jade snatched back her phone. God forbid she missed a single text from Ernesto. Sure enough, she immediately began typing away.

"Hey, girl," I finally said.

Jade raised a finger. *Wait.*

"Wow," I said, crossing my arms when she finally put down the phone.

She smiled wide. "What?" Even her eyes seemed to smile. It was cool, on the one hand, seeing her all cheesed out and whatnot, but I couldn't help but be worried that she was going to turn into one of those girls who only had time for their guy.

I handed her the METCO pamphlet.

Jade turned it over. "What's this?"

"Read it."

The pamphlet included information about the history of the program, contacts, and biographies of alumni, along with stuff about the *W* towns—Wellesley, Wayland, Weston, Westburg. White towns. Towns where the schools were real good, where there were enough computers for everyone in a grade to be using one at the same time. Truth, the laptops in the computer carts at my school were always breaking. Kids were always stealing letters off the keys—especially *F*, *U*, *C*, and *K*.

The pamphlet also bragged about all the extracurricular clubs, from fencing to fashion. But Jade just scanned the cover, then flapped it at me. Her phone buzzed. "Okay, so what exactly is this I'm reading?" she asked, glancing at a new text.

"I got into that program, METCO. I guess my folks signed me up forever ago, but before you say anything—"

Instead of looking upset though, Jade looked . . . impressed? "Sounds fly."

"*Fly*? Who says 'fly' anymore?" I laughed.

She smirked, checked out her phone again, which had pinged a second time, and then looked back up. "Girl—so you're really changing schools?"

"I kinda don't have a choice. My mom is being super aggy about it all." I didn't want Jade to think I'd been seeking out this opportunity, or was like, dying to leave Boston. "I wanted to tell you about it last night—"

Bzzzz. Her phone. Again.

How could she not be upset? And I realized that I *wanted* Jade to be upset. I *wanted* her to want me to stay.

"So, that's it?" I asked.

"Whatchu want? A bunch of balloons to fall from the ceiling?" Jade's smile disappeared.

"No . . . It's just— Forget it."

"Well, I think it's cool, that program. Damn. And," she added, "I got some news of my own."

"What's that?" My head was stuck on Jade thinking METCO was cool. Even though, well, wasn't she going to ask me about the school? Wouldn't a best friend want to know basic things like, when I'd leave? Hello?

She shut her eyes for three long-ass seconds. "Ernesto said he loved me."

"In a text?" Whoa! "For real?"

"No! Yes. He said it. Last night!"

My stomach did this fluttering thing. "That's fire."

"Yeah." And I swear she looked all . . . dreamy. Gah!

"So happy. For you." I didn't know what else to say. It *was* true. I wasn't jealous—not of what he said. It was more like, my best friend was sitting right in front of me, but she couldn't have felt further away. Like . . . it didn't matter to her at all if I went to school twenty-two miles away. Yeah, I'd looked it up.

The bell rang. Jade stood up and gave me a side hug. "Anyway, congratulations. 'Bout the new program. That's whatsup. Look, I gotta get to art."

"Thanks," I said. "Later."

Yeah, but who knows when, later.

After school I brought the boys to the library so I wouldn't have to deal with them complaining about Mom hiding their video games for a second day in a row. We stayed until the sky turned the color of cement. When we walked into the living room, Mom was going *nuts*. She was hunting through a bunch of papers and envelopes, looking wildly at each handful, then flinging them to the floor.

"Mom!" I grabbed her by the shoulders, but she pushed me away, so hard that I fell backward onto the couch. What the—

"I can't take this anymore!" she yelled, and began pacing the living room.

"Mom?" I said hesitantly, not wanting to get her even angrier. "Why don't you just sit down? Maybe I can help you find—whatever it is?"

Benjamin and Christopher had immediately booked it down the hall and were now poking their heads around the sheet that divided the living room from their bedroom (which was really the dining room).

Mom's eyes were totally swollen. It looked like she'd been

bawling for a month straight. I remembered her crying last night. *What* was up?

"Mom?"

"I need to find a paper that belongs to your father. A pay stub. It's important."

I jumped up. "I can help." I went to the chair by the door and picked up a pile of mail that I assumed she hadn't looked through yet.

"Don't touch *anything*, Liliana!" She yanked the letters from my hands, and they flew everywhere.

"Mom. Chill." I squatted to pick it all up.

"*What?*" She glared at me.

"Calm . . . down . . . ?"

Why did people hate it when they were told to calm down? Still, I was about to take it back, when Mom said, "You want me to *calm*— Do you even know how much— Do you think—" She was so *un*calm that she couldn't even finish her sentences.

I reached for the remote control and shut off the television. Then I kind of wanted to turn it right back on. The silence sucked. So did arguing with my mom.

"Look, Mom, it's been a minute since Dad left, and yeah, he's unpredictable—he's done it before. But you're . . . you're kinda scaring me . . . and the boys. You're acting . . . kinda craz—"

Her hand flew up, ready to slap me. And my hand flew protectively to my cheek as if it already stung.

"What the hell—" came out of my mouth before I could

stop it. I cringed, waiting for her to slap me. Truth: she'd only ever hit the boys and me on the arms or legs before, and that was only when we did something really bad, like steal money from her purse. I'd never seen her this riled up.

"Malcriada," she said, raising her arm in the air once more.

"Well," I said, narrowing my eyes, "you're the one who raised me, so then that's on you."

This time I *knew* she would actually slap me, so I ducked out of the way, snatched my backpack, and headed out the door.

"Where do you think you're going?" she bellowed after me.

I was charging down the hall, pushing open the door to the stairs.

"Liliana! Get back here!"

I took the stairs two at a time, holding the rail so I wouldn't fall on my face. Fury surged through me. Why was she like this? No wonder my father kept taking off!

Outside I glanced up at the apartment, and there she was, head stuck out the window, hair all crazy like a witch's or something.

"Liliana! Get back in here right now!"

No way. But where to go? Not Jade's. Mom would just march over and drag me back. The library was closed already. I could go to the corner store. And then it dawned on me. Damn. My phone and wallet were on the counter. It was dark. Suddenly I could barely breathe. I hated this. Being cornered. Out of control. Not knowing what was next.

I hadn't even grabbed my jacket. Stupid! I checked my pockets for money. Nada. I avoided eye contact as I roamed up the street, especially with that sketchy dude with the mustache in front of Lorenzo's Liquor who always catcalled at me and Jade. I walked around until my skin prickled with cold. September could be like that—unpredictable. Like my life, apparently.

Finally I had no choice. I had to head home, and face . . . more unpredictability. But when I cracked the door open, Mom was asleep in front of the television. I turned down the volume. Had the boys even had dinner? I peeked behind the curtain. They were sleeping hard, sprawled out like they owned the world. I felt a pang in my chest. They were okay. At least there was that.

I filled a coffee mug with Froot Loops and milk, grabbed a spoon, and tiptoed to my room. Out the window, Jade's lights were off. The moon was bright. Bright like a diamond. No, that was from a song. Bright like a Home Depot bulb? I thought, *I should write that down*, but I didn't feel like writing. Or reading. Or painting my nails. Or working on my cardboard buildings. Ugh. My head began to throb. I wolfed down the cereal and tried to fall asleep.

But I couldn't.

Because all I really wanted to do was talk to my dad. Look, I wasn't stupid. I knew Dad wasn't a saint. Yeah, he had a day job, delivering soda crates, but I knew he had side stuff going on too—gambling, selling car parts, and whatnot. A couple of his friends had even been arrested, mostly for stupid stuff—theft and drugs here and there, but nothing really bad like murder or whatever. Dad was a hustler. A businessman of the streets, I liked to think. And he was smart. Really smart.

And now he'd been gone for twenty-six days. Yep, I'd been counting. I legit counted every time. And when he did come back, he was like recharged or whatever. Last July when he came back from a five-day stint to who knows where, he was in the best mood for, like, the rest of the summer. Every morning he'd bring my brothers and me someplace fun, like swimming at Revere Beach or to get pastries at Au Bon Pain or to some program at the Children's Museum. Dad had friends who worked everywhere, it seemed—the Prudential mall food court, the big library downtown in Copley Square, the welcome center at one of the Harbor Islands. So we'd visit his friends and get something free, even if it was only a soda from a concession stand. On really hot days he'd take us to the movies and we'd sneak from room to room, show to show, until my skin prickled with goose bumps from the air-conditioning. But this time felt different. . . . This time I got to thinking, What if he wasn't just skipping town? What if he was gone for good?

My mind kept racing. Was this insomnia? And now I was crying—I had to get a grip. Sometimes I wished I could just . . . just . . . unzip myself from my own life and start over, somewhere where no one knew me, or my shady father, or my depressed mother, or my "best" friend. Escape it all.

It's a scary thing, though, to get what you ask for. Right?

JENNIFER DE LEON

* * * *

The next morning the couch was empty and Mom's bedroom door was closed. Didn't even open when Christopher spilled cereal all over the place and Benjamin screamed, "I'm going to tell Dad!" We all froze, stared at the frosted squares on the floor, waiting for Mom to come charging out, but nada. The deep dark state must be near sea bottom. To be honest, after last night, I was glad I didn't have to see her before I left for school. Gave me the day to think. Then she wasn't there when we got home. I let the twins play as many video games as they wanted.

Mom must have gotten a quick job. Sometimes she got calls from other ladies in the building to join them for a day's work, usually doing something like helping a white lady in Brookline reorganize her closet or label a hundred jars full of homemade jam or whatever. My mom was the queen of random jobs. Once, she got a job from this lady who needed help making party favors for her four-year-old son's birthday party. No joke! These jobs paid in cash, so Mom was happy. Thing was, she didn't have a high school diploma. So it was hard for her to get steady work and still be home for us after school or at night or whatever. Plus, there was some issue with missing paperwork—something about she lost her original birth certificate and stuff in a fire when she was younger.

Dad was the one who'd had—HAD—a real job, like, one he went to every day, at a soda company warehouse. They even gave him a special belt that protected his back while he worked. You would think we would have gotten tons of free soda, right? WRONG. That company was mad cheap. Employees couldn't even take a soda for their break, or they'd be fined, or even fired.

I microwaved some instant hot cocoa for the boys and me, then pulled the half-finished bakery from under my bed. I'd used an empty cereal box for the walls, painted them pink with some old nail polish. Made the walls nice and glossy. Now I cut up a tissue box and used those pieces to create some windows and a door. I flipped through some recycled revistas for a picture of a brick wall (which was really hard to find, in case you're wondering). As I was writing *Yoli's Pasteles y Panadería* on a rectangle of cardboard—I was going to glue it onto the front of the store—Benjamin came into the kitchen for more cocoa and asked what I was doing.

"What does it look like I'm doing?"

"You know what you should do?" Benjamin opened the refrigerator and stuffed a slice of cheese into his mouth.

"What?" I rubbed the glue stick on the back of the little sign.

He chewed with his mouth open. "You know how they have those wires at the top of buildings so robbers won't jump over the walls?"

I looked up, picturing the barbed silver spirals that covered so many of the stores on Centre Street. "Hey, shut the fridge!"

"You should do *that*," he said.

It was actually a good idea. "But what would I use?"

He didn't answer. He shut the refrigerator door with his hip and ran back to his room.

Hmmm . . . I'd have to think on that one.

I was writing in my journal, ready for bed, when Mom finally came home. I expected her to head straight to the kitchen to heat up some frijoles or whatever. Instead she knocked on my door real soft. That made me instantly nervous. For years I'd tried to train her to actually knock on my bedroom door instead of barging in—so why was she finally doing it *now*?

"Come in," I said, closing my journal and sitting up straight.

She perched on the edge of my bed. "How was your day?"

I shrugged. I got it. I got it; she was under a lot of stress. But she was going cray-cray. Still, I knew I probably should apologize for swearing the night before. Just as I was about to, she surprised me again by saying, "So . . . listen. I'm sorry about what happened." She looked away. "I really am. It's just that there's a lot going on and I don't know what's going to happen." And then—gahhh!—she was crying again!

No lie, I felt bad for her. "Dad's not coming back, is he?"

She cried harder. "I don't know, mija. I just don't know."

I rubbed Mom's shoulder. She cried it out for another minute, then pulled a tissue from her jeans pocket and wiped her nose. "Liliana . . . ," she began. I knew what she was going to say.

"Mom," I said. "I'll try METCO." We both knew that meant, *I'll do it, but I'm throwing in that "try" because I'm stubborn and we both know that I'm stubborn because I'm your daughter so let's just leave it at that. K? K.*

"Ay, mija," she said, hugging me tight. Then her phone buzzed. It was probably Tía Laura. She'd been calling from Guatemala like every other day since Dad had left. Tía Laura had raised my father, so she was more like his mother than his aunt, which made her more like my grandmother than my great-aunt. She was sweet and all. Dad loved her a lot. I could tell from the way he made us clean the apartment like crazy whenever she visited, or how he insisted on Tía Laura getting the best seat on the couch. Mom glanced at the phone screen and bolted out of the room.

Huh. Lately, every time Tía Laura called, my mom took the phone into another room, and on top of *that*, she whispered. Something was up. Something was *definitely* up. And not just me, now going to METCO.

And after one more week of skyscraper-size butterflies in my stomach, I was on my way to Westburg High. When my alarm went off that first morning, it was still dark outside. I wouldn't say I was 100 percent excited or 100 percent nervous. I was more like that scared emoji with all its teeth showing. Everyone else was still asleep. I kissed Mom goodbye on the forehead, and she opened her eyes long enough to smile and whisper, "Good luck, mija."

"Thanks," I said, pulling up her blanket. I looked at the empty other half of the bed. Dad didn't even know I'd gotten into METCO.

I was heading for the front door, when there Mom was, in her wrinkled white robe.

"Jesus, Mom! I thought you were a ghost or something."

"Here," she said, handing me a warm ten-dollar bill. "I don't know what they'll have for lunch over there."

She looked so sleepy.

"Thanks, Mom," I said.

* * * *

Most of the twenty or so other kids on the bus were asleep. The few who were awake listened to music on their phones or did homework. I could never do that—read or write on a bus. I would throw up all over everyone. I didn't recognize anyone. They were mostly Black and apparently from all over Boston, not just my neighborhood. I wondered how long they'd been in the program. Some looked my age, some older. Were any starting *today*, like I was?

I was supposed to meet my METCO "buddy" at school, some girl named Genesis. Miss Jackson had explained that the buddy was usually a junior or a senior, also from Boston. The buddy would do stuff like show me where to sit at lunch and whatever. But last night, Genesis had texted to say that she was going to be absent on my first day—she'd meet me on Tuesday instead. So I was on my own. Great. I also had something called a host family, like a backup family in the suburbs. I wondered who my host family would be. Were they rich? The pamphlet had said: *In case of a bad snowstorm, if the buses can't get out of Westburg, it might make more sense for your child to spend the night with his/her host family.* Now I was worrying about snowstorms—staying with some rich suburban family sounded totally awkward!

Yet I must have dozed off, because all of a sudden the sky was pink and orange and we were in the suburbs. I wiped drool off my chin with the back of my hand, hoping no one had noticed, and stuck a piece of gum into my mouth. There was actually traffic out here! Except no one was honking or cussing anyone out. People used their blinkers. Let each other turn at intersections. Crazy-nice cars too. Expensive-looking. The neighborhoods all had big houses. BIG houses. I also saw things I knew the words for but had never had a reason to name: sprinklers, landscape truck, dog trainer. No joke—a van with the words CANINE ETIQUETTE and paw prints painted on it drove past us. Who says "canine," anyway?

We drove down one street lined with pastel-painted mansions, photo-shoot-ready lawns, and driveways dotted with abandoned basketballs and scooters and everything. People just left their stuff outside overnight? NO WAY that would happen on my street; it would be like putting up a STEAL ME sign. I saw a man jogging. An old lady power walking with her elbows out to the sides. A teenage guy delivering newspapers. Like, real newspapers. I thought newspaper delivery people were extinct or whatever. And they were all white. Allllll white.

My stomach started to cramp up. Did these white kids all really have their own cars? Were they all really allowed to drink beer and wine in front of their parents? Did they hang out with their boyfriends and girlfriends in their furnished basements (or was it "finished"?)? Okay. Maybe Jade and I had watched *Mean Girls* way too many times. But still.

Finally the bus swerved through a maze of mini rotaries, over speed bumps, and boom, we were at the school's entrance. I followed the rest of the METCO kids off the bus, trying not to check things out too obviously, like, *Hello! I'm the new kid.* The air smelled cold, like the ice-skating rink at

Stony Brook. My elementary school always took field trips there, I think mostly because it was within walking distance. But man, that smell—did this school have its own rink? Dang. The school itself was huge. A janitor—even he was white!—rolled blue bins toward a dumpster. I could hear birds cawing, the roar of an industrial lawn mower, and the growling of a bus tackling one of the speed bumps in the parking lot. Speaking of, there had to be a hundred speed bumps.

As I walked in the front doors, a girl with long, thick red hair was stopped just inside, trying desperately to peel gum off the bottom of her sneaker. *Try scissors,* I wanted to say, but I didn't know this girl, and what if she told me to just mind my own damn business? That's what happened the last time I'd tried to be friendly with a white girl. Truth. That girl's name was Melissa, but everyone called her Missie. She was tiny, but boy she had the biggest dirty mouth. She cussed out teachers left and right and held the record for most suspensions. Once, when I tried to help her pick up books she'd dropped in the hall, she told me to mind my own damn business. So, yeah, Missie was the only white girl I'd ever spoken to for more than five seconds. Some people might find that surprising, but it was true. I mean, duh, I'd SEEN white people, especially in Jamaica Plain. That was another thing. White people called it JP, but we call it Jamaica Plain. Well, I used both now, to be honest.

So I gotta admit, I was so surprised when the redhead girl looked up and said "Hi" that I looked around to see who she was talking to. I took in the gold and silver trophies displayed on the walls, protected by Plexiglas. Everyone else seemed to be headed to classes, so she must have been talking to me.

"Hey," I said back.

Redhead girl was now using a pencil to pick at the gum. "Shit! Any idea how to get rid of this stuff?" Her tone seemed friendly enough. She wobbled over, trying to keep the gum area of her shoe from touching the ground, and extended a hand. "Holly."

Suddenly I didn't like how she was staring at my outfit and backpack. "Happy first day," she added. Was she being sarcastic? And how did she know I was new? My cheeks went hot. I didn't know what to do, so I adjusted my backpack. Not that there were any real books in there yet, just notebooks and new pens and highlighters I'd bought over the weekend with Mom's CVS ExtraCare bucks. I scanned this Holly person up and down—loose jeans, white T-shirt, baby-blue flannel tied around her waist—and walked away. Yeah. Totally mature. Not that I knew where I was going or anything. As I turned the corner, I could hear her say, and pretty loudly too, "Okaaay . . ."

Around the corner I slowed down. What was my problem? I'd just thrown this girl I didn't even know some major shade. Nice. More and more sleepy-eyed kids began to fill the hallway. I needed to get my schedule at the main office, so I needed to backtrack, and risk bumping into the redhead girl again. Can you spell "awkward"?

I managed to get to the office without any red-haired-girl encounters. Phew! A lady wearing pastel everything—even pastel-pink frosted lipstick—looked up as I walked in. "Good morning, honey." She eyed me up and down. "Where are you from?" I opened my mouth to answer (I was going to say *Boston*), but then she lowered her voice to a whisper. "Ah, you must be our new METCO student."

I nodded, forcing my shoulders back.

Clearly ready for me, she held out a half sheet with my schedule, saying, "Oh, you'll want to check in with Mr. Rivera. He's the METCO faculty adviser, right down the hall. Oh, wait. He's at a district meeting today. You can catch him later in the week; he'll set you up with diagnostic exams and all that good stuff. But for now, you're in a general schedule. Probably won't change much." She looked me up and down once more. "That about covers it. Have a good first day!"

Wow. She'd basically had an entire conversation without me saying a word. Jade would think that was funny.

Jade—where was she right at this moment? Probably just leaving for school, and here I was, on another planet.

The bell rang. I had no idea where I was going, but I tried to look like I did, joining the flow of kids in the hall.

Eventually I found the right classroom. Geometry. To my surprise, not everyone was white—there were like three Asian kids. I sat down at an empty desk, and the teacher handed me a textbook. "Welcome," he said after asking me my name. I flipped through the book—the answers to all the problems were in the back! In Boston the teachers ripped out those sections. Huh. And this math teacher's breath didn't stink. Okay. Class number one, not so bad.

At the bell I pushed through the hallway and found my next class. And the next. And the next, and then the principal made an announcement over the loudspeaker that there was a community meeting in the gym. I only knew where that was because everyone started walking in the same direction.

The gym—whoa—was total state-of-the-art. They even had a climbing wall. The basketball nets looked brand-new, probably were. Dad would have been so psyched. He *loved* basketball, was always saying if he were five inches taller, he'd have had a chance. He used to take me to the courts on the corner of Jackson and Centre, taught me how to dribble, control the ball with my hands. How to breathe before taking a shot. "All the little things add up, Liliana," he'd say. He never cared that I missed half my shots, just kept showing me how to get better.

I shook my head hard. *Stop. Thinking. About. Dad.* I climbed into the bleachers and looked for a space to sit. Technically there weren't any assigned seats, but you wouldn't know it based on how kids bunched together almost instantly.

The only other time I'd been surrounded by this many white people, Dad had taken me with him on an errand, I think it was in Back Bay, and we stepped inside a building where everyone was white, even the security guard. I remember feeling like *everyone* was staring at us. Dad had knelt down beside me and whispered, "Don't ever let anyone make you feel like you don't belong in the world. ¿Entiendes?"

Did I belong in *this* world? Which made me think—Dad. What world was *he* in? I nearly tripped. *Focus! Find a place to sit.* I searched for the METCO kids, which wasn't difficult—they were the only other brown kids in the bleachers. I tried not to be obvious as I headed over to them. A couple of guys in puffy black jackets huddled over a phone while some girls with fake nails carefully pulled chips from crinkly bags, then deposited them into their lip-glossed mouths.

"Hey," I said to a girl eating Doritos. She had black frizzy hair, and her eyebrows were penciled in real nice. She looked like maybe she was Puerto Rican. Maybe mixed. Definitely Latina. Whoever she was, she didn't respond, just kept chewing.

I didn't know whether that was an invitation to sit down or not, so I just stood there, feeling like an idiot.

"You lost, little girl?" one of the puffy-coat guys asked. Half of the row started laughing. I bit the inside of my cheek.

The girl with the Doritos crunched dramatically.

Now I thought I might actually throw up. No one would remember *that* or anything.

"Hey," I said again, trying to recognize someone—anyone—from the bus ride. "Are you guys in METCO?"

"Who wants to know?" So Dorito Girl did speak, after all.

"I'm new."

"Yeah, we know," she said, a tiny smile surfacing.

Another girl made room for me, and I sat down. But then they all went back to talking, or not talking, or crunching or reapplying lip gloss. Not exactly the world's most welcoming bleacher row. Finally, I couldn't take it anymore. "Wow," I said. "Y'all are mad friendly to the new girl. Whatsup with that?"

A guy in a red hoodie with a silver earring in his left ear laughed louder than I expected. "You're funny."

"I'm Liliana," I said.

"Rayshawn." He stuck out his hand. "And that's Patrice, Jo-Jo, Alfonso, Shanice, Kayla, and this here"—he paused and pointed to Dorito Girl—"is Brianna." Everyone either raised a chin or smiled.

"Hey," I said.

Rayshawn took a gulp from a can of AriZona iced tea. You could have drinks during school here? Then he said, "So, it's your first day, huh?"

"Yeah. I've been in METCO for, um . . . like three hours," I said.

He laughed again. "Yo. You *are* funny."

Then, I swear Dorito Girl started eyeballing me. Was there something weird with my clothes? We both had on jeans, T-shirts, and hoodies. My hair was curlier. Longer. Gelled to cement-level perfection. Caramel skin. Except mine was getting redder by the second. When was this stupid meeting going to start, anyway? Why did class always start on time but these kinds of things never did? Three teachers were fussing with the podium's microphone. Maybe it was broken. And what was a community meeting anyway?

A lady went to the podium and introduced herself as a college counselor. Finally! For the next several minutes she talked about the importance of extracurricular activities on your college application and how after the meeting there would be sign-up sheets for various clubs and whatnot. I tried to listen. I mean, I was interested, but I was kinda shook by Dorito Girl. When the bell rang, no lie, I couldn't leave fast enough. On my way out I sensed someone staring at me, a guy in an orange-and-black soccer jersey—number thirteen—and sweatpants, long dark bangs. He was cute. Like, ridiculously cute. For a white boy.

So, I smiled at this white boy.

He immediately looked away. My stomach dropped.

I WANTED TO DIE. I would pin this morning as one of the most embarrassing ones of my long-ass life.

* * * *

Next on my schedule was lunch. Holy shit! The lunchroom was like a food court! An entire row of food stations lined the walls—a salad bar, an oatmeal bar, and a yogurt bar. And pizza. Even gluten-free. Crazy, right? My brothers would have gone nuts. Me? Uh-uh. Getting food meant having to sit somewhere, and, yeah, total cliché, but I had no one to eat with. No way was I going to go over to the METCO group again. Not today, anyway. I thought about eating my ham sandwich out at my locker; I had packed one real quick right before Mom gave me the ten bucks for lunch; I could use that money for something else. So instead I just roamed down the halls and took bites of my sandwich until the next bell rang. Problem solved.

It was past four o'clock when the bus dropped me home. First thing I did was knock on my bedroom window; I needed to talk to Jade. No response. I turned on lights in the kitchen and living room. Mom and my brothers would be back in an hour. Mom had signed them up for an after-school program at the YMCA, as I wouldn't be able to pick them up anymore. I peered into the fridge. Nothing but hardened rice in a pot. Ugh. For the next hour I must have knocked on my window a dozen times. Nada. Jade wasn't answering my texts, either.

I actually *tried* to do my homework, but to be honest, I didn't have the energy to read through each teacher's course intro packet (syllabus, expectations, rules, and procedures), never mind the actual assignments. So I left a note for Mom—they must have stopped at the store—and tucked myself under my comforter. I was wiped. Outside, the wind pushed hard against the window as I replayed the day in my mind, from the food to the fashion at Westburg. I was not going to think about the METCO kids' dis. Instead I thought about how most girls wore Converse or Uggs, even if they dressed in skirts or leggings. Some had holes near the toes. For kids with so much money—well, kids whose parents had so much money—I wondered why they dressed so crummy. Super-faded jeans, wrinkled T-shirts, mismatched socks, and sweatshirts. It was totally the opposite at my old school, where, just saying, the first day after Christmas vacation everyone showed up like it was a fashion show, displaying their presents all over their bodies. Crisp new jeans, new sneakers—unlaced, of course—new puffy coats, new nails and jewelry and hair. Weaves especially. Then, after a week or so, everyone went back to dressing how they normally did, the crispness in the jeans having softened, the nails having chipped.

I yawned and glanced at my alarm clock. Only 6:12 p.m.? Man, getting up at five was brutal. I considered not setting the alarm. What would happen if I missed my bus? No way I could get to school. But Mom would flip. I yawned again. I could hardly keep my eyes open, but the image of the METCO kids clustered on the gymnasium bleachers crept in anyway. Dorito Girl and her nasty attitude. What was her issue? I yawned once more. I'd never gone to bed so early, but here I was, shutting off the bedside lamp, and at the last minute, yeah, I clicked the alarm on for the next morning. Maybe Dorito Girl was just having a bad day. Maybe the next day she'd be nicer. Maybe.

When the alarm buzzed at 5:10 a.m., I hit snooze so hard that I knocked the clock over, along with the stack of books on my bedside table. Ten more minutes. I needed ten more minutes. Even though I'd gone to sleep at an abuela's bedtime, I was still mad tired. But when I finally hauled myself up, got ready, and went into the kitchen, I discovered something great—

Mom had gotten me a new phone! She had a free upgrade on her plan! And—wait for it—it was charged and everything. She'd left it with a note explaining that she wanted a reliable way to communicate with me throughout the day. Truth: I *was* gone for most of the day. *And* my old phone never charged properly after I'd cracked the screen, so. Yesss!

At school there was no redhead girl scraping gum off her sneaker in the lobby. But there was another girl. She was definitely Latina. Tall. Flaca but with some curves. Hard to tell because she was wearing a Westburg hoodie that maybe belonged to someone else—her boyfriend? It was huge. Her hair was pin-straight like she'd spent the last twenty-four hours getting every single hair to obey her command. She had a blue streak down the right side. I couldn't decide if she looked cool or like a punk witch.

This girl headed straight for me, stuck out her hand like she was a teacher, not another teenager. "Good morning. I'm Genesis Peña." Ah, my METCO buddy.

"Hi," I said, hesitantly shaking her hand.

"You're Liliana, right? From JP? Welcome to Westburg. About yesterday—sorry I wasn't here. I had a college interview. Anyway, I'm from Roxbury. I spend Monday through Friday here in Westburg, though, with my host family cuz I have so many after-school activities. So I'm only ever on the bus on Monday mornings or Fridays after school, unless I stay after on Friday for theater club or prom prep." She paused only long enough to take a breath, then barreled on. "Don't look so scared. And yeah, I'm a fast talker. At least that's what they say. Thing is, I'm kind of nervous. Not to talk to you! It's just, I'm working on my Single-Choice application to Yale, and it's got me kinda rattled."

"Single-Choice?" I interrupted at last, wondering how she had so much energy so early in the morning.

"Single-Choice Early Action program. It's like early decision."

"Oh, right." *Say what?* I was thinking.

"Anyway, I really hope I get in, because I don't want to have to go through the whole general college application process, you know? I mean, I guess I already did. SATs, SAT IIs, the essay, interview, and don't even get me started on how long it took me to put together my CV."

"CV?" My throat went dry.

"Curriculum vitae. It's another way of saying 'résumé.'"

I'd never heard someone like me—Latina, I mean—talk like that, like she was white. But not completely. It's hard to explain. I was barely following what she was saying. It was as if she was talking in English but in an alternate version. At least she wasn't throwing me dirty looks like I was going to take away her Doritos or something. Genesis started moving down the hall, so I just trailed behind her as she pointed in different directions—the computer lab, dance studio (there was a dance studio?!), library, Writing Center. Hold up. A Writing Center? A whole room for writing? So I had to ask, "What kinds of things do they do in the Writing Center?"

"Liliana." Genesis slowed down. "You for real?"

"I mean . . . besides the obvious."

Now she nodded. "Well, you can also sign up to tutor other kids or help them with their English papers."

"Oh." I had imagined beanbags and dim lighting and gel pens in mugs.

"Don't look so disappointed. It looks great on your CV."

Genesis waved at every single teacher who passed us. One actually stopped to say, "Just to reiterate, I really urge you to apply to my alma mater. They're well endowed, lots of financial aid," and another asked, "Hey, Gen. How's the Yale application coming?"

"It's coming," she replied.

"What did she call you? Gen?" I asked.

"Yeah."

Genesis sure was a talker, kinda like my dad, actually, and she knew every corner of the school. She *did* ask me about myself for one second—like, literally. "So, tell me about yourself. What makes you *you*?" Is that what a college admissions officer sounded like? What was I supposed to say? *I hate funerals. I am afraid of cats. After my class read* Night *by Elie Wiesel last year, I vowed never to get a tattoo.* I could tell Gen how I love making buildings and houses and stuff out of cardboard—how I used Styrofoam peanuts for loaves of bread for the bakery—about the building that's a Pentecostal church by night and a carpet store by day. But would Genesis really want to know any of this?

"I love writing," is what I landed on.

Genesis raised an eyebrow. "Guess you should check out the Writing Center, then."

When it seemed she'd shown me everything but the plumbing, she led me down some basement stairs to see "the best bathroom in the building."

As soon as she pushed open the door, Genesis completely changed her script.

"Move, people!" she practically yelled. The girls who looked like freshmen immediately scrammed. The rest just shifted out of the way until she passed, then reclustered by the mirror. She shooed away two girls standing beneath a small window up by the ceiling. They rolled their eyes but stepped away as Genesis climbed on top of the heater and shoved the window open. Back down, she pulled a big purple bottle of hair spray and a JUUL from her backpack, then passed the JUUL to me with a "Hold this." Whaaa? I slipped it up my sleeve fast in case a teacher walked in. Just what I needed, to be the girl who got kicked out of METCO on her first (okay, second) day. Mom would KILL me.

Genesis, pulling her skirt up at the waist, making it two inches shorter, shot me a look. "Don't be so paranoid. Teachers never come in here. They have their own bathrooms."

Who *was* this girl? One minute she was parading down the hall like the next class president, and now she was unzipping her hoodie and . . . oh. She wasn't so flaca after all. Her black top was so tight, it had to be a kid's size. Her waist was tiny. I looked at my own reflection in the mirror: magenta cardigan over a white V-neck and jeans. Sleepy face. My gold necklace that said LILIANA sat crooked on my chest.

Genesis blasted the hair spray at a few stray hairs. "See ya, Gen," a girl called out as she left the bathroom.

"Listen," she said suddenly, voice low as she aimed the hair-spray nozzle at me.

I ducked. "Hey! Watch out."

"Don't make any friends here."

I gaped at her. "What? That's your welcoming advice?"

Genesis laughed. "You're funny."

"Thanks." I straightened my necklace.

"It's just—you seem smart."

I didn't know what to say to *that*.

"But for real, you know what I mean. Girls here will be nice to you to your face. You know, 'Hi. Oh, you're so lucky you speak Spanish. You must get straight As in that class' or 'Can you teach me how to put on eyeliner like that?' But then behind your back they'll be all, 'Oh my God, I can't believe she wore that' and 'Why does she even come to school here?'" She pressed hard on the aerosol button, and a cloud of grape-scented spray filled the space between us.

I coughed.

"Trust me. Don't trust anyone." She lowered her voice even more. "Especially the white boys."

Wow. Okay. Immediately I thought of the guy in the auditorium, the one wearing the soccer jersey. White. Boy. I switched the conversation to METCO, fast.

"So, we have meetings? With someone named Mr. Rivera? What's he like?"

"Yeah, he's the METCO faculty adviser. He's all right. And yeah, you missed our first meeting, probably our only meeting. He's one of two teachers of color at the whole school, so he's pulled in a million directions."

"Oh."

"Here's the deal. Just stick with the METCO kids," Genesis said, her gaze back on her own reflection.

"About that . . . Well—" I coughed again. Man, that hair spray was lethal! "Anyway. Yesterday I tried to sit with them, but they froze me out."

Genesis frowned. "How?"

"I mean they were nasty. The guys made fun of me and

the girls just stared me up and down. It was . . . embarrassing."

"Oh, come on. They're just testing you." She patted down an invisible hair.

"I mean, except for this one guy named Rayshawn. And *testing me*? You for real?"

"Trust me, they're cool. Listen, we have to stick together. I'm telling you."

Someone in the far stall flushed the toilet.

"Okay," I said. "Well, I'd better get to class."

"Wait." Genesis held out her palm.

"Oh. Right." I handed her the JUUL. "See you at lunch?" I hoped I didn't sound desperate.

Genesis gave her hair one final blast. "Oh . . . sorry. I won't be there. Theater club. We skip lunch to rehearse."

"Oh." Great. Another day of feeling like an outsider to the outsiders.

"Don't worry. Like I said, just stick with the METCO kids. You said that Rayshawn was nice. He's cool. Just sit near him." Genesis tore her eyes from the mirror. "Okay, you can go now because I have to pee, and I can't pee while anyone else is in the bathroom. It's a thing."

With teachers, I tried my best—I really did—to answer their constant questions and comments. *How are you adjusting so far? You do know where the tutoring centers are located, right? You'll probably find the work more challenging here than in Boston. That's where you're from, right? Where are you from?* Man, they made me feel mad dumb. Weren't teachers supposed to do the opposite? And not for nothing, but was this *really* the school my parents wanted for me? Dad had always talked about how we should be proud to be Latinos and all that, so why had he and Mom signed me up for this school full of white kids? Where the teachers practically held my hand.

I had to take these stupid diagnostic exams first thing—even though I'd already been placed in the college-prep classes. The English one required a writing sample, and when the bell rang I wasn't quite done, which had *nothing* to do with the fact that I might miss lunch. So I asked my new English teacher if I could finish up my essay during lunch, and get this: She simply told me to leave it on her desk when I was through. No questions. No pass. Nada. My teachers back in Boston would have wondered what I was up to. They would have taken their purses with them even if just to the vending machines down the hall. And especially their laptops, hello. But here? I mean, students didn't even have locks on their lockers. Here, the teacher just vanished, leaving me to write and write, and no one cared how long I took.

Unfortunately, lunch wasn't over by the time I was done, so I had to go to the cafeteria after all. Dorito Girl gave me a look like she wanted to chew me alive. So I walked right past that table. (It wasn't like anyone was making room for me to sit down or anything anyway.)

But—ugh—now I had to walk by the cute guy from the day before, who was sitting with his friends. Talking with their mouths full of food. One of them copying the other's homework. I willed myself not to look up, especially if that guy was also looking up. But that thing happened where your body does the exact opposite thing than your brain is telling it to do, and so I did. I looked up. And sure enough, the guy, still wearing a number thirteen jersey but in a different color, was downing a carton of chocolate milk into his mouth as he watched me from the corner of his eye. I watched him right back, thinking about what Genesis had said about staying away from the white boys. No white boys, and nowhere to sit.

I'd just taken a bite of my sandwich—ham again—walking the halls again, when I heard "Liliana? Liliana Cruz?"

I swallowed quickly. "That's me," I said, turning.

A man in a navy-blue suit and a tie with clouds on it rushed over, hand extended. "Hello! I'm Mr. Rivera, the METCO director." With his salt-and-pepper hair, he kind of reminded me of a much younger Don Francisco, the old guy from the variety show *Sábado Gigante* who Mom and Dad watched every Saturday night. "I was hoping to run into you, set up a time to talk. How's it going? I know it can be an adjustment. Did you get a school tour yet? Finding your classes okay? Meet your buddy yet?"

Wow, I didn't know which question to answer first. "I'm good," I said. If I said anything more, he'd probably fire off a dozen more questions.

"Great. Listen. Stop by my office—it's next to Guidance. You can't miss it. It's by the sneaker in the lobby. You know, the one worn by Larry Bird—"

I stared at him. Who?

"You know, Bird, one of the greatest Celtics players of all time. He visited the school once—"

"Oh yeah," I said. So *that's* why there was a random sneaker all propped up in a glass box like it was a Viking helmet or something.

"So swing by. We can chat." Mr. Rivera's walkie-talkie made a static sound. "I have to run to an appointment. But listen, definitely check out the student lounge in the METCO office." His walkie-talkie *fizz-fizz*ed again. "See you there!" And he was off.

I sent Jade a text: **legit eating lunch by myself. In hall.** ☹

She replied: **4real? Lol. Taking test. Call u later?**

I finished my sandwich, then headed for the shoe shrine. I wanted to know where it was, you know, in case I actually went to a meeting. It couldn't be worse than eating lunch alone in the hall, right?

At home, because I was supposed to be doing homework, I decided to organize my closet. No lie—it always makes me feel productive. So I took out all my summer clothes and put them in trash bags, which I stuffed underneath my bed. I found an old sweatshirt I hadn't worn in like a minute. It had my name spray-painted in hot pink letters across the front. Mad cheesy. I used to *love* that sweatshirt. I held it out, the pre-Westburg-me sweatshirt. I tried it on. Nope. Barely fit over my chest. I gave a laugh. Genesis might wear it! Then I was thinking about how people called her "Gen." Had *she* called herself that first? Liliana. Liliana Cruz. Maybe I needed to change things up. New school . . . new name? Not change-change it, like when you get married or have to go into hiding under some witness-protection program or something, but change, like revise. Like, to Lili. Yeah. Lili. It *was* technically part of "Liliana." I said it a few times: "Lili Cruz, Lili Cruz. Hi. I'm Lili Cruz." Not bad! Truth, I sort of felt like I was getting a makeover, or at least a significant haircut. Like, a fresh start. And no way was I cutting my hair. So Lili it was. Welcome to Westburg, Lili.

Doing proofs in geometry is not the most exciting thing in the world, in case you didn't know. I couldn't stop daydreaming—I saw number thirteen get off the bus this morning, same time as me, and, yeah, he gave me another look. It was the kind of look that stayed on my skin, if you get what I mean. That was, until he'd looked away.

My teacher was in the zone, writing and labeling and talking. I had to get a grip. I grabbed my pencil and started copying the proofs. How much longer? I glanced at the clock over the door, and that's when—insane!—I saw him, soccer jersey guy, walking right past the doorway. Suddenly I felt wide awake. Electric awake. Like, I had to get into that hallway. Maybe he would still be out there. Maybe I would have the guts to actually talk to him. I raised my hand.

"Yes?" my teacher asked, looking annoyed.

"May I have the bathroom pass?"

He lifted his Expo marker in the air, a gesture I took as

"yes." So I hopped up, my heart thumping fast-fast-fast, and proceeded to walk out of the room.

"Miss Cruz?" the teacher called after me.

"Yes?"

"The pass?"

"Oh. Right." I took the wooden block from his hand.

Turns out I didn't even need it because just then the fire alarm went off and everyone, even the kid taking a nice siesta in the back row, bolted from their seats and into the hall, talking and laughing and saying "Thank you, God" while teachers standing by the red Exit sign ushered us all outside. Normally a fire drill in the middle of class is dope, but dang, I had missed my chance to, you know, see soccer jersey guy. Definitely needed to learn his name.

Kids clustered on the grass, but I didn't see anyone I recognized, so I closed my eyes and lifted my face toward the sun—warm enough that I felt like I was being recharged, like a cell phone or something. I was standing there, my face all upward, when I heard someone clearing their throat. Then, "Hey. Hi."

A guy.

I opened my eyes, and there, not two feet away, was soccer jersey guy. He stood directly in front of the sun so I could hardly see him, but by the way he shifted from one foot to the other, it seemed . . . maybe he was as nervous as I suddenly was, even though *he* had come up to *me*.

"Hey," I said back, thunder in my chest.

"You're new here, right?"

"Yeah." *Say something else,* I willed myself. *Tell him you moved here from Boston. Tell him you're lit about the fire drill because you were in math. Don't tell him you love his face.*

"Where are you from?" he asked before I could get any of the above pried out of my brain and into my mouth.

"Jamaica Plain," I said.

He cocked his head.

"Boston," I quickly added, pulling at my necklace.

"Cool."

He stared at his feet, then mine, then me. I tried to see what he saw: tight jeans, black sweatshirt zipped halfway, a purple tank top, a fake gold necklace that said LILIANA sitting on my chest. I could see him see me, and it was terrifying and exhilarating at the same time.

"Dustin," he said.

"What?"

"My name. I know, it's confusing. My parents were really into Dustin Hoffman back in the day. Sad, but true."

Say something! Anything!

"You know. Dustin Hoffman. As in, the actor?" he went on.

"Oh yeah." I smiled. I had no idea who he was talking about.

Thankfully, another guy approached us. He snatched Dustin's phone from his back pocket and proceeded to shove it into his own boxers, yelling, "Hey, loser!"

Dustin's eyes widened in an *I can't believe you just did that* way. "Give me my phone, you shit!" Then he lunged at the guy, but it was awkward because of where he had, you know, stuck it.

The guy finally reached into his boxers and pulled out the phone. "Hey, take a joke!"

"Dude!"

"Who are *you*?" the guy now asked me, a hint of irritation in his voice.

"Liliana. I mean, Lili."

This guy definitely wasn't subtle in checking me out. He stared right at my boobs and didn't stop until I zipped my sweatshirt practically up to my chin.

He kinda smirked at that. "Steve," he said, reaching out his hand, which I did NOT shake. Ew.

"Hey," I said instead.

"What are you?" he asked.

I narrowed my eyes. "Excuse me?"

He rephrased his question. "Where are you from?"

"Boston." I answered quickly this time.

"No, I mean where are you from-from?"

"What?" Did he ask everyone this, or just METCO kids? Never mind. I knew the answer to that. Jerk. Plus, by the way, he stunk. Literally.

Dustin thought the same thing, because he gave him a shove, saying, "Steve. Seriously. Go take a shower. You reek."

Steve grinned. "Nope. No shower until after tomorrow's game. Call it superstition. But it works." He then tried to stick his armpit in Dustin's face, but Dustin shoved him again, harder.

"You're sick, dude."

The Steve guy moved on to torture someone else. Dustin shrugged. "He can be a real douche."

"No kidding."

"You'd never know it, but he *does* have a brain. He's actually really smart."

I put my hands in my pockets, not sure how to respond.

"He was on teen *Jeopardy!* last year. I'm serious."

"Huh." Is it shallow to admit I couldn't stop noticing how cute Dustin was? His eyes. There were flecks of green in them. I. Could. Not. Stop. But then I had to, because the vice principal, gripping a megaphone, instructed us all to return to the building. "False alarm, folks! Someone pulled the alarm." This set off a round of booing. Except from me. Except from Dustin.

He just kept looking at me, so . . . "So I guess the fire drill is over," is what I brilliantly came up with. I wanted to smack myself. Students were filing back inside. I swore I saw the crowd make room for the basketball players, Rayshawn at the center.

"Yeah. False alarm," Dustin said. He cracked his knuckles, breaking into a huge grin.

"Yeah," I said.

"Yeah," he repeated, his huge grin huger.

"Wait—was this *you*?"

His jaw twitched.

"You pulled the alarm?" I whispered. *He pulled the alarm?*

He brought a finger to his lips.

The vice principal stepped toward us, clapped his hands. "Let's go, folks!"

I pivoted. "I guess we have to go back inside," I said. Oh, I was absolutely brilliant.

"I'll walk you back to math," Dustin offered.

"Thanks," I said, heading for the door. Was this actually happening? "Wait. How did you know I was in math?"

Dustin held the door open. He was so close that I could smell his shampoo. Or maybe it was his ChapStick. Either way, it smelled fantastic.

Again Dustin grinned. "I knew you were in math because I saw you sitting there. You looked bored."

"So . . . then you decided . . . to pull the alarm?" I asked, keeping my voice low.

"Yeah. How else was I going to get to finally talk to you?"

"Oh . . ."

"Plus you leave right after school. You take the METCO bus, right? You're a freshman, right?"

"Yeah . . . you?" I blushed.

"Junior."

"Oh."

"So, anyway, I had to find an excuse."

"Um, you could have come up to me in the hall? Cafeteria? Ever considered the obvious?"

"Boring. Unoriginal."

"True," I agreed. Very true.

*   *   *   *

So, that happened.

I know. I KNOW.

We exchanged numbers, and after that, boom, he sent me three texts in a row. Back and forth—all chill. But then in his last text he invited me to his next soccer game this Thursday. *I know!* Of course, my very first thought was that Mom would say no because she was always going for Strictest Mother of the Year. Not that I wanted to give her more to worry about. But going to a school soccer game should NOT be something to worry about. I would just have to figure out how to play this.

The first thing I did when I heard Mom and my brothers coming home was swing open the front door and offer to help with the bags. You know, get on her good side. But my brothers already had the bags, and were nonstop yakking . . . about cooking? Seems there's this chef's club for kids at the Y, and they actually *liked* it. Like, they were talking about making dinner . . . that night. *My* brothers! Mom was nodding encouragingly. Dad would have been dumbfounded (vocab word). And so psyched to know they could actually boil water without burning down the kitchen.

They were mad excited as they unloaded the groceries. Christopher looks more like Mom, so his eyes were all bright, but Benjamin totally has Dad's exact eyes, sort of gentle and smiley, if that makes sense. Food I'd never seen them eat before piled up on the counter. Benjamin looked so happy, taking out some chili sauce. Christopher was saying, "Don't forget. We have to wash our hands first!" Whaaa? Where *was* I?

Mom gave them each a kiss on the cheek, then disappeared into her room. I decided to wait to bring up the soccer game. Thing is, when she tucked away in her room like this, it was like she wasn't even home, she was checked out. Like, my brothers actually wanted to do something besides play video games, and she barely noticed. Dad, he would have been all over it, asking them a million questions, making them explain everything so they could feel like big deals. But Dad didn't know about the cool chef's club. Didn't know I ate sandwiches in the hall at this fancy school he apparently wanted me to go to. The thing with my dad is, if you talked to him about something, he always had an idea about how to fix it. What would *he* have to say about METCO? About Dorito Girl? About being froze out even by kids *like* me?

After Benjamin and Christopher made chicken with chili sauce and broccoli (it wasn't bad), and took off for their room to play video games (without washing any dishes!), Mom came into the kitchen, adjusting the belt on her robe. She seemed calm, at least. So I took my chances. "Mom. I want to ask you something."

She stifled a yawn. "Por favor, Liliana. Vaya. What is it?"

"Okay." I went for it. "Can I stay after school tomorrow . . . for a game?"

"No."

"Mom! You didn't even ask about what game or how long it is and if there is an after-school bus. Which there *is*, by the way."

She began opening and closing her fists. This is what she

did when she felt stressed—she must have read about it in one of her magazines.

"Liliana. I can't be worrying about where you are. Just . . . just go to school and come home. Please." Yup. Just like I figured. "I've got enough to worry about with your father in—" She stopped short. In? IN? Wait, wait, wait—did she know where Dad was?

"In *where*? Where *is* Dad?" I blurted out. She knew! I could tell!

Mom, suddenly pale, reached for the table as if to steady herself, then plopped into a chair.

"Mom?" I said, sitting beside her. "Just tell me."

She looked at me so long, if I'd had a timer, it would have been a straight minute. It really would've.

Finally she took a deep breath. "Bueno . . ." She nodded, as if to convince herself it was okay to say more. "Your father . . . he's in Guatemala."

I sat stiller than still. Guatemala? *Guatemala?* What was he doing *there*? But I didn't utter a syllable and risk her clamming up.

"Because . . . well. At first, and I'm sorry to say this, but I thought he was with another woman. There have been times, Liliana, when part of me wished that were actually the case."

Whaaa? "Mom!"

Mom held up a hand. "Escucha. He got into some trouble. He didn't do anything wrong! This you have to believe." She lowered her hand. "At first, though, even I really thought he had done it."

I grasped her arm. I was trying not to freak. "Done what? What are you talking about? And why didn't you tell me before!"

"Oye. So, he and some of his friends went to a bar one night after work, and then they stopped for burgers at Wendy's. No big deal, right? Then some old guy started in on them. Calling them spics and other stuff, telling them their days were numbered. One of your father's friends got mad. He—maybe he'd had too much to drink, I don't know. But he started pounding on the old man. The manager called the police." Mom paused to inspect a worn spot on one of the place mats. She rubbed a finger over it, frowning, then went on.

"Once the police arrived, things got worse. Your father's friend really got into it with one of the cops. Your father stepped in. How could he not? But then the old man started hitting your father!"

I couldn't believe what I was hearing.

I wanted her to stop.

I didn't want her to stop.

"Anyway, de verdad, this is all on video, so they know it was self-defense, but they didn't care." She wiped at her nose with her robe sleeve.

"But, Mom, I don't get it. What does this have to do with him being in Guatemala?"

She closed her fists, opened her fists, closed her fists, nodded, then whispered, "Liliana . . . your father was deported."

I gaped at her. "What! But he can't be deported. How can

he be deported? He's a US citizen! Right? Right!" I wasn't hearing correctly. I couldn't be hearing correctly. *Could* I be hearing correctly? But then I *saw*. Mom looked scared. For real. *No, no, no.*

Then she said it. "No, Liliana. He isn't."

I slumped back in my chair. Oh my God, what did this mean? Were . . . were . . . I had to ask. "Is he— Are you . . . undocumented?"

Mom plucked a napkin off the table and pressed her face into it. I couldn't even do that. Honestly, I felt paralyzed, like someone had just covered me in cement. My father . . . my mother . . . my *parents*—they were undocumented. I had no idea what to say. And now Mom was sobbing.

I don't know how long we sat there, Mom crying into the napkin and me just staring at the wall. The room felt like it was closing in. I brought my hand to my chest. Breathing? Okay. I was still breathing.

And as I sat there, so many images, so many pieces of the past that I never quite understood, came into focus, and suddenly made sense.

Like the time when I was eight and we got separated by a crowd at the South Shore mall. After she found me, Mom grabbed my shoulders, shook me hard, and told me that if anything should ever happen, I should call—not her, not Dad, but my Tía Carmen in Lynn.

And the time at a New Year's party at some friend of Dad's in Everett. Someone shouted that an immigration cop was on his way up the stairs, and everyone ran out the back door. Dad held my hand so tight, I thought it was going to snap off. We never stepped foot in Everett again.

Oh my God. Mom's obsession with paperwork and envelopes and bills and filing . . . and her freak-out *just the other day* when she couldn't find some letters! No wonder she was always a minute away from a nervous breakdown.

And . . . oh! Ohhhhh. Her inability to get a real job.

It all made sense now. Oh man.

After Mom went to bed, I texted Jade. No answer. I knocked on the window three times. Nothing. *C'mon, Jade, where are you?* I mean, holy shit. My father was *deported*. My father was deported. My father was *deported*. Was he coming back? *Could* he come back? What if he never came back? Would we have to move to Guatemala? Gahhh! My brain was in overdrive. No. Dad would find a way back to us. But would he have to hire a coyote? The first time I ever heard this word, I thought it was a reference to an *actual* coyote, as in the animal, but I'd since learned that in this case "coyote" refers to a person you pay mad money to sneak you across the US border.

My purple notebook stared at me, practically begging me to open it. Funny. On the bus home I'd been imagining writing all about Dustin. . . . Yeah, some people fantasized over the dessert they were going to eat later on; I fantasized over what I'd write about. But now Dustin seemed a million days ago. I picked the notebook up, put it down, picked it up again, and wrote *Today.* I wrote *Today.* I wrote *Today* like seventy-five times all on top of each other until I tore a hole right through the page. Plus my hands were doing this old-person-shaking thing. Dang it. Where was Jade? Her grandmother *never* let her stay out this late. I paced the room. My father had been deported. My father had been *deported*. Okay. It had *never* occurred to me that my parents weren't citizens. I mean, why *would it*? And where was Dad staying, anyway? Was he getting food? Was he scared? Was he with family there, or did he have to like, *hide*? I had no idea. And how did they even actually deport you, anyway? March you to an airplane going to the country you came from, and push you on? Are you *handcuffed*? Oh my God! Thank God Jade finally replied to my text.

Me: **can u come over NOW**

Jade: **k . . .**

I raced to the bottom of the stairs so Mom wouldn't hear the buzzer. "You okay, girl?" Jade asked as I swung open the building door. Then she gave me a hug.

I held on to her. She smelled like Ernesto's cologne.

"Not really."

Jade stepped back, really looked at me. "Liliana, what's going on?" She wore summer on her body, a jean skirt and a peach halter top, hadn't even taken the time to put on a jacket; it dangled in her hand.

"Nothing good. Come on up. I'll tell you everything," I whispered.

"Yo, I can't. My grandmother will flip if I'm not back in five minutes. Spill!"

I looked up the stairwell, then leaned in close. "So . . . my father . . . he's been gone for a minute because . . . he was actually deported."

Her hand flew to her mouth. "No. . . ."

"Yes. He got sent back to Guatemala." Now I bit hard on my bottom lip because an ugly cry was coming.

"Shit—your *dad*?"

"I know."

"You for real?"

"*Yes*, yo."

An ambulance siren blared in the distance. Jade put on her jacket and crossed her arms. "That fucking sucks, yo."

We talked for a few more minutes, but I don't remember what we actually said. All I remember is that I felt a little better. Jade hugged me one more time before she left. As I looked out into the dark street, my head felt fuzzy. I prayed that Dad was okay wherever he was now. A streetlight flickered, then burned out. I must have stared at this street a thousand times, but that night it looked darker than all those other thousand nights stitched together. Yeah, pretty ironic.

Dad, he was never scared of the dark. He said you needed dark so that light could be light. One was nothing without the other. The hard times, he said, made you stronger. And, you know how you *hear* that stuff, and it all feels totally cliché? But then when you *need* it, it's weird, yeah, I know, but it kinda helps. Still, I pictured Dad kicking a pebble down some lonely road somewhere thousands of miles away from our home. I sent him a hug in my mind, told him to keep going. And you know what? I kinda didn't need to actually talk to him to know what he'd say to *me*. He'd tell *me* to keep going. He would tell me to stay focused, give METCO a shot, dig in my heels at Westburg. *You do you,* Dad would have told me. So that's what I decided to do. No matter what.

8

With my new You Do You attitude holding my Where Is Dad Now panic attacks at bay, I admit I was psyched to see it was C day on the school calendar. This meant I had a double block for my English elective, Creative Writing. On my way into the classroom, I spotted Dorito Girl and another METCO girl—named Ivy, I think—clustered in front of the lockers. Ivy looked up and sort of smiled, but then Dorito Girl pulled her elbow and they were off. Fine, then. Maybe I'd make them villains in a story. For real, it would be great to roll up my sleeves and *write*. Except, no lie, Mrs. Grew didn't exactly send out the creative vibes. At least not to me.

As I slid into a seat, I did a double take. Rayshawn was there, in the far back corner. Huh. I would have guessed he'd pick weight lifting or study hall—seemed more his thing. But there he was, in his navy-blue hoodie and basketball shorts. Different earring. His eyes were closed.

Mrs. Grew was telling everyone to settle down. Ha. Rayshawn couldn't have been *more* settled. Then she told us to take out some paper as she scribbled on the board. I couldn't resist peeking back at Rayshawn. He was pulling out a thin notebook and a pen missing its cap from his backpack. His earring caught the light coming in from the window and sparkled, but *he* looked totally beat. I turned back to the board.

Describe one of your worst fears and a time you overcame it. Show. Don't tell.

"You have thirty minutes," Mrs. Grew said, looking at her watch.

They didn't play at this school. We were getting right into the work.

Everyone around me started writing feverishly, stopping only to click their mechanical pencils, releasing more lead. I stared at the pale lines on my paper. My worst fears? Well, I had a bunch, including two new ones: that my father would never come home, that my *mother* would also be deported, and that the boys and I would be left without our parents. Okay, that was three. And then there was that Jade and I wouldn't stay best friends until we were one hundred years old, that I would mess up this opportunity to go to a school that had all these resources—including a pool. But right that very second my worst fear was writing this essay. That's right. I had writer's block. Bad.

"Is there a problem, Miss Cruz?" Mrs. Grew called out.

I shook my head, sank down in my seat. Began to write. I wrote *something, something, something* along the first two rows. Total waste of lead. But at least I *looked* like I was writing.

Barely fifteen minutes later, one girl raised her hand.

"Yes, Paula?"

"Can I share?" she asked. My eyes bugged. She was *finished*?

Mrs. Grew nodded.

"Then me," said a kid in the front row.

"And me," said another.

Really? These kids were all amped to share. Maybe they got extra credit for participation or something? I dug out the class syllabus and scanned it. YUP. Participation counted for 25 percent of your grade. I kept reading the fine print. Oh, wow. It also said that at any time the teacher reserved the right to collect writing prompts and count them as a quiz grade. I looked at my *something, something, something*. That wasn't even F material. My bad for not reading the syllabus.

"Of course! Anyone can share," Mrs. Grew was saying, clapping for our attention.

Paula cleared her throat. She didn't stand, but her voice was loud, as if she was standing anyway.

> *A Time I Overcame a Fear*
>
> *When I was younger, I was afraid of the*
> *ocean. Everything about the ocean. I was*
> *scared of the waves. Seaweed and all the*
> *animals in it. I thought that if I went in,*
> *I would get pulled out to sea and drown.*
> *I was a good swimmer, but I only swam in*

pools. Every time I went to the beach with
my friends, I would always stay on the sand
and make up a reason why I couldn't go in
the water. I wanted to get over the fear. The
next time I went to the beach, I promised
myself I would go in the water. A few weeks
later I got up one morning. It was sunny and
my dad planned a day to go to the beach.
Once we arrived I felt like running back, but
I knew I had to face my fears. Right at the
edge of the water, I stood there, counted
one . . . two . . . three . . . and I ran in the
water! It felt good not to be scared anymore.
I was happy I faced my fears.

Wow. That kind of sucked. People slow clapped. More hands flew up. Double wow. I desperately wanted to ask for the bathroom pass just to escape from all this eagerness, but before I could even raise my hand, a kid charged to the front of the room.

"Jeremy D.," Mrs. Grew said in a low, disapproving tone. "Next time, please wait to be called on."

He ignored her and started right in, no dramatic pause like Paula, no waiting for a nod from the teacher, no anything. "My Favorite Video Game," he said so loud that the class across the hall probably heard him.

Mrs. Grew placed her coffee mug on a high file cabinet and said, in an eerily calm voice, "Just . . . just, go."

My Favorite Video Game

*On the cover of the game it said there are like
eighty-seven bazillion guns in the game. It is
a good game for people who like killing, guns,
humor, and fantasy. Now I only have three or
two friends that have the game and another
friend might get it for Hanukkah. Anyway,
the game is great.*

The class cheered. Mrs. Grew jotted something down on a pad on her desk. Maybe she was writing *something, something, something* too. For the next few minutes, Mrs. Grew talked about imagery and the power of three in writing. I stared out the window at the parking lot—the *senior* parking lot, according to the green sign. Whoa. Like, as in high school seniors? And the parking lot was full! Jeez. My family didn't even have a car, hello.

"Now I want you to take a look at what you've written. See if you can substitute abstractions and generalities for more specific language, sensory images, as we discussed last week. Remember, we have another hour," Mrs. Grew said now, looking right at me. I swallowed.

"Miss Cruz? Can I check in with you in the hall, please?"

Could she see all the *something, something, something* from where she stood? I followed her nervously.

Outside the door, Mrs. Grew turned to me, her eyes two watery pools of blue and gray, like wet marbles. Sensory imagery! She put her hand on my shoulder. More sensory: Why did teachers smell like either potpourri or coffee? "Liliana." She said my name as if trying on the word. "Where are you from?"

I hesitated. She *knew* I was in METCO. From Boston. So what did she want? My exact address? "Jamaica Plain," I said. "Hyde Square."

She nodded, but I could tell she didn't know where that was. "Feel free to express yourself fully here. We *want* you to succeed. Okay?"

Huh. Maybe she was nice after all. "Okay," I said, and smiled. And I decided right then to write about Jade and one of the most fear-inducing nights of my life.

I filled three whole pages about the night when we were six or seven and Jade's father came tumbling into their apartment, the whiskey practically oozing out of his pores. Our moms were eating pan dulce in the kitchen. The twins were asleep in their carriers by Mom's feet. But as soon as Jade's father burst in, everyone scrambled, as if on cue. Jade grabbed the Barbies we'd been playing with and shoved them under a couch cushion. In the kitchen I could hear the gathering of plates and saucers, a kitchen chair scraping the linoleum. "Shut off the TV!" Jade's mother called from the kitchen, even though the TV wasn't on.

Look, I had seen Jade's father drunk a hundred and one times, but never quite like that, with bloodshot eyes and his head twitching to the right, like he was trying to use his shoulder to get something out of his ear but couldn't. He stormed into the living room. His fly was undone. "What's this mess? Who are all these people in MY house? Get out! Everyone, get out!" And then he was off. He punched the wall. The plaster made little clouds, like the wall was coughing. In the kitchen, my brothers started crying.

"We were just playing," Jade tried to explain, frantically scooping up all the Barbie accessories from the rug.

"I'll help you," I told her, my voice wobbling. We snatched up tiny pairs of high heel shoes and sparkly skirts, and deposited them into a shoebox.

Her father lurched toward us. "Don't talk back to me!" he yelled, and—whack!—he slapped the back of Jade's head. "Do you hear me?" Jade was using every ounce of strength not to cry.

"Leave them alone," Jade's mother said, coming out of the kitchen, her face as white as the beat-up wall.

My mother gripped her necklace, her eyes darting between the babies fussing in their carriers and me. "Get your stuff, Liliana. Now."

But I couldn't move. I just stared as Jade continued desperately, madly, scooping up miniature jean skirts and frilly scarves. Her father hit her again. The side of her arm. Then again. Her ear. The more he hit, the faster Jade's fingers grasped at Barbie sneakers, Barbie bathing suits.

And then Jade's mother charged. She leapt onto his back like a pro wrestler. "Leave. Her. ALONE!" she screamed, which set the babies off screaming. And Jade kept picking up Barbie stuff. Not crying, just clawing, clawing, clawing tiny shoes out of the carpet.

The neighbors downstairs—or maybe it was upstairs, it was hard to tell—began to bang on the floor, or ceiling. Jade's mom became a wild dog then, barking at Jade's father as she clung on to his back. In my essay I said that she actually looked like a human backpack. It was true. Oh, and her black hair flung around like a mop.

I could tell my mother didn't know what to do. Her eyes pleaded with me. *Get up*. She couldn't leave with the babies and leave *me* inside the apartment with this monster. I was so scared, but I couldn't leave Jade. How could I?

"Jade! Come with us!" I begged. Now her mother was the one who was clawing—clawing at Jade's father's eyes. He circled and punched at the air, at anything in his way. Jade had just wiggled past him, racing for the door, when he suddenly kicked out. Jade went sprawling, falling right onto the glass coffee table. Shards flew everywhere. Blood flew everywhere.

I couldn't believe how shiny the blood was.

"Jade!" her mother yelled. Both mothers ran toward her.

More knocking sounds.

Jade was drenched in blood and glass. Seconds later cops burst through the apartment door. Then it seemed like everyone was screaming in Spanish. The rest was a loud blur.

On my final page I wrote about everything that happened once the police showed up. How they immediately called for backup and an ambulance, how the sirens grew louder and louder until they stopped right below the apartment window. The sound suddenly stopped, but the orange and white lights still swirled like a disco ball, hitting every surface of the living room, including the framed photo of Jade and her parents that had been taken at Sears. I knew it had been taken at Sears because our family had been next in line, waiting for our turn. In the photo, Jade's father looked like a totally different person. He still had his ponytail, but his skin was softer, his teeth so clean and white as he smiled into the camera. The three of them were dressed in plaid—red, white, and black.

I described how the cops handcuffed Jade's father and told him to "Shut the eff up!" (I thought I might get points taken off if I used an actual swear word.) I described how the paramedics placed Jade onto a white stretcher, how I could see that Jade had a hundred bits of glass speckled across her skin and sticking out from her T-shirt. The paramedics gave her an injection of something they said would make her feel better. After that Jade's father was deported (I know that now, but at the time I just knew he had been taken away), and Jade's mother had a nervous breakdown and started using drugs and hanging out with even sketchier dudes.

Jade's grandmother had raised Jade ever since. Her father was still in Honduras as far as I knew.

I wrote until my hand hurt. And at last I was done. Mrs. Grew noticed, because she came over and asked if she could read my pages. "Sure," I said with a shrug. She took them to her desk while I read the syllabus front to back, trying not to watch her. When she was finished, she remained seated, looking into the distance. It was not an A for Your Essay look.

Maybe I shouldn't have mentioned the police? I stared at the prompt written in green marker on the board. *Describe one of your worst fears . . . overcame it . . .* Oh, wait. I hadn't written about that. I had written about a time when I *was* afraid, but not a time I overcame it! NOT the same thing. Ugh.

I felt so relieved when the bell rang. My classmates zipped backpacks and bolted out the door, one guy asking another, "Dude, what'd you write about?" The other answering, "Not making the traveling team. I was so afraid I wouldn't make the cut, so we hired a private coach for a month before tryouts." *What the—?*

Mrs. Grew stood up at last and handed me back my essay. "Liliana. I hope this is fiction."

My throat tightened. I managed to nod.

She squinted as if suddenly seeing me through a new lens. Just then another teacher interrupted us—thank God! I escaped into the hall. On my way out I crumpled up the pages, then slammed the wad into the nearest trash can. No, it wasn't fiction. So what? So this happened to my best friend. And yeah, I was fearful. So I didn't exactly follow the prompt, but I mean, weren't writers supposed to write about the worlds they knew? I blinked hard, fighting back tears. No way I was going to let anyone see me cry.

I checked to make sure Dustin wasn't in the hall. But then I *wanted* to see him. Maybe that'd make me feel better. I reached for my phone, sent him a text: **hey**.

He wrote back right away: **finishing up lab. Want some cat intestines?**

I replied: **all set thx** ☺. At least he put a smile back on my face.

Hey, meet at outside bleachers for lunch?

My stomach dropped. In the best way. **K** ☺, I replied. I was about to text Genesis next, ask her what was up with Mrs. Grew, but up ahead I heard kids laughing. They were surrounding Rayshawn, who somehow had a blazer (teacher's?) over his hoodie and was sashaying down the hall, tossing out pink detention slips and letting them fall like confetti. Kids were dying-laughing. As I walked past them, someone said, "Yo, Rayshawn! Do it again!" And so Rayshawn did it again. And everyone laughed again.

A teacher in the hall actually clapped before taking the pink pad from Rayshawn and saying, "That's enough. Thank you for the performance, brother. But keep that energy for the court. Season is just getting started. All right. Now get to class."

Whoa. Did that teacher (white) call Rayshawn "brother"? Rayshawn either didn't hear or pretended not to hear. But he *must* have heard it! Others moved on to their classes. But it all really . . . bugged me. As I walked to my next class, I tried to figure it out. Aside from a white teacher calling Rayshawn "brother," it was like . . . Rayshawn was their entertainment and they held the remote control. Yeah, it bugged me.

I texted Genesis. **Hey girl. Where r u?** Immediately she wrote back: **theater club . . . all ok?** I responded with the brown-skinned thumbs-up emoji. But what's the point of having a METCO buddy if they're never around? So I texted her again and asked: **what play are u in anyway?** She replied: **the Emperor's New Clothes**—which I thought was mad random. She read my mind because she added: **i play one of the spoiled daughters lol**. I sent her an emoji with stars in its eyes and stuffed my phone back into my pocket. Good for Genesis.

After checking my hair in the bathroom mirror, I walked to the field, and sure enough, Dustin was sitting in the top row of the bleachers. He waved his sandwich in the air—ha. I had mine too. Ham and cheese. His was bleeding purple, so PB&J. "Hey," he said when I got to the top. "Table for two?" He took a little bow. Aw . . . We sat so our thighs touched, even though there was space for like, a thousand more people. And I tried, tried, tried not to obsess over whether or not I had a piece of ham stuck in my teeth. But I couldn't. So I talked mostly with my hand over my mouth. I told him about Mrs. Grew. He said not to worry about her. That she was officially now Mrs. Ew. I laughed. Took a sip of water. Screwed and unscrewed the cap about fifty times. When we finished eating, he gently pulled my sleeve, and I scootched up and sat even closer to him. He put his arm around me and we sat like that, tucked into one another, the half hour wrapped around us, the fresh air on our faces, until the bell rang.

When Mom asked me how school was, I said that it was whatever. No way was I telling her about Dustin, hello. She muttered something about how it would get better, but then went back to staring at the television. She was beyond obsessed with the news (understandably, hello), in Spanish *and* English. She watched all the channels and brought home three different newspapers, hunting for information on what was going on at the border. She didn't even watch her telenovelas at night. And she hardly left the apartment anymore, and *never* at night. If we ran out of milk, too bad, the boys ate their cereal dry in the morning.

One of the top stories on the news: a rival gang shoot-out at a nearby park. A bystander had been killed. We knew the gangs did their thing, and we knew not to wear certain colors in excess, but still. Knowing this happened just three blocks away wasn't exactly comforting. Then, as if that weren't bad enough, the news switched to an image of the president and "the wall" on the southern border, like between the US and Mexico. Whaaat? An actual wall? For, like, hundreds of miles? Mom began praying superfast in Spanish, her eyes screwed shut.

I draped a wool blanket over her. "Can I get you anything?"

"No thanks, mija." She didn't take her eyes off the TV.

"You hungry?"

She shook her head. I didn't bother asking if she'd made dinner; she'd never even gotten out of her pajamas. Dang. That meant she took the twins to school like that. Double dang. I checked in on them. No surprise, they were playing video games, firing their remote controls, making gun sounds, *pat-dat-dat, pat-dat-dat.* I told them to turn down the volume, but they only lowered it a little.

Everything felt so cramped all of a sudden. The rooms, the walls, the apartment building, the streets. Even the air. Which was weird, because you'd think the place would feel bigger with one less person in it. But it was as if Dad's absence was sucking up all the oxygen. Thing was, if Dad had been home right then, he'd probably be wrestling with my brothers. They capital *L* Loved to wrestle. Dad would pull one of their mattresses into the living room, and then the three of them would really go at it. The boys would jump from the couch onto the mattress, aiming right for Dad's chest. They got all kinds of wild. Drove Mom bananas. She'd have to leave the apartment and go do laundry or something because she was sure that one of them was going to get hurt and then we'd be spending the rest of the day in the emergency room. *I* thought it was pretty funny. Sometimes I even recorded it on my phone, and then we replayed it in slow motion. *That* was really funny.

Huh. Probably my brothers were playing so many video games now because Dad wasn't around to play with them.

"When's dinner?" Christopher asked. Good question. I went into the kitchen. The sink was full of dirty dishes. Great. But I washed and dried them and put them away. Then I stared into the cupboard. Cooking . . . wasn't exactly my strength. I had only ever made rice once before, and it had come out more like soup. Mom said I had added too much water. See, my parents never followed recipes. They always just eyeballed amounts. I'd tried to do the same. But ended up with rice soup. So this time I measured and timed and stirred, and twenty-five minutes later, the rice was done. It looked like rice! Until I tasted it. Bland-o! It wasn't savory like when Mom made it. Then I remembered that Mom put onions and tomatoes and other stuff in there. Bouillon? Garlic? Salt! I could add those things now.

I took the pot off the stove, cut up a tomato and an onion, and stirred them in. Then I opened a bouillon cube and mashed it using a fork. Why are those things in cubes, anyway? Ohhh! They'd make good little presents if I made a Christmastime miniature room; I'd have to remember that. I got out the big container of salt and was sprinkling some in when Benjamin burst into the kitchen, shouting "You need to sign my reading log!" He scared the heck out of me, and I accidentally poured way too much salt into the pot.

"Benjamin! You just made me spill it!" I tried to scoop the cloud of salt out, but it was already sinking, dissolving into the rice.

"*Me?* It's not my fault you can't cook."

I gave him a dirty look.

"So, can you sign it?" He waved a green paper at me.

I scanned it. "Did you actually read for thirty minutes?"

"No."

"Then I'm not going to sign it. Go read."

"You're such a—"

Beep! Beep! Beep! What the—the smoke alarm! Christopher barreled in with his hands over his ears, followed by Mom, the blanket around her shoulders. "What's going on? Liliana!"

"I was making rice—" I looked around frantically. Damn! I'd never turned off the stove. I switched it off, grabbed a dishrag, waved it at the alarm, and braced myself to get yelled at.

But Mom was peering into the pot, an enormous smile on her face. Then she took a bite. "Oh, Liliana." She gave me a *Thanks for your help; this rice stinks* look. And so it was worth it—the annoying smoke alarm and all. Mom opened the windows and the door that led to the basement stairway. She even opened the refrigerator! Then she spooned out the top layer of the rice—where, according to her, most of the salt would be. She added more water to the pot and a bunch of frozen chicken thighs from the freezer, and she set it all to simmer. "Come get me in half an hour," she said, heading back to the living room. "Don't forget."

"Okay," I said, turning toward Benjamin. "*You* can start reading now. And don't stop until I say."

He put on a protest pout, but got his backpack and sat at

the table. "You know," he said. "I *am* taking a cooking class. So I *could* help you with the rice next time."

"*Now* you tell me?"

He grinned and opened his book. "Oh yeah," he said. "I also thought of something you could use for the barbed wire above the panadería you're making."

"Yeah?" He was actually thinking about me outside his universe of video games and reading logs? Aw . . .

"The inside of a pen. You know, for the spirals. Just pull it loose a little bit."

"Benjamin! That's a great idea! Thanks!"

And once the rice and chicken were done, and I'd eaten a bowl and a half—it was pretty good, and only a little too salty—I knocked on my window three times for Jade. She wasn't home. Thought of texting Dustin, but then remembered he had a game. So instead I went right to work on Yoli's Pasteles y Panadería. I took apart an old pen and used the silver spiral just like Benjamin had suggested. It was perfect.

With Mom watching news nonstop (which made me worry about Dad nonstop), school was *almost* a relief. On the ride in, I noticed there wasn't a single pastelería in Westburg, only Starbucks and one bakery on Main Street called—you guessed it—Main Street Bakery. And it sure didn't advertise sillas y mesas for rent on a handwritten sign in the window like at Yoli's. I guess Westburg customers didn't need to rent any tables and chairs. And that, folks, was my takeaway on that morning's bus ride to school. Oh, and Dustin texted me eleven times, just sayin'. He really wanted me to go to a game. I really wanted a different mother. Joke, joke. But . . .

In third-period World History—I couldn't *believe* it—we were starting a unit on Central American immigration. It was part of a larger unit on immigration as part of a year-long theme of Reading Like a Historian. Guess who finally read that syllabus? I noticed that this school gave unique names to their courses, instead of the basic English, art, math, history, etc. Like, there was one senior English course called American Rebels and Romantics. And yeah, Central American immigration. But ugh, why couldn't we just study the Civil War or the Vietnam War or some other war? There were enough of them. At the same time, I *was* kinda curious. Maybe I could learn more about, I don't know, how my family got here—about Dad? At the same time, I didn't want the extra attention on me, because, sadly, it didn't seem like there were any other METCO kids in the class. So I *knew* the attention would be on me. Because, yeah. Double ugh.

Our teacher, Mr. Phelps, started things off by holding a class debate. First he projected this onto the whiteboard from his computer:

> *The United States federal government should*
> *substantially increase its legal protection of*
> *economic migrants in the United States.*

He read it out loud a couple of times. All I could hear was the hot hum of his laptop. Why was he showing us this? Because of the president's Build a Wall obsession? What kind of wall, anyway? And who would actually build it? Okay. If getting our brains spinning was his goal, he'd succeeded.

As if he'd read my mind, Mr. Phelps tapped his keyboard, and up came a picture of the president wearing a blue suit and red tie and speaking into a microphone. A speech bubble said:

> *We want a great country. We want a country*
> *with heart. But when people come up, they*

have to know they can't get in. Otherwise it's
never going to stop.

WTF?! I glanced around, but no one else seemed as outraged as I was—or else they had freakin' good poker faces. Next Mr. Phelps played a short clip from a documentary about child migrants trying to flee Central America to the US by climbing cargo trains that traveled up through Honduras, El Salvador, Guatemala, and Mexico. In the clip, two teenage boys were lying on top of a massive train, the wind flattening their hair, the sun in their eyes, as they tried desperately to hang on tight as the train blasted through a tunnel in a mountain. I gasped out loud. The clip ended right before the train moved into the darkness.

This time everyone moaned. Someone shouted, "Oh, come on! You can't do that! Play the rest of the video!"

Mr. Phelps looked all smug, like his unit "hook" had worked. Well, it had. We were interested. Invested. Sitting up.

He then explained how the debate would work. We would argue for or against these quotes. Simple. Hands flew up left and right. Not mine! One kid said, "Who can't get in? You mean immigrants? Look, we're all immigrants. Seriously, we should just give the country back to the Native Americans." I nodded. I mean, she had a point.

"Yeah, but . . . then what happens to all of *us*? There are like, half a billion people in the United States. Where are we all supposed to go, huh?" a girl in the front row asked.

Another student raised his hand. "Well, those quotes you

showed kind of raise a good point. If people think they can just, like, keep getting in, then yeah, it's never gonna stop. You know what? We *should* build a wall."

A guy in the back—I'd seen him hanging around with Dustin—jumped in next. "Well, I don't know about the wall. And I'm not against immigrants or whatever, but they should come educated, and like, without any diseases."

Diseases?!? Wow. Dustin had some whack friends.

"Totally," two other guys joined in.

"That's *totally* unfair. Didn't *Europeans* bring over small-pox or whatever?" a guy by the door asked.

"Whatever. We're talking about *today*," the girl beside me said.

"Don't *whatever* me," Door Boy said.

All the voices started to blend in, and I couldn't tell who was saying what. I just know that the next comment was from the kid in front of me. "I'm sorry, but this is just . . . wrong. You can't deny people their human rights. They go through all that trouble to get here, and then what? We spray tear gas on them when they're steps from the border? Or we're just going to send them back?"

If I slouched any lower, I'd fall out of my seat.

Then Mr. Phelps did something I abhorred (vocab word). He called on me directly. "Miss Cruz, do you have anything you'd like to add?"

Oh crap. "No," I said fast.

"You sure?" He was so aggy. I dug my nails into my thighs.

"Yup." Now everyone was *staring* at me.

Mr. Phelps squatted beside my desk like he was my personal coach. Gahhh! "The class may seem hard now, but stick with it," he said in a low voice. Then he stood up and clicked to the next screen, some pie chart with statistics. Humiliation complete. I flipped up my hood.

Hard? I was used to hard. Like two weeks' worth of laundry in one day because Mom never left the couch anymore. Like standing over Christopher and Benjamin until they brushed their teeth *and* flossed. But explaining my perspective on immigration to a bunch of white kids in a richie-rich school? That wasn't hard. Nah. That was just annoying.

Okay, to be totally honest, it wasn't just annoying. And okay, maybe it was hard. But hard in the sense of, why did *I* have to talk? Be the one to make like, an official statement or something? God. I *didn't* know everything. But—but, but, but—I *did* want to be there, in that room, part of that discussion. It's just that, well, I wasn't used to being the only brown person. At my old school I was in the majority. Besides Missie, the minority consisted of like one Irish kid named Casey, who everyone called Casper.

Was it like this for *everyone* in METCO? How would I even know? It wasn't like the other METCO kids were exactly winning awards for going out of their way to be helpful. Well, except for Rayshawn. But he was always surrounded by other kids, or at basketball. And there was Genesis. *She* seemed to weave in and out of groups—METCO, theater club, Honor Society—like it was nothing. She fit in. I bet *she* didn't get asked for her *perspective*. But she was always mad busy. Then again, she *was* my buddy.

Time to buddy up.

* * * *

I asked Genesis to meet me in the library during study hall, and by "asked" I mean "begged" over text: **PLEASE, GIRL**. I found her at the round table by the window. She had just added a second blue streak to her hair and was taking selfies, messing with the filters on her phone, adding all sorts of graphics and whatnot. I stood there waiting for her to, well, acknowledge me. She didn't. She was swiping away at her phone. Finally I couldn't help it, and butt in, "Look, I need to ask you something."

"Sure. What?" She sucked in her cheeks. Press.

"So how do you do it?"

"Do what?" Now she was pouting her lips, holding her phone at arm's length. Press.

"Like, go back and forth? You, like, cruise around, acting like yourself, but also, at the same time, kinda white—and then what? You go home and eat arroz con gandules and plátanos fritos and call it a day?" There. I'd asked it. She was the first person I'd ever spoken to like this, *could* speak to like this.

Her eyes softened suddenly, went younger, despite the fact that she was wearing fake lashes.

And she put her phone down.

"Lili," she started.

She nodded to me to sit.

"Listen, girl. And I mean, hear me. You have to get this right." She tapped the table with a fingernail. "So . . . this school right here is like the world. What I mean is, you have to act a certain way. Or, more like, you have to *carry* yourself a certain way—in order to get what you want, and what you need." She looked me head-on. "When I first got here, I was all 'This place is whack. I'm going back to Boston.' But even after a whole bunch of shit happened, I realized that I didn't *want* to go back. What for? I had so many more opportunities here, and I'm not bullshitting you. I really did. You do too."

She paused at last, but before I could even open my mouth to respond, she went right on. "What I'm saying, Liliana, is that you have to stick it out. It's not perfect, and yeah, some kids and sometimes even some of the teachers say racist shit, but just take it all in stride or whatever. Get yours. Do *you*. They have this many AP classes at your old school?" She didn't give me time to answer. "Don't get it twisted. I love being Latina. I wouldn't trade my identity or my situation for anyone else's, and that's facts, girl. Here, it's actually an *advantage* to be different."

"It is?" I wasn't quite following.

"Yep. Think about it. There are like twenty METCO students and a thousand resident students. There are only like three other Black kids in the whole school who *aren't* in METCO. And everyone thinks they are anyway. So, look. *Work* it. Raise your hand in class. Speak up. Do your assignments. Don't give them an excuse to say that you're just another lazy blah, blah, blah. You get up at what, five a.m?"

I nodded.

"How many non-METCO kids start their day that early? Lazy, my ass."

I nodded again.

"And the other thing—you have to get *involved*. Join a club at least. Rayshawn said they mentioned a ton at the gym the other day. There has to be something you like. It really does look good on your college applications; they love that shit. And volunteer for something. Like, last spring I went to Guatemala to do Habitat for Humanity."

My mouth literally fell open. "You've been to Guatemala?"

"Yeah. It was tight."

I was speechless. Genesis had been there? And I hadn't? And that's where my dad *was*. I felt some kind of way. I really did.

"And I'm trying to go to Sweden this summer. Some program that Guidance told me about . . . ," she was saying, but I was stuck on Guatemala. You could do volunteer projects in *Guatemala*? What if I did something like that—but Genesis interrupted my thoughts by slapping her hand on the table.

"Oh shit. I think the deadline is coming up! Come to think of it, you wanna help me with the essay? You like writing, right?"

I nodded yet again.

"Thanks!" Then she gave me an *I'm serious* look. "Liliana, here's what I'm saying. Make the system work for you. You won't remember these fools twenty years from now when they're calling you up trying to get internships for their kids at the TV station you're working at, writing scripts and shit. You'll be spinning around in your chair in your corner office, being all like, 'Who are you?'"

We both laughed. Truth, I really appreciated her telling

me all this. And, maybe because she'd been to Guatemala, I had the urge to tell her about Dad. But I knew I probably shouldn't.

So instead I asked, "Hey, Genesis?"

"Yeah?"

"So, what do you tell your mom when you want to stay after school?"

She gave me a look. "That I need to stay after school."

"Fine. Okay, but what about when people ask you, 'Where are you from?' I swear, like three people have asked me that since I started here."

Now it was Genesis's turn to nod. "No doubt. Say, 'I'm from my mother.'"

I laughed. "Okay. What if they ask, 'What are you?'"

"Then I say, 'I'm Puerto Rican. What the fuck are you?'"

I laughed again.

"For real, though. Everyone is from somewhere," she said.

"True." Take Dustin, for instance. He was from Westburg. And I was from Boston. And yet, in school, it didn't matter. When we hung out, I only wanted the time to last longer. And so now a new thought was brewing. I'd need to join a club. Stat. Hmmmm. "Okay, listen. I'll help you with your essay. But first, can you do me a favor?"

She was turning a photo of herself black-and-white, all artsy. "What do you need? I gotchu."

"Do you think you could talk to my mother about after-school stuff, extracurricular stuff? She's overprotective—like, mad extra."

Genesis looked up and grinned. "Yeah. I can do that for you."

"For real?"

"For real."

A burst of giggling came from the stacks to the right. I looked over and saw Brianna, a.k.a. Dorito Girl, all close and personal with another student, a white girl. I nearly fell out of my chair. Brianna's hand was on this girl's waist, and the girl was stroking Brianna's hair. "Yo," I said. "Genesis?" She was taking another selfie.

"Yeah?"

I glanced back in a look-over-there way, but Brianna and the girl had vanished.

"Nothing," I said quickly. "It's . . . nothing."

"What?" Genesis pressed.

"I just thought . . . I saw a mouse."

"WHAT!" Genesis yelped like her feet were on fire, her phone clattering onto the floor.

"Ladies!" the librarian hissed, giving us a very stern finger-to-lips, quiet-in-the-library gesture. End of conversation.

I met Dustin at my locker before lunch. This time I came prepared with a peanut butter and jelly sandwich—officially eliminating the possibility of ham teeth. Nice, right? But trailing behind Dustin was Steve. Wait. Was he coming with us? As if reading my mind, Dustin tapped Steve on the shoulder and said, "See ya after lunch, dude." I laughed. But

Steve . . . not so much. He stiffened and shoved his hands into his pockets. "Ditching me for a girl again? K, loser." He didn't even look my way—just stalked off. Now he'd be the one alone at lunch instead of me. A part of me wanted to call out to him. What was the big deal if he joined us? Then I heard him mutter, "*Someone's* got jungle fever." Whaaa? But before I could say anything, Dustin took my hand and squeezed it once, pulling me toward the doors. And I let him. Lunch was officially becoming my favorite part of the day.

As I grabbed the mail after getting off the bus, I could hear music coming from Jade's bedroom window. She was probably working on some art project. I could tell from the loud bass—always meant she was in the zone. I unlocked the apartment door. Shocker: Mom was on the couch, half-asleep.

"Mija," she mumbled. "How was school? Don't forget to take out the trash. And can you go pick up some dish soap? We're out." She yawned, pulled the blanket up to her chin, and closed her eyes again.

"Sure, Mom." I held in a sigh. Dad would hate seeing Mom in this state.

"Oh, Liliana. Your friend called. Genesis." Woo-hoo—Genesis had kept her promise!

"What did she say?" I asked, as if I didn't know.

Mom yawned again. "You know what she said."

Busted. A smile crept onto my face.

"Listen," Mom said. "You can stay after school for activities, but only because it will help you get into college. ¿Entiendes?"

I nodded. "Thanks, Mom." I kissed her on the cheek.

To this day, I have no clue what Genesis actually said to my mother, but it worked. It capital *W* Worked. And so I decided to sign up for art club with Mrs. Davila. Genesis had told me that Mrs. Davila let you work on your own individual projects, and because the club was voluntary, I could sign up and then not go, or go and do my homework, or whatever. Mrs. Davila was cool like that. Anyway, I could work on my cardboard buildings *and* hang out with Dustin, hello, before taking the late bus home!

Late bus = awesome. Now I just had to ask Dustin for his schedule.

Yeah, I was saying "awesome" a lot more since I'd started METCO. Whatever.

Genesis had also told me to keep up my grades because even with great extracurricular activities on my CV or whatever, I still had to have a good GPA. So I was going to double down on my homework. And you know what? I think Dad would have been proud. I mean, at that very moment he was trying to get back to us. I could *sense* it. Least I could do was make it worth it for him. Do my part. Get my education. And what was the big deal if I hung out with a boy named Dustin at the same time? Bonus!

I turned off the living room light, lowered the volume on the television (another reporter going on about the wall), and got the trash. I know it sounds obvious, but the trash *stunk*. Like, I had to hold my breath while carrying it to the bin outside. When I opened the lid, it was even worse. It reminded me of the time Dad carried home a whole pig from the market in Hyde Park. Like, the *entire* thing. He spent all morning making some dis-GUST-ing stew that made the entire apartment reek for like a week. My brothers and I were dying-laughing when Dad took the pig's snout and tried to put it on his nose, then on Mom's. I'd grabbed the disposable camera from the kitchen drawer and taken a picture. For real, it was one of the best pictures I have of him. Where was that photo, anyway? I dropped the lid on the bin, dashed back upstairs, and looked all over my room. Nada. Grrr. But I spied my purple notebook.

And all of a sudden I was writing. About the pig stew. Then about all the times we went to Castle Island in Southie, how we'd sit on a blanket and eat sandwiches Mom had packed. We were never allowed to eat out at Sully's, even though the hamburgers and French fries smelled soooooo good. Too expensive, Dad said. But he *did* always let us get ice cream. In fact, that was his sure way to get us to leave him and Mom alone for a while. When we'd come back, Christopher and Benjamin all hyper and begging for more money so they could get a second ice cream, Dad would have his arm around Mom's waist, and she'd look all girly like they were on a first date or something. It was kind of gross and kind of cool at the same time, you know, for your parents to be in love and all.

Page after page filled up as an explosion of Dad memories broke through. Like, when we showed up at a party without him, everyone would always ask, "¿Y tu papá?" Sometimes he'd arrive later, sometimes not at all. But when he did, he was that guy—the one who'd open bottles of Coronas by banging the bottle cap against the edge of a countertop, the one who held the rope for a piñata, the one who pulled Mom away from the other women and danced salsa with her on the lawn or the porch or in the driveway, wherever the party had space for a dance floor, and he'd twirl her and dip her and hold her close.

The more I wrote, the more I was smiling and the sadder I got, which, yeah, makes no sense. Plus I couldn't get this image—this image of my dad trying to scale over this giant wall, and sliding down, and trying again—out of my mind. My dad, all by himself. Without us to help, trying to climb this wall. Stop! I switched to working on Yoli's Pasteles y Panadería. I glued a picture of a three-tiered cake from a magazine onto the window, and boom, that building was done. Then I started on Lorenzo's Liquor Store. In red marker I wrote *ATM Lotto* and *Money Orders* on teeny pieces of paper for the front window.

Mom called from the living room. "Liliana? The soap."

Shoot. I'd totally spaced. "Sorry! I forgot."

"It's okay. I'll get it. I need to pick up your brothers, anyway." I heard Mom lock the apartment door.

A half hour later, she and the boys were back from the YMCA. At least Mom had done that one thing, pick up the boys. Well, actually, I think technically a parent *had* to pick up their kids, so that didn't even count. No one felt like cooking, so we ate Cup O'Noodles for dinner. Again. At least I had the option of staying after school now, which meant spending less time at home. Where Dad wasn't.

For five weeks now. Eight hundred and some odd hours. I wasn't even going to do the math for the minutes.

A week later, I stood at the entrance to the cafeteria, scanning my options in dread. Dustin's coach wanted the team to eat together in the gym now and go over drills or something. Steve was probably happy about *that*. He threw total attitude when Dustin hung out with me instead of him—on Friday I overheard him say to Dustin, *She's got you whipped!* but Dustin just fake-punched him in the arm and we went to the bleachers anyway. Sooooo, no more Dustin lunches; I took a deep breath and headed for the METCO table. Points for trying, right?

"Hey," I said, remembering Genesis's advice. "Is Rayshawn coming to lunch?" I avoided Dorito Girl's eye.

A guy with a blue hoodie looked up. "Who wants to know?"

"Me."

"Hey, don't you hang with Genesis?" one girl snarked.

"I know Genesis," another girl said. "Genesis Peña, a senior, right?"

"Yeah," the first girl said.

Dorito Girl gave one of her eye rolls. "Pffft. She's a total gringa."

"Whatever," I mumbled.

JENNIFER DE LEON

Maybe that was why Genesis didn't waste her time with them.

I reached for my phone. Was secretly hoping I had a text from Dustin. Jade. Even Mom! Just so I could do something with my hands. No luck.

I put my phone back in my pocket.

I was heading out of the cafeteria for my hallway loop, feeling like a total loser, thinking I'd maybe beg the secretaries to let me sit in there, when I spotted that girl Holly, the one with the gum on her sneaker from my first day. She was last in line for ice cream. I took a deep breath, grabbed an ice cream sandwich, and stood in line behind her. When it was her turn to pay, she said, "Oh, fuck. My money's in my locker." She stepped aside to double-check her pockets. This was my chance.

I quickly paid for my ice cream sandwich.

"You want half of mine?" I held it in the air.

Holly paused, as if I'd asked her a trick question. "Why? What'd you do to it?"

I laughed, perhaps a little too loud, a little too eager. "Nothing. I swear. It hasn't even been opened. See?" I handed it to her.

"Thanks," Holly said, opening it, then breaking half off. "It's Liliana, right?"

Now it was my turn to pause. "How'd you know that?"

"I'm your METCO host sister or whatever. I tried talking to you on your first day, but . . ."

But I was a total jerk to her. *That's* why she had been

trying to talk to me that morning. Nice, Liliana. "About that—" I started.

"Whatever," she interrupted. "Everyone skitzes out on the first day. Wanna come sit?" She bit into her half of the ice cream sandwich.

What? Come sit? "Sure," is what I said.

I followed Holly, who joined a group of three other girls, ones I recognized from the halls. The three stared, expressionless, at me. They looked like triplets. Same height, same pale complexion, same brown hair parted down the middle. Maybe they were sisters.

Holly motioned for me to take a seat. *Thank you, God.*

I finished eating my half of the ice cream, the ham sandwich stuffed back into my backpack. The other girls just chewed their lunches and stared, chewed and stared, until my left leg started bouncing like it does when I'm all anxious. Luckily, the others couldn't see that from where they sat.

"So how do you two know each other?" one of the triplets asked at last.

Holly's mouth was full but she answered anyway. "I'murhmhosidoor."

"What?"

She wiped her mouth with her napkin. "Sorry." She cleared her throat. "I'm her host sister."

"For METCO," I added. The other girls glanced away.

"Yeah," Holly said. "I was trying to welcome her to the school on her first day here, you know, like a normal person, but then she freaked out."

JENNIFER DE LEON

"I didn't freak out—"

Holly tilted her head.

Okay, busted. "Well, maybe just a little. Like you said, first day weirdness."

Holly smiled. Unscrewed her water bottle and took a long sip. Man, people really loved drinking water here.

"Well, anyway, I go by 'Lili,'" I added.

"You *go* by 'Lili'? Do you need a talent manager? Because I could use an extracurricular activity on my résumé," Holly said, thankfully in a joking tone. "Need all the help I can get to get into Stanford."

"Stanford?" I tried not to make it sound like a question even though it was a question. Yes, I'd heard of Stanford, but in a general way. Like, I knew it was a college, but I didn't know much else.

"It's in California," Holly said.

"California," I repeated, like an idiot. Obviously I knew where California was, not that I'd been there, but I could identify it on a map, hello.

"Yeah, California. As in three thousand miles away. That way I can live as far away from my annoying brother as possible."

I wasn't sure how to respond.

"Kidding," Holly added. "Sort of."

"Right." I folded my ice cream wrapper into fourths, then eighths. The brown-haired girls were now ping-pong talking about everything from how annoying gluten-free wannabes were, to whether or not a certain teacher would drop the lowest quiz score, to guys—guys with names like Aiden, Jackson, and Ryan. "Ryan is a douche," Holly said, and crossed her arms. My mother would say *She has a mouth on her* or whatever. It's not like I wanted to be this girl's best friend or anything. But I needed somewhere to sit. Speaking of sitting, from the corner of my eye I spotted Steve play-pulling this girl Erin—I recognized her from Mr. Phelps's class—onto his lap. She jumped up and jabbed his shoulder, but he pulled her onto his lap again. *He* was the douche.

"So. Lili—" Holly interrupted my thoughts. "What do you think of Westburg so far?"

"I love it," I lied.

"Yeah, fucking right you do," Holly said, one eyebrow raised. "Westburg is boring as hell."

I laughed out loud. So, not best friends forever, but we would get along fine.

So get this. On Saturday morning, like crazy early, like, the sun was hardly up, Mom—with zero notice—woke me up to inform me that my tía Laura and her husband were coming to visit from Guatemala. As in, that day. Um . . . what? Once it actually woke up, my brain started churning. Obviously this had something to do with Dad. Then my brain stopped churning as Mom gave me clean-my-room orders. "I want it spotless by the time I get back from the airport." She straightened piles of mail on the kitchen counter and then wiped away a few stray crumbs with the side of her hand. Whoa. The kitchen was practically gleaming.

"Why? They're not even going to see my room."

Luckily, it was my brothers' room they would be staying in, not mine. The twins would be sleeping on the pull-out sofa bed, and they were actually excited about it. Phew. I'd dodged a major one. No way I was going to give up my room, not even for old people. Does that make me a terrible person?

"Just clean it, Liliana." My mother sounded exhausted. How could someone who slept so much be so exhausted?

"Okay, okay." I hesitated, gauging her mood, then asked, "So, Mom, does this have something to do with Dad? It does, doesn't it?"

Mom suddenly got *very* busy taking down a fancy crystal sort of bowl thing she'd gotten way back when she and Dad got married, one that she, like, never took off the top shelf of the cupboard, and started polishing it.

I tried a different tack. "How long are they staying?"

"Liliana. Por favor." She set the bowl in the center of the counter. Began arranging a bunch of bananas in it, moving it to the left, then the right.

"Fine," I grumbled, and went to clean my room.

I heard the front door close a few minutes later. Mom had left for the airport. So, yeah, technically I *was* cleaning my room—folding shirts, arranging my hair products on top of the bureau, but I was also talking to Dustin. *Talking*, not even texting! A few minutes of chillin' on my bed, phone glued to my ear, turned into a couple of hours. You know how that happens. Don't lie.

Suddenly I heard voices and laughter. Shit! I told Dustin I had to go, then bellowed, "Benjamin! Christopher! Shut off the TV!"

My brothers for once listened. Even they knew what was expected. Whenever relatives from Guatemala visited, my brothers and I had to be on our best behavior, like fake children or something. We wore clothes we never usually wore, like corduroys and collared shirts, like we were going to take a family portrait at Sears or something. Smile. Sit up straight.

Give the guests something to drink. If there were kids, we had to play with them. Share our toys. When they left, we had to offer our toys to them—to *keep*. Yes. It was ridiculous. I learned not to show off my best stuff—the newer Barbies, or the bottles of neon pink and yellow nail polish. Yep. I really am a terrible person!

Luckily, Tía Laura and her husband—honestly, I keep calling him "her husband" because I forget his name, Rodolfo or Refugio or something—were childless. I mean, not exactly lucky for them, but lucky for me, because maybe the fact that she had had no children of her own was the reason why Tía Laura had agreed to take in my dad when he was little. Dad's real parents were killed in some war. I don't really know much about it—it wasn't something Dad ever talked about.

"Hola," my mother called out in her fake TV voice from the front door. *Here we go.* I yanked a brush through my hair and headed for the living room. I just wanted to get this part of their visit over with so I could get back to Dustin. But— wait. They probably knew something about Dad, so maybe I should stick around a while?

"Hi," I said, hugging my aunt and uncle. "Bienvenidos," I added like a good daughter. Then we all stood there like a bunch of idiots just smiling and nodding at each other. Sorry, but it was true. It was mad awkward that my father wasn't there, and I was sure everyone else was thinking the same thing.

"A la gran . . . ," Tío R. was starting to say as he gave me a once-over that kind of gave me the creeps. He was old and freckled, and he had tufts of white hair pushing out of his ears. He was short, but not as short as Tía Laura.

She was soooooo short. The same height as Benjamin, who was the slightly smaller twin. For real, Tía Laura looked like a miniature person. I hadn't seen her in probably three years. Her black curly hair had white roots showing, giving her head a skunk-like look. And now she had a missing tooth. I tried not to stare.

Tía Laura squealed in agreement. "Liliana! You look like a woman!"

I never knew what to say to comments like that, especially because then everyone just stared at my body.

"Do you need help with your bags? Moving them to your room?" I asked to distract them. Plus, look at how polite I can be, Mom! I gestured toward their maroon suitcases. Somehow this question ignited giggles.

"She's so funny—" Tía Laura said.

"Verdad," Tío R. chimed in, shaking his head. "Those aren't jobs for girls."

My mouth fell open. Mom didn't even notice. "Por favor, sit down," she was telling them. On the coffee table: Ritz crackers on a white plate arranged in a circle, a block of cheese and a small knife in the center. The cheese still had the clear wrapping on it. Then she turned to me and mouthed, *Get the boys.* They were taking *forever* to get dressed.

"And get drinks for everyone," my mother whispered next, giving me the *You should have already thought of that* look.

A few minutes later I returned holding glasses of iced tea, the ice cubes clinking and popping. First I set one in front of Tía Laura, who promptly handed it to her husband. I gave her the second glass as my brothers scampered in, all decked out in the clothes our mother must have set out for them—checkered sweater-vests and white button-downs, khakis and shiny shoes like for church, even though it was Saturday.

"Gracias," Tía Laura said. Tío R. didn't say anything, just started patting the top of Benjamin's head like he was a dog. My brother looked like he wanted to evaporate. Christopher began eating cheese and crackers like he was in a cheese-and-cracker-eating contest. Mom glared at him and he cut it out real quick. It was hard not to laugh.

"So, Liliana." Tío R. crossed his legs and leaned back on the couch. "Do you have a boyfriend?"

I practically choked on the cracker I had just bitten into. Dustin-Dustin-Dustin! "Uh . . . no." *Please change the subject. Please change the subject.*

As my mother offered Tío and Tía napkins, in a no-nonsense tone she explained, "Liliana is not allowed to date until she is eighteen." Saved by Mom! But—wait—eighteen?! *Eighteen?* I decided to let that go for now.

Benjamin and Christopher snorted. I wished I could aim the remote at them and turn them off.

But Tía Laura's eyes grew mischievous. She leaned forward. "But my Sylvia. You dated well before that, didn't you?" She took a dainty sip of tea, staring down my mother, who sat like a saint, her hands folded on her lap.

"Memory can get fuzzy with age, no?" Mom said it like a statement instead of a question.

"Not mine," Tía Laura responded, holding back a smile.

Oh snap!

Here's the thing. Tía Laura had had no formal education in Guatemala. She could not read or write her own name, but my dad said she remembered every little detail of *everything*. Like this one story she'd told me about Dad. *Your father, oh. When I first started taking care of him, he was like a bird. So whenever I ate a piece of pan dulce, I would only nibble around the edges, save the inside part, the soft doughy part, for him. I'd walk to the school at recess and stick my hand through the fence and pop it into his mouth or sneak it into his hand. I did this a couple of times a day, and before I knew it, he was growing. Then one day, I handed him the ball of pan dulce like always, except this time, I lingered by the fence. And your father, bless him, walked up to a little kid, littler than him, and gave him the ball of pan. I started crying right there on the sidewalk, but they were happy tears, you know?*

I loved Tía's stories. Maybe she was so good at remembering everything—and I mean everything: songs, dichos, proverbs, and especially juicy memories—because she also seemed to save everything, including the napkin she'd just folded into fourths and tucked inside her bra.

"Let's get you settled," Mom said now, changing the subject from dating. Ha—now we were *both* off the hook! Of course this made me crazy curious about when she *had* started dating. "Do you remember where everything is? The kitchen is yours. The bathroom, too. Anything you need, we can get."

"Sí, sí. But first, gifts!" That made Christopher and Benjamin sit up real straight. Tía Laura pointed at her suitcase. Tío R. unzipped and searched and dug and unzipped some more, before finally taking out a few items. My brothers were practically panting, but if they were hoping for some kind of Guatemalan version of video games, they were about to be super disappointed. Tío R. handed a wooden toy to Tía Laura, which she then handed to Benjamin. It was some kind of a wooden spinning top with a picture of a Mayan temple painted on it. "Gracias," Benjamin mumbled. Mom's jaw twitched.

"And for you, Christopher.! Tía Laura gave him a miniature chicken bus painted in bright orange, blue, and yellow, with the word GUATEMALA written across the front of it. Little papayas, watermelons, and bunches of bananas had been glued to the top of the bus. As someone who appreciated miniatures, I thought it was cute, but Christopher, not so much. Maybe he'd let me take the fruits off for my bodega.

Still, he hugged Tía Laura and Tío R. "Muchas gracias." My mother beamed.

"Wait!" Tía Laura suddenly yelped, as if we were all going to get up and leave. She pushed Tío aside, rummaged through the suitcase herself, and unwedged about a pound of white tissue paper. Then she took forever opening all the layers, until she got to the center—a magnet of the Guatemalan flag. She placed it triumphantly into my mother's hand. Squeezed. "For you, Sylvia."

"Oh, how pretty," Mom gushed, like it was jewelry or something. Well, it was sort of practical, unlike the enormous—I'm talking how-did-they-fit-in-the-suitcase enormous—wooden fork and spoon wall pieces they'd brought last time, which hung in our kitchen to this day.

Tía was already rustling through more tissue paper. "Last but not least, for you, Liliana." She passed me a royal-blue-and-purple textile thing. I held it up, planting an *I love it* look on my face. Was it a purse? A belt? A headband? "A holder for your water bottle," Tía Laura declared.

I did *not* look at Christopher, who was one glance away from hysterical laughter. "Muchas, muchas gracias," I said. When I got up to give Tía Laura a hug, I stepped on Christopher's toe. On purpose.

After Mom finished the grand tour (even though my aunt and uncle had been there before, and hello, there were only five rooms, six if you counted the bathroom), Tía Laura gently led me by the elbow into the hallway. She stood so close that I could smell her old-country smell, like what every relative from Guatemala's suitcase smelled like: burning firewood and sweet corn and dirt after the rain. And a hint of Head & Shoulders shampoo.

"Como te pareces a Fernando," my aunt said, running her palm along the side of my face. "¡Igualita!"

Unexpectedly, the sound of my father's name brought tears to my eyes.

"Don't cry, mija," she murmured, and squeezed me tight.

She leaned in even closer (which, I'm telling you, was hard to do because she was already mad close). "No matter what, he will always love you, mija."

What the heck did *that* mean?

"Thanks?"

She dropped her voice down to a whisper. "He is trying really hard to come back. You must know that. You have to believe that he will make it back safely. Si Dios quiere." She made a cross over her chest.

I froze. *Safely?* And why did he need prayers? How exactly was he planning to come back?

"Tía?" I asked. "What do you mean, *safely*?"

"Laura!" Tío R-something called from down the hall.

Tía Laura's eyes widened.

"Tía, please?" I begged.

She pressed a finger to her lips, then turned to catch up with my uncle.

Later, while Tía and Tío were taking a jet lag nap, I approached my mom in the kitchen. She was stirring batter for a Magdalena cake. The empty box sat crookedly on the counter. On the front a white hand presented the finished cake on a pink platter. I wondered if it would be a better cake than the one I had for my birthday last year. I cleared my throat. "Mom?"

"What is it, Liliana?" She poured the batter into the Bundt pan; it looked delicious. I reached for a spoon to lick what remained in the mixing bowl.

"Tía Laura said something about Dad making it back *safely*."

A flicker of worry crossed my mother's forehead. She suddenly got very busy pushing buttons on the oven.

I didn't want to add to her stress, but I had to know. So I pressed. "Well, she said that Dad needed prayers . . . to help him *make it* back. What did she mean by that?"

"Oh . . ." My mother pushed at the temperature buttons so many times that the oven started beeping.

"Mom! You bake at three-fifty. Not five hundred." Even *I* knew that! I moved her hand away and adjusted the temperature, set the timer.

Ignoring me, Mom reached for the Bundt pan. It slid from her hand and started careening off the counter. I caught it just in time. "Mom! Tell me what's going on!"

"Not now, Liliana." She wiped her hands on the embroidered towel—a gift from Tía from three years before—hanging from the refrigerator handle. "Finish the cake?" She opened the oven door for me before leaving the kitchen. A moment later I heard her bedroom door click shut.

13

Safely, Tía had said. Tía, who was visiting for whatever reason. *Safely.* The thought began pricking at me. What if things weren't as simple as straightening out paperwork? Would Dad have to sneak across the border to come back? *Literally* climb an actual wall? No, no. My dad was smart. Street smart. He'd find a way to get back to us without putting himself in danger. I mean . . . right? But Tía had said *make it back. . . .*

So Mom wasn't going to dish the info. Fine. I'd just have to get it out of Tía Laura. But first, I peeked in on my brothers. They were sniping at each other about who knows what in the living room. Poor kids. They basically escaped to the video game world probably like I did with making miniatures, or writing. Right before I walked in, I overheard Benjamin say to Christopher, "How long are they staying here? And when's Dad coming home?"

"Hey!" I called out. Benjamin glanced up.

"What?"

"You guys want to . . . wrestle or something?" I had a flashback of Dad pretending to wince in pain as one of the boys pinned him down, and I gave my head a shake.

Christopher narrowed his eyes. "Seriously?"

"Yeah," I said, all enthusiastic-like. "We can . . ." I paused to think of a way to make it more fun. . . . Ah! "Put pillows in our T-shirts and wrestle sumo-style. Want to?"

They looked at each other and with their twin ESP thinking came to a silent decision, because Christopher picked up the remote control. "Maybe later."

I tried.

An hour later, in the kitchen, Tía Laura was drinking beer, a fan of cut limes in front of her. Tía *liked* her beer. And she was talking nonstop and sort of yelling-laughing to my other aunt on the phone. Mom had gone to the corner store to get stuff for dinner. Tío R. was taking a pre-dinner siesta, not to be confused with his jet lag siesta. He'd eaten half the Magdalena cake for lunch. He sure was comfortable here!

"¿Con permiso? Tía?" Normally I wouldn't interrupt an adult on the phone, but it sounded like she was about to get off.

She didn't hear me, just kept talking a mile a minute.

"Tía?" I repeated, louder.

She turned and blinked at me as if trying to remember who I was. Maybe she was more buzzed than I thought.

"Te llamo después," she said into the phone, and hung up, just like that.

She popped a thick wedge of lime into her mouth and sucked on it, smiling with her eyes as I joined her at the table.

I actually really liked Tía Laura. Usually I caught like

80 percent of what she was saying. Her Spanish was fast and full of slang, and she was funny. I liked how her whole body laughed when she laughed. Her arms would fall to her sides, and she'd lean over like she was about to fall, but at the last second she'd straighten herself up and let out an enormous laugh that was, no lie, contagious.

"Tía? So . . . by any chance . . . have you been in touch with my dad?"

"You know . . ." She paused to take a sip of her beer. "You should talk to your father before—"

WAIT. It was possible to *talk* to Dad? Had Mom talked to him? How often? And she didn't she let me, or the boys?!?! *Slow down, slow down*—I needed to play this cool.

"If I knew his number, I would love to talk to him," I said, as in HINT, HINT—do *you* want to call him, like right now, and pass me the phone? I picked up a knife and began to cut a lime peel into tiny pieces.

But Tía stayed quiet, set down the now empty beer can. I got her a second from the refrigerator.

"Gracias, mija." She cracked it open, letting loose that great little hissing sound.

I eyed her. "Tía, can I ask you something?"

She shrugged. "Ask or don't ask, but don't ask whether you can ask, mija."

I picked at a hangnail. "Okay, well . . . What did you mean when you said you hoped Dad would make it back *safely*? Is he in, like, danger? Is this why . . . you're here?"

She twanged the pull tab on her beer can. "I'm here to

get money, to bring back to Guatemala, sí, for your father."

Got it. Money. So . . . did that mean she got to *see* him? That she'd *seen* him?

And *of course* that was when Mom barged in the front door, yelling, "Come help with these bags!"

Tía whispered, "Mija . . . he is paying a coyote to help him cross."

Boom.

14

"Earth to Lili." Holly poked me in the arm.

"What? Oh—sorry!" I gave my head a shake, trying to refocus on whatever it was Holly was talking about. But my mind was on the bomb Tía had dropped the other night. Dad had hired a coyote. Normally I was not so bad at compartmentalizing home and school, but this—this was *major*.

"Am I *boring* you?" Holly now verbally poked. "You're like spacing out here!"

"I know. I'm so sorry. I've just got a lot on my mind. My aunt and uncle are visiting from Guatemala, and they're kind of . . . making me crazy." So—not true, but not *entirely* a lie. What Tía had said *was* making me crazy, worrying.

Holly now looked at me, her lips pursed. "*You* need a break, is what's up. Why don't you come over after school?"

"You mean to your house?"

"No. Not my house," Holly said, throwing some snark. "Come over to my cardboard box under a bridge. Yes! To my house."

Sunlight pushing through a tall window in the cafeteria made her hair glow. And she'd just invited me to her house.

And suddenly I was wondering how big her room was rather than how you even *hired* a coyote. I wondered what snacks she had in her kitchen. Of course I wanted to go! But, hello—my mother . . .

"I'm not sure I can, because my aunt and uncle—well, they need lots of entertaining." I looked over my shoulder. It was a weird thing that I'd caught myself doing all day. It wasn't like I was worried Dad would show up with a coyote in the hallway or anything, but—I don't know. I felt nervous now, like down to my toes, ever since Tía had told me about my father.

Holly nudged me. "So? It doesn't have to only be *you* doing the entertaining."

"I—I mean, I don't know," I stammered. "My parents are kind of strict." *That* was not a lie! Translation: my parents had never let me go to someone's house besides family or family friends that they'd known for years.

"So, they won't let you go to a friend's house? That's weird." Holly instantly grimaced like she regretted what she'd said. "Sorry. It's just that, going to your friend's house is kind of, I don't know . . ."

"Normal?"

"Yeah." Holly shrugged.

I picked up my lunch tray. Normal? What *was* normal? I bet it didn't involve worrying about whether Border Patrol was going to catch your dad.

I faced Holly. "You'd think. But okay, thanks. I'll ask." Then it dawned on brilliant me. I didn't have to ask! I'd just let Mom think I was going to art club like any other day. Yes!

But the more I thought about it, the more anxious I got. What if I missed the late bus home? So just in case, I decided I *should* tell Mom about going to Holly's. But, of course, of all days, I'd flippin' left my phone at home. I KNOW. So, during study hall I asked for a pass to the nurse, said I had a headache. No lie—except it wasn't the type an aspirin would help. Then the nurse told me, as I had hoped, that I needed to call my mother to get permission to take aspirin. When my mother picked up, I spoke in Spanish for the whole call. Times like these, I really loved being bilingual.

"Liliana? What's wrong? What happened? Where are you?" That's Mom. Instantly hysterical.

"Fine. Nothing. School. I left my phone at home, so I'm calling you from the nurse's office."

"Oh." Mom paused. "So what's the matter? Are you *sick*?"

I quickly reassured her that there was nothing wrong.

"Nothing? You called for nothing? What *is* it, Liliana? I'm late."

In the background I could hear her scrambling—the faucet running, the microwave beeping. She was probably getting ready for another interview. All of a sudden she's been trying to get work as a housekeeper—said it paid more. And now I understood why, and why it was so difficult for her to get a job. Probably everyone wanted to see papers! How much money did Dad even need anyway? I bet a lot. And, even with Tía and Tío there now, Mom was still losing it. Just yesterday I found my sock drawer rearranged by color—by *color*.

"Well, my new friend here, this girl Holly? She and her family are my host family. I told you about the METCO host families. So, she's really nice. She has red hair. Anyway, Holly asked if I could come over to her house to study for a big test in bio we have next Monday, and you know I really want to make a good impression on my new teachers here, and this test is going to suck. I mean, it's going to be really hard, so everyone is studying extra for it. Holly's mom can drive me back to the school so I can catch the late bus to Boston. I'll be home by seven. So can I go?"

"Fine."

"Really?"

"I have to go, mija. Ahorita."

"Okay." *My mother had said fine!* What universe was I in?

"Wait!" she yelled just as I was about to hang up. The nurse was giving me a look like, *You know, I haven't heard the word "aspirina" once during your entire conversation.*

"Yeah?"

"Call back right away and leave the girl's name and address and phone number on my voice mail. Just in case. I won't pick up."

"Okay."

"Don't forget."

"*I won't.* Good luck."

"Love you."

"You too." I hung up.

I thanked the nurse, told her I no longer needed aspirin, and returned to study hall, where I couldn't focus on my math homework. The numbers all translated to money, which got me thinking about how Tía Laura and Tío R. had flown all the way to Boston to collect cash to bring it all the way back down to Guatemala for Dad, I guess because wiring the money was too dangerous. But the plane tickets alone had to be mad expensive, so how much did a coyote cost? Couldn't exactly pay that with a credit card, hello. And money was the *easier* part! I mean, Dad would be trusting his life to a *stranger*—even if that person was the best smuggler around—with his actual life. And, *actually*, how far away *was* Guatemala from the US border? I didn't even know! And all of a sudden I *had* to know. I closed my math book and again asked for a pass before heading to the library.

On my way there I passed the METCO office and overheard two girls laughing. I slowed down, peeked inside without trying to be mad obvious. They were eating Halloween candy from a bowl in the shape of a pumpkin. I recognized one as Ivy. But the other part of me was on a mission. Guatemala.

Score. One of the library computers was free. I sat down and Googled "Guatemala." Up came:

- a Wikipedia article and map
- photos of volcanoes
- news articles about people looking for disappeared family members
- a recipe for tamales

"I love tamales!" I yelped. The librarian gave me a disapproving look. "Sorry. . . . Charley horse," I said, as if that would explain my tamale outburst. I clicked on the map. Dad was *there*. Huh. I knew Dad had come to the US when he was eighteen, but I never thought about how he'd gotten into the US to begin with. Mom had come to Boston from El Salvador two years after him. They'd met at a party, and that was that. I kept scrolling. Countries that bordered Guatemala: Mexico, Belize, El Salvador, and Honduras. Next I read some quick facts:

- home to volcanoes, rain forests, and ancient Mayan sites
- capital is Guatemala City and boasts lots of museums
- the old capital, Antigua Guatemala, features preserved Spanish colonial buildings
- Lake Atitlán, formed in a massive volcanic crater, is a major tourist attraction
- Guatemala is roughly the size of Louisiana

Jeez, I hadn't known *any* of this. I wish I'd asked more questions about Guatemala. I had sort of wondered why Mom and Dad never took us there, you know, to visit, especially since we had tons of relatives and everything was less expensive. (Mom and Dad were always comparing US prices to things "back home.")

JENNIFER DE LEON

I clicked on "Images," and up came dozens and dozens of photos of coffee fields, villages, women wearing traditional dresses and skirts made of a zillion different colors, kids as young as my brothers carrying big baskets of vegetables on their heads, a blond lady overlooking a huge lake while meditating on a yoga mat, a giant cross in front of a giant church, a Mayan ruin called Tikal, skyscrapers beside an old fountain, a couple getting married on a cobblestone street in Antigua with plump clouds and pink skies behind them, and a rug on a street made entirely of colored sawdust! I couldn't stop scrolling. Why hadn't Dad ever told me about any of this stuff? Once in a while he went all nostalgic—telling us how the chicken tasted much better there and how people looked you in the eye more—but then he'd go back to doing whatever he was doing. Or maybe . . . maybe it was that I never asked him to tell me more? Maybe he didn't think I was interested? Dad—I'm interested!

Suddenly I felt the presence of the librarian behind me. "Can I help you search for something?" she asked. Her tone reminded me of those annoying salespeople who followed me down the aisles, probably thinking I was going to steal something.

"Oh . . . no, thank you," I said, immediately clicking on the *x* in the corner of the screen. Oh God. Now she probably thought I'd been looking up porn or something.

"I see that you were reading up on Guatemala." Again with the tone! She sounded like I *had been* looking up porn.

I legit didn't know what to say.

"Are you writing a report?"

"Sort of . . . I mean, it's . . . extra credit." Good save!

"It's nice to see students take advantage of extra credit," she enthused. "But—" She glanced at the clock. "This period is almost over. I can leave some books and resources on reserve, and you can pick them up later if you'd like. Good for you. To learn more about these people."

These people?

On my way out of the library, I headed to Mr. Phelps's class, "these people" still running through my head. I was the first one there. Mr. Phelps sat on a stool, hunched over his laptop, his glasses about to fall off the tip of his nose. Mr. Phelps was kinda growing on me (even though he still went overkill on asking if I understood the material and all).

He was really ramping up the immigration unit. Like, he'd added all these books to our extra-credit reading list, and he'd been showing us parts of documentaries about immigration but from different points of view. One was about the women who leave their children in Honduras and Guatemala and El Salvador to come to the United States to work as maids and housekeepers and stuff, and send the money back. It was crazy sad to see how they were sometimes separated from their kids for their entire childhoods, missing their kids' birthdays, graduations, everything. And here I complained when Mom made me call Tía Rosa on her birthday. And she was only in New York. Plus, I had both my parents with me—well, I *used* to—unlike the kids in the documentaries. I guess I'd always known why my parents had moved to the United States. I mean, *in general*: They wanted a better life. But I didn't really understand what they'd had to go through to come here, leaving their own country, language, family, friends, everything. *Everything.* I'd been so clueless!

"Excuse me, Mr. Phelps?" I said.

He looked up. "Oh, hello, Lili."

"If this is a bad time, I can ask you later," I said quickly.

"No. Please. Sit." He shut his laptop. "What can I help you with?"

"Well, remember how you were saying that we could get extra credit for reading a book on immigration?"

"Yes!" Dang, teachers got so excited when kids showed like a speck of interest in anything.

"Well, there was one book you mentioned, one about a boy who travels on top of a train from Mexico to the United States?"

"Guatemala."

"Huh?" I froze. Guatemala?

Mr. Phelps shook his head. "No, not Guatemala, my bad. Honduras. The boy's name is Enrique. The book is about his journey from Honduras to North Carolina." His tone grew gentle. "He was searching for his mother."

"Oh—"

Mr. Phelps was now practically sprinting for the bookshelf. He ran a finger along a few spines. "Here it is!" He handed me a paperback. The cover showed a boy—about my age—perched on top of a huge train. He could have been—my dad? As a teenager? I blinked hard.

"This the one you were thinking of?" Mr. Phelps prompted.

"Yeah. Thanks." *Enrique's Journey* by Sonia Nazario. I shoved the book into my backpack. I didn't want anyone else seeing it. I *was* born here, and I didn't have to prove it to anyone, but it was just easier for me to slide the book into my bag and not make a big deal.

"Lili, I'm glad to see you're interested."

I stayed quiet, balanced my weight on my heels.

"Honduras, I don't know. But Guatemala is actually a beautiful country."

"You've been there?"

"I have! When I was in my twenties, I traveled in Mexico and Guatemala and part of South America." He pushed his glasses up, looked as if he wanted to say something else, or worse—*ask* me something. But he didn't. Instead he told me, "Don't forget. You only get extra credit if you write a response to the book. Minimum of two pages. There's more information on the class website."

The bell rang and other students began to trickle in.

"Right. Okay. Thanks." I paused. "One more thing, Mr. Phelps?"

"Yup?"

"So, do people really make it? I mean, do the people who ride the tops of those trains or hire smugglers, do they really make it across the border?"

His brow furrowed. "Some do."

JENNIFER DE LEON

"Ah, okay. Good to know. Thanks," I said, keeping my voice chill. The rest of me? Not so much. Was he looking at me funny? What if he guessed why I was asking? I found a seat in the back row and took out my homework.

On my way to meet Holly at her locker after school—I gotta admit, I was excited to go to her house, be a *normal* kid—I peeked into Dustin's last class, hoping to catch him. But no luck. I hate not having my phone! Then I stopped at the library. Sure enough, the librarian had set out three books for me on Guatemala. But they were nothing like the ones Mr. Phelps had in his class. These books were . . . basic. Mostly factual and showing photos of exotic birds. I checked out two just so the librarian wouldn't feel bad, but I knew what I was reading first, for sure.

Not twenty minutes later, and faaaaar away from Guatemala, I was stepping through Holly's front door. The smell reminded me of a dentist's office. Well, a mix between a dentist's office and pumpkin pie. Her house was massive. Like, it would take a hell of a lot of cardboard to make even a miniature replica of *that* house. Everything, and I mean everything, was a shade of tan—the paint on the actual house (three stories), the enormous front door, the wall-to-wall carpeting, the tiles in the kitchen. Even the towels in the downstairs bathroom were tan. A wooden-framed

JENNIFER DE LEON

photograph of Holly and her little brother, Max, faced me when I sat on the toilet. In the photo they were laughing so hard, their eyes were nearly shut. I had to hit the bathroom as soon as we got there. Yeah, I was so worried that my pee would be loud that I ran the faucet. Even the bathroom had mad space. And no dog, thank God. Dogs basically freaked me out. Most of the ones I knew lived behind metal fences with BEWARE OF DOG signs. No thank you.

Holly and her mother stopped talking the second I stepped back into the kitchen. The floor was so clean, it could have been in a Clorox commercial. Every detail competed for my attention—like when Holly's mom kept calling us *girls*. I mean, obviously we're girls. But she used it like this: "Would you girls like some snacks?" And she waved toward the island—yes, they had an *island*—in the center of the kitchen. Still, Mrs. Peterson seemed nice enough. Though—ha! She had beige hair! When we were driving here she had asked Holly about her day and then had let Holly play whatever playlist she had on her phone. When a rap song full of swears came on, Holly blasted the volume, and her mother didn't even ask her to turn it down! My mom would have gone ballistic.

On the kitchen island were bowls and platters full of pistachios, chips (the expensive kind where every chip was a different shape), apple slices and cheddar cheese cubes, crackers with flecks of real wheat in them, a dark kind of peanut butter or something on the side, and two empty glasses.

"Thank you for the snacks," I said.

"Would you like some milk, Lili, or juice?" Mrs. Peterson asked.

"Mom. Seriously?" Holly said, sighing dramatically and dunking her hand into the bowl of already-shelled pistachios. "We're not in kindergarten."

I rushed to say, "Oh . . . no thank you, Mrs. Peterson. Water is fine. I can get it."

Holly's mother beamed at me before turning to Holly. "Well . . . Lili certainly has better manners than you."

"Whatever." Holly dropped a handful of pistachios into her mouth. For a skinny white girl, Holly ate like she was anything but. I mean, she wasn't anorexic-looking or anything, but she was thin. Thinner than me.

I ate a chip and looked out the big bay windows that banked the far side of the kitchen, showing off a wide, landscaped yard backed by dozens of tall trees that probably housed some fairy-tale land. I legit felt like I was in the woods, like when we went on a field trip to Blue Hills last year. The glossy leaves glistening in the massive yard—it all looked so perfect, I half expected Bambi would step out between the trees. My brothers would have loved it. And *I* found myself hoping for at least one huge snowstorm this winter. Preferably midweek.

"So how are you liking Westburg? And METCO?" Mrs. Peterson asked. "And you poor thing, the bus ride is so long! Tell me where you're from again, honey. And do you miss your old school? It's perfectly normal, you know."

I didn't know which question to answer first. And I didn't have to, because Holly's mother kept going. She held the horseshoe charm on her gold necklace while she talked. "When I was in high school, my family moved across the country. Can you imagine? It was an adjustment, but in the end, I was so glad we moved to the East Coast. I just fell in love with Cape Cod and the islands. We spend at least a week on Nantucket every summer. You should come with us next time! Anyway, is there anything else I can get you, Lili? Something sweet or savory maybe? I'm a decent cook but not the best baker. Although you're probably used to some great cooking from your mom and all. You know what, though? I can make some mini PB&J's?"

Wow! Her mom was mad extra.

"Mom! Please stop." Holly turned to me. "Sorry. I don't know why she's trying out for the Martha Stewart award right now." She turned back to her mother. "Can you, like, go now?"

I glanced uneasily from Holly to her mother. If I ever spoke to my mother that way, especially in front of a guest, she would probably pinch my arm and lecture me about who the mother was. Instead Holly's mother reached for a bottle of hand lotion inside a coffee-colored wicker basket— of which there were half a dozen on that floor alone—and squirted some onto her hands. Cloves. That was it. The smell was dope.

As she rubbed the lotion into her cuticles, she told Holly that the pizza menu was in the drawer, and she'd be in her office if we needed her. Then she disappeared down the carpeted hallway. Her *office*. No lie, I had never been inside a house that had an *office*. I was actually dying to get a tour, but then I thought that might be rude to ask. So Holly and I hung out in her room instead.

Correction: suite. She even had her own bathroom! One that her uncle wasn't stinking up on the regular, either.

"You even have your own bathroom!" I pointed to it as if Holly might not have noticed it before now.

Holly didn't respond; she was too busy dumping out the contents of a pink wicker basket onto the rug. This family was seriously into their wicker baskets. "Fuck! I thought my charger was in here. I swear. If Max took it again, I'm going to kill him in his fucking sleep."

"Must be a really good charger." I sat cross-legged on the rug.

Time was suspended in Holly's room, in her gigantic house, in the intoxicating smell of the pepperoni pizza her mother had allowed us to order for no special reason. "Look in the cash drawer for smaller bills," her mother had instructed, her voice coming from down the hall, from her *office*. How cool would that be—to have my own office one day? I pictured myself spinning in a black leather chair, writing at my wide desk, pink and yellow Post-its fluttering around like confetti.

"What does your mom do, you know, for work?" I asked Holly.

We were eating slices right from the box. A string

of greasy cheese hung from Holly's lip as she answered, "Consulting," as if that meant anything to me. I was too embarrassed to ask more, so I just reached for another slice of pizza.

Holly was scrolling through different playlists on her laptop. Everything from Taylor Swift to Cardi B to Fetty Wap to old-school hip-hop. I liked how she played music. I mean, she didn't just hit play. She changed it up like a DJ or something.

I hesitated before taking the last slice of pizza. I felt like I should wrap it up in a napkin and bring it home to my brothers. At my house, ordering pizza was something that was reserved for nights like, well, when Dad got a bonus at work, or for my birthday. It was never casual, never, *Well, the pizza menu is in the drawer*.

Suddenly a loud sound, like an earthquake or something, came from under the floor. "What's that?" I yelped.

Holly laughed. "You kill me. It's called my dad coming home from work. You know, parking his car in the garage."

I still found it hard to tell when Holly was being sarcastic. It seemed to be the general way she talked. About everything. Truth, I had never been inside a house with a car garage attached to it. Holly's house had a *triple* car garage. What the heck would they need a third space for anyway?

A minute later, a sweaty boy, maybe eleven or twelve years old, wearing hockey gear head to toe, appeared at Holly's door, sticking his middle finger up at her. "Hi, butt-face."

"Get out of here, Max!"

Holly's brother eyed me up and down. "Hey."

Holly charged across the room and slammed the door in her brother's face. Then she turned up the music even louder.

Holly was shouting over the music about what an idiot her brother was when we heard—barely!—a knock at the door.

"Ugh! It's probably my dad," Holly shouted. "He always has to say hello when he comes home." She said this as if it was the worst thing in the world, to have your dad come say hi when he got home.

Another knock. "Coming, Father," Holly sing-songed, hopping up to open the door.

"Hello, Lili," he said after giving Holly a hug.

"Hi," I said, back to feeling awkward. He looked like a principal—a suit and tie and everything. No—like a superintendent. "Nice to meet you, Mr. Peterson."

"So, girls, how was school?" He smiled warmly at Holly.

"Fine. Um . . . what do you want?"

"What do you say we light up the fire pit out back? We can make Oreo s'mores?"

"Yes!" Holly slapped on the top of her laptop.

I was stunned silent. She'd just been totally rude to her father, and now he was basically rewarding her with dessert? "What are Oreo s'mores?" I asked at last.

"Oh my God. The best thing ever. S'mores, but instead of graham crackers we use Oreos. Insanely delicious. Come on."

"I'll be there in a sec," her father said. "Let me change out of my work clothes." He disappeared down the hall.

Sounded great to me. Holly led me down the wide curve of stairs to the pantry—a room *just for food*! She grabbed off the shelves—marshmallows, chocolate bars, and of course, Oreos.

She was just handing me the Oreos when Mrs. Peterson appeared out of nowhere, holding her cell phone. "Oh, here you are, Lili." She gave me a careful look. "I don't mean to alarm you, but, well, honey, your mom is looking for you. She sounds very concerned. I assured her you were fine but—" I could hear my mom's frantic voice pushing through Mrs. Peterson's cell phone.

My brain was instantly exploding. Dad. Had something terrible happened? Thoughts were wheeling in every direction.

"Mom?" I practically whimpered into the phone. I squeezed my eyes tight, silently praying this had nothing to do with Dad.

"Liliana! You were supposed to call and leave a message! I had to call the METCO office to track you down. You were supposed to call back!"

"Mom, stop freaking out," was the first thing out of my mouth, my lower lip starting to tremble. Now, like dominos, my thoughts flipped backward. Holly's annoying brother. Greasy pepperoni. Listening to music. You know, normal teenage stuff. Isn't that what Holly had said? Going to a friend's house after school was *normal*. Yes, unless your name was Liliana Cruz and your mother thought the only trustworthy people in the world were your teachers and family members. And even then you never really knew. Then I was back in the nurse's office, me clutching her phone, asking Mom for permission to go to a friend's house. Oh shit! Oh shit, shit, shit. She was right. I was supposed to call her back immediately and leave a message on her voice mail. I was supposed to give her Holly's address, phone number, names of her parents, yes. I totally forgot. Damn!

"Excuse me? This is not a joke, Liliana. You get home right now. Do you hear me?"

"But we're going to make Oreo s'mores."

"Make qué?" Mom yelled. I pulled the phone away from my ear. I was sure Holly and her mom could hear every single word. They were both staring at me. My shoulders pinched. "S'mores . . . but instead of graham crackers, we use—"

"You get your butt home *right* now. I don't know these people. ¿Entiendes?"

She had to be kidding. Basically, my parents—correction, my *mother* was the most paranoid person on the planet. Here I was, inside a picture-perfect town, at my perfect friend's perfect three-car-garage house eating perfect (and healthy, if a little bland) snacks (except for the pizza, and now—well, not now—the s'mores). And I was just trying to be what every other teenager in America was: normal. But I couldn't be. Of course Mom was a basket case. I got that now. But at the same time, did she have to ruin *everything*?

And what difference did it make whether I was at Holly's house or at art club?

"Fine," I said, and clicked the phone off and handed it back to Mrs. Peterson.

"Everything okay, honey?"

"Yeah," I said, breathing hard. "I just have to go home now is all."

"Right *now*? But what about the s'mores?" Holly sounded like a little kid. And I felt even worse.

It was dark by the time I got home. Mr. Peterson had insisted on driving me, which was super nice of him. His car was nice too, and *not* beige. A black Lexus with caramel-colored leather seats and a sunroof. But I couldn't really enjoy the ride because I was picturing Mom exactly as she was when we arrived at the apartment—standing, arms folded tight, at the top of the stoop. Really? Had she been there since we'd gotten off the phone? My brothers' heads poked out the second-floor window, Benjamin's mouth in a perfect oval, Christopher giving me a thumbs-up. Maybe one of them would fall out the window, and all the attention would shift away from me. I thanked Mr. Peterson at least five times for the ride as he looked toward my mom, slightly concerned. I said a fake cheery "Bye" and scrambled out of the car as he was saying I was always welcome to visit.

"Liliana!" Mom pulled me up the steps as soon as Mr. P. pulled away and squeezed me to her as if I'd been rescued from a war.

"Hey, Mom," I said in my most good-girl voice. From the corner of my eye I could see Tía Laura and Tío R. coming down from our apartment, probably about to take their nightly walk. "I had a really nice time at Holly's. We got a ton of studying done, and then we listened to music and ate pizza. I'm fine. Really." But I wasn't. My stomach was in knots because I *knew* she was going to lay into me. But what did she think could possibly happen on a suburban street in Westburg on a weekday afternoon? She *had* overreacted.

Sure enough, once we were inside, the lecture my stomach was in knots about began.

"What were you thinking, Liliana!" My mother's eyes were wild. "What if something had happened to you on the way to this girl's house? I had *no* idea where you were. None. I can't just call the police. You *know* that! Dios mío. I don't need this on top of everything else. You need to use your head."

The police? Was she serious? Then she launched into lecture, part two.

"Or what if, God forbid, you all had gotten in a car accident? At least you're okay. And who else was at her house? Does this girl have any older brothers? Older friends? You can't trust anyone, you know."

Now she was pacing. "You know what? No more TV. Nada. Forget it. From now on you just come home after school and do your homework, help me, play with your brothers. I'm serious. You have to be careful, mija. Just because men aren't sitting around on their stoops in that rich town waiting for little girls to come home after school doesn't mean they're not lurking around somewhere else. Men are men. You have to be careful! ¿Entiendes?"

Me (finally): "I was at Holly's house. We weren't even outside! I told you that! But sorry I forgot to call back with her number. Anyway, Holly's family is super nice. They're not serial killers or anything. God! They have a three-car garage. What did you honestly think could happen? And what do you mean I can't stay after school anymore? You think I'm going to get killed in *art* club? Wow. Oh, and by the way, Holly's family is my HOST FAMILY. Do you even know what that means? You don't!"

Now my mother's eyes were filling with tears—and I instantly felt horrible, wished I could take it back. I'd said that to be mean. I'd sounded like . . . I knew what I'd sounded like. Like I was better than her, like I'd crossed an invisible line of knowing something she didn't, and rubbing her face in it. I waited for her to let me have it. Instead she just stared past me, one single tear on the verge of sliding down her cheek. No lie—this was kind of worse.

"Por favor, Liliana. Just go to your room."

"My pleasure," I mumbled.

When Tía Laura and Tío R. return from their walk, I heard Tío R. ask Christopher and Benjamin to turn down the volume on their video games. I could just imagine their little faces. They had nowhere to play with Tía and Tío here. We were all on top of each other. I thought of Holly having her own bathroom—that sure would be nice—especially as Tío R. had just come out of our only one, and yikes. I decided to hold it for a while instead of going in next. After dinner, while Mom and my aunt and uncle played cards at the kitchen table, I went to take a shower.

On my way, I caught a glimpse of Mom's face. She looked worried, and it didn't seem like it had to do with the card game. So while the hot water fell over me, I came up with a new building idea: Sylvia's Salon. Yes! Mom would love it. I rinsed super quickly and got dressed. Then I pulled the shoebox out from underneath the bed, the one with my cardboard scraps and magazine cutouts. First, I made a floor foundation (a heavier piece of cardboard). Then I noticed that the foundation had a tiny grease stain on it, so I covered the "floor" with plain white paper and drew tiles on it. Just like the tiles from the first time Mom took me with her to a hair salon, I realized when I was done. I'd sat on one of the plastic chairs in the waiting area and had watched as Mom was transformed—her hair pressed into thick, smooth curls; her eyebrows shaped and waxed; and her nails polished and shined. The whole time, she and the other ladies spoke in Spanish. Mom always seemed relaxed, almost floating, in a way I only ever noticed when she was in a beauty salon.

Next I glued on four walls, pressing each edge to the next, waiting for the glue to set in. Then I made little seats at a table, and even a small bouquet of flowers to put on it, drew miniature magazines on the table. It was getting late. Still, I kept going. I thought of Mom coming to this country all alone, not knowing English, working so hard to get by and then raise us with Dad. And it wasn't like once they'd gotten here, they stopped working, stopped striving. Hello—signing me up for METCO, which Dad didn't even know I'd gotten into! I wished I had money to send her to the salon. Before I knew it, it was eleven o'clock. And yes, they were *still* playing cards. I was halfway done with the miniature building.

I wished it were this easy to make her one in real life.

After the Holly house disaster, I tried my best to, you know, (a) not give Mom any reason to flip and (b) convince her to let me stay after school again. I cooked pasta and meat sauce one night. I didn't even complain when Tío R. just sat at the kitchen table criticizing everything I did: too much salt, add cut-up fresh tomatoes—don't just use the sauce from the can!—and no, Christopher and Benjamin shouldn't help. They were boys. Well, I thought, if boys weren't supposed to be in the kitchen, then why was *he* there?

I helped Mom bring in grocery bags. The mail. And on Halloween, I even volunteered to take my brothers trick-or-treating around the neighborhood. They dressed as wrestler zombies, which we had to explain to Tía Laura and Tío R. I guess they don't celebrate Halloween in Guatemala or whatever. I convinced my brothers to give me ten pieces of candy each because if I hadn't taken them around the neighborhood, they wouldn't have gotten *any* candy. It must have all worked, because Mom started letting me stay after school again. Days and weeks went by, and no progress on Dad's situation. With each day, I imagined the president's wall getting higher. Pretty soon it would be so tall that even Dad wouldn't be able to find a way over it.

While I was picturing Dad climbing up a too-tall wall, Holly jolted me back to the present, hopping happily over to my locker. "I have an orthodontist appointment!" Okaaay . . . a little weird, to be this crazy happy to be going to a dentist. "I'm getting my braces off!" she added. "I've had them for two years and three months." Ah. Now it made sense; I'd be psyched too. She shut her locker. Her brown-haired "triplet" friends—Elizabeth, Shannon, and Lauren—walked up. They were nice enough and all, but I hadn't become friends with them like I had with Holly.

Lauren smiled at me, but it was vacant. I got the feeling she didn't like how Holly was hanging with me all of a sudden.

"Hey," she broke in. "Do you want to come to Starbucks with us? We have this period free." The others nodded on cue.

I'd been to Starbucks once, but only to use the bathroom. A coffee costs like five dollars in there. And coffee is nasty, anyway.

"No, thanks. I'm good," I said.

Lauren glanced at one of the other girls. "I meant Holly," she mumbled.

Whoa. Was Lauren throwing me shade?

Holly instantly gave her a *What the fuck?* look. "Lauren—"

Lauren quickly backtracked. "I mean, sure. Why don't we all go?" Then she gave a little gasp. "Actually . . . I could use your help, Lili."

"Mine?"

"Yeah!" Now she looked all excited. "I have a three-page paper due in Spanish, and I haven't even started it yet. My treat at Starbucks if you help me? Pretty please?"

Holly choke-coughed as I gaped at Lauren.

"I mean, you speak Spanish, right?" Wow. Lauren was *oblivious*.

"Yeah. But I don't write it that well. Actually, I take French."

"You do?" Lauren asked. "But why wouldn't you just take Spanish? It'd be an easy A."

My jaw clenched. "Well . . . do you get easy As in English?"

Lauren went all pink, like on her neck and everything. "I didn't mean . . . I wasn't . . ."

I didn't mean to give her attitude; I was just answering her question. But Lauren legit looked like she was about to cry. Oh, great. I could see the headline now: METCO STUDENT MAKES LOCAL GIRL CRY. What the—

"Ha!" Holly grabbed my arm. "No class is totally *easy*. Speaking of class, let's go, Lili. And, Lauren, no Starbucks for me, thanks. Later."

"Later." Blinking hard, Lauren tucked a piece of hair behind her ear and stalked away, Elizabeth and Shannon by her side.

When Holly and I were alone, she said, "Seriously. What is wrong with her?"

I didn't want Holly to make a big deal out of it. I didn't want it to be a *thing*. Lauren had assumed I could and would help her on her Spanish paper. So? This wasn't the problem.

I even remembered something Genesis had said during her pep talk in the library. I mean, why *wouldn't* I help her? That wasn't it, though. What bothered me was that she was only going to invite me to Starbucks *after* she realized I could be of help to her. Ugh. So, yeah. This was a whole lot to explain to Holly, so I just said, "It's whatever."

But of course, it wasn't.

I wanted to see Dustin. Disappear in one of his big hugs. We usually met after school, before he left for practice or games. But today they were playing a team an hour away, so he'd left school early. On the bus ride home I sent him like a million texts, even though I knew he couldn't answer. But later he replied to every single one. I know! We got on this big back-and-forth about women's sports vs. men's sports and how it's the media's fault that women's sports don't get as much attention, and so it's a perpetuated cycle. I couldn't get over how easy it was to talk to him. He wasn't like any other guy I'd hung out with. I mean, it may sound weird or totally dorky, but I really liked . . . Okay, I'll just say it—his mind. I liked how he taught me stuff just by telling me about stuff he did. Like, he geeked out over rock climbing. So I learned all about different climbing grades and names of grips and holds, like pinch grip and pocket grip, because he and his brother went to the White Mountains one weekend.

And yeah, he did talk a lot about sports, but he could tell when I was getting bored, and he'd switch it up. He had no clue I'd rather talk about sports than about my family, any day. What? Was I supposed to tell him about how Tía Laura actually went through my closet while I was at school and "borrowed" a sweater because she was apparently freezing? Welcome to November in Boston, Tía. I admit, it *was* mad funny the other night when she tried on one of my old puffy coats. She looked like a blue marshmallow, but she sashayed around the apartment, thanking me repeatedly. It was pretty sweet.

Speaking of sweet, there Dustin was at my locker the next morning, with a fresh blueberry muffin for me! He'd stopped at the bakery on his way to school. He was going on about how this bakery used only Maine blueberries in their muffins, which was why the muffins were so good, and I mentioned that my brothers loved to cook. "You have brothers? You never talk about them—"

"Two," I said, thinking, *Please don't ask me about my family.*

"I have three!" he said, all happy. "Mine are older, in college and grad school. Another is married. How about yours?"

"Almost nine." *Please don't ask. . . .*

"Twins? That must be fun!"

"Er . . ."

"Lil?" He pretend-elbowed my arm. "You okay? You've gone one-syllable on me."

"Yes. I am." I grinned. "See? That was three words."

"Ha—but each just one syllable!"

Now I pretend-elbowed him.

A teacher coming down the hall called out, "Good game yesterday, Dustin."

I could see Dustin's Adam's apple twitch. Impulsively I reached out and touched it. He turned, and I swear he was going to lean in and kiss me, but the teacher was now two feet away. Dustin gave him a high five. I mean, it would've been rude to leave a teacher hanging like that, even though no one high-fives anymore.

After that, though, something shifted. There was more charge to every text, every glance, everything. And it was dope. And then, later, instead of our usual good night emojis—the sleepy one, the smooch-faced one, the monkey with his hands over his eyes—he wrote: **Come over this weekend?**

I stared at those four words in happy disbelief. Then the happy collapsed. Yeah, right. Like my mother would go for *that*. No dating until I was like, ninety, and plus, I think she was convinced I might get pregnant just by talking to a guy. I flopped back against my mattress, *so* annoyed.

You there?

I sat back up, said I'd check. Then, **sorry, family plans**, is what I told him.

Thing was, if Mom had known that I was hanging with Dustin, she probably would have pulled me out of METCO altogether. Or taken me to Bible study class like the one my cousins in Chelsea went to on Saturday mornings. I went with them once, and *that* was a blast. Not. A sweaty pastor in a too-tight suit sputtered proverbs in Spanish, after which we all descended to the church basement for punch and sugar cookies while the men played tambourines and guitars and the women sang church songs. Yeah, not happening again.

What did happen: going to the basement with Dustin.

It was during study hall. He texted me, asked me to meet him at his locker. Then he led us toward the stairs. On the way I spotted Genesis. She and two other kids were pinning theater performance flyers on the bulletin board. "Hey," I said with a wave. She didn't wave back, just watched as Dustin and I pushed through the double doors that led to the basement stairway, an odd look on her face.

We took two flights of stairs down, and then kept going . . . to the storage rooms? "The basement?" I managed a small smile. He responded with a bigger one.

We found a secluded spot behind a row of old lockers. Dustin leaned against the wall and pulled me close, so close that I could feel his chest rising and falling. If I looked up, our lips would touch. Maybe. Maybe I was crazy about him. And now he took my hand and squeezed it tight. He dipped his head.

"Hey," he said.

"Hey," I said back.

And then we weren't saying anything at all.

Yeah . . . so I was kinda loving my social life lately. And yeah, it was a major distraction from worrying about Dad, and like, basically being tethered to my room because Tía Laura and Tío R. were so flippin' loud with their card playing— usually Thirty-One or poker—and the phone calls they had with relatives on speakerphone. Why, oh why, did they have to use the speakerphone? I will never understand. But yeah, it was all a welcome distraction.

But there was something I was *not* loving. Believe it or not, keeping up my grades was hardest in Creative Writing class. I mean, I *could* have worked harder on my assignments, but five a.m. was killing me—so much that sometimes I fell asleep in my clothes. I *did* finish reading *Enrique's Journey* for Mr. Phelps's class, at least.

At my locker I pulled the book off the little shelf to give back to Mr. Phelps. Man, was that book gutting. I just kept imagining Dad riding the tops of the freight trains. And *thousands* of people did this—not one train, but as many as thirty!—to get through Mexico. . . . If people knew that it sometimes took over a year . . . If they knew that some folks went for days and days without eating . . . knew how migrants kept scraps of paper wrapped in plastic tucked into a shoe—scraps with telephone numbers of relatives in the US . . . If people knew these things, would they still assume immigrants just came here to cause problems?

I yanked out all the Post-its I'd written notes on for my "review" of the book. The orange squares fell to the ground like confetti. There were a *lot*. Maybe I wouldn't pick them up. Maybe let some other kids find them and read them. Yeah, right. They'd step on them and leave them for the janitor. So I squatted down and picked them up one by one, and—no lie—it was like I could feel the weight of the words on the paper, bringing back scenes. I remembered how one father wrapped his eight-year-old daughter's favorite hair band around his wrist before starting the train journey north.

I wondered what my dad might be holding on to.

(Okay. That wasn't exactly a distraction from the situation with Dad.) Weekends? They were unpredictable, depending on Mom's mood swings.

Mrs. Grew didn't have *swings*. She was on permanent full force. She took off points for EVERYTHING—spelling, grammar, everything. Today she didn't even say hi to the class, just wrote on the whiteboard: *Write about a meaningful trip you've taken and explain why it was so meaningful. Use sensory details.*

I wrote about my family's vacation together, last April break. We drove down to Houston to visit my mom's cousins. In a van we'd rented by using a Groupon, we drove and drove and drove, dipping down through states I'd only ever seen on a map—West Virginia, Tennessee, Louisiana. Instead of stopping at Pizza Hut or McDonald's, like everyone else I knew did, Mom had packed enough homemade food into the cooler to last us the whole trip—pan con frijoles, hard-boiled eggs, arroz, pollo asado, plátanos, and tortillas—and some Vietnamese spring rolls on the side. We ate at the picnic tables at rest stops, where puddles with gasoline rainbows dotted the parking lots. Even though it took forEVER to get down to Houston, I loved those days in the van, the windows down, my hair all crazy blowing in the wind, me listening to music on my headphones, Benjamin and Christopher asleep with their mouths open, Mom talking to Dad or reading her magazines while we all passed around a bag of chips. So that's what I wrote about.

Mrs. Grew was suddenly standing right in front of me. "Miss Cruz."

"Yes?" I set down my pen.

"Care to share your story?" She sounded genuinely interested, but still, no. I mean, there was no way I was going to share!

"No, thank you," I said. But in case she was legit going to give me an F, I quickly handed her my pages so she'd know I'd actually written something. Mrs. Grew walked back to her desk, frowning. I tried not to look back at Rayshawn, but of course, I did. He gave me a look I couldn't figure out. Did he feel bad for me? Did he think I was pathetic? Or was he just sleepy?

In the hall after class he tapped my shoulder. "Hey."

"Oh, hey. Hi."

"Don't let her get to you. You know, Mrs. G. And just so you know, it's not just METCO kids she's mad awkward with."

"She's whatever."

Rayshawn gave a half smile. "So, it's been about two months now. How you liking Westburg?" When I didn't answer, he pressed. "Welllllll?"

"Sorry . . . Guess I'm still bugged out by Mrs. Grew."

"Right."

"Fine. It's okay," I said. "Well, some of it."

"Like Dustin?"

My face went all hot. "Yeah."

He smiled, or smirked. It was hard to tell. "Why don't you come sit with the METCO table at lunch sometime?"

"Me? Uh . . . they weren't exactly the best welcoming committee my first couple of weeks here."

"You know how it is."

"No . . . I don't."

"They're just waiting on you."

"For what?" Now I was the one smirking.

"See if you last. If you stay."

Whaaa? They were waiting until . . . Huh. I'd never thought of that! I hadn't even remembered that METCO kids could start the program but then quit anytime they wanted. Yeah, like my parents would let me—but it was technically possible.

Rayshawn put his hand on my shoulder. "It's not that

deep. They're just probably sick of opening up to people, only to have them leave. You feel me?"

"Do a lot of kids leave?" Actually, I could understand why. Too-early mornings. Aggy teachers. Long days.

"Yeah, actually."

One of his basketball buddies bounced up and play-flicked him in the head.

"Later," Rayshawn said to me.

"Later," I said to the back of his head.

18

Just when it seemed like Tía and Tío would *never* leave, all of a sudden they were leaving, heading back to Guatemala. *They must have all the money they need,* I thought, again wondering how much "all the money" could even be. That made me kind of excited, kind of nervous. The Sunday before their flight, Tío R. surprised us all by making pepián. It was totally something Dad would have ordered in the Guatemalan restaurant in Waltham that we used to go to sometimes on special occasions. I'd never tried it. It was a stew the colors of an army jacket. And it took hours—apparently—to make, which meant Tío R. was in the kitchen for like the whole afternoon. He roasted tomatoes, crushed pumpkin seeds—even had Christopher and Benjamin help. *Even* though he'd said earlier that men didn't belong in the kitchen!

Mom had to go to the grocery store three different times because he kept asking for certain ingredients like dried chiles and green beans, but not all at the same time. Mom didn't complain, though. Somehow having these smells in the apartment put her in a good mood. Or maybe it was because we were all together, chopping and cutting and mashing and focused—finally—on something good that had nothing to do with getting Dad home. Jade came over for dinner and after one bite said the pepián was mad good and could she take some in a Tupperware to her grandmother, who was working late cleaning an office building. Of course Mom said yes. I wished they hadn't waited to make Guatemalan food until they were *leaving* for Guatemala. That pepián was right up there with Vietnamese.

Once Tía Laura and Tío R. left, my brothers would get their bedroom back. But it also meant that things were getting real. I still had so many questions. So after they were finished packing, while my brothers were out playing on their scooters, my great-aunt watching them, I joined her. Dustin sent me a text, but I ignored it—I know! Tía drank her beer from one of those free plastic cups from the bank. Tío R. was smoking cigarettes with a couple of old dudes down the street. The streak of pink in the sky caught my eye. When I was little, Dad had told me it was the sun saying good night in sun-language. *Good night, Dad.* Then I sat on the steps beside my great-aunt.

Tía Laura must have seen me looking all thoughtful, because out of nowhere she said, "Don't worry too much about your mother. She has depression, but it will pass. The sun falls before it rises once more. Así es." She paused. "And don't slouch, mija." Why were people always telling you not to slouch?

So. Yes. My mother was depressed. I knew that. And it wasn't going to pass until my father came home. So I asked,

"Tía, I need you to tell me. Dad's going to make it, right?"

She sighed. "Only God knows." Well, that didn't exactly make me feel better. She pulled a lime wedge out of the cup and began sucking on it, then pulled it out of her mouth and waved it at me. "But I'll tell you one thing. Your father is smart—hard working and smart."

"You always say that."

"Well, it's true. When his parents died, may they rest in peace, he was only nine. He made it three more years in school and then insisted on dropping out and working to help support the family. There was no budging him."

"That doesn't sound very . . . smart to me, Tía."

"No?"

"No."

"Well, your father found a job at a university. He cleaned the bathrooms, swept the floors. He didn't mind. He talked to the students, and after their final exams, they would give him their books and notebooks. Your father taught himself a college education when he was only a teenager. And he got paid! *That* is smart."

I picked at a crumbling corner of the stone step. "I guess. But—and I'm not trying to be rude or whatever—but then why did he *have* to move to the United States?"

She took another sip of beer. "Well, that . . . is a longer story. This was back during the war—"

My phone vibrated. Dustin. I put the phone in my pocket. A war? Did I know about a war in Guatemala? I knew Dad's parents had died in a war. . . . But I didn't want to sound like an idiot, so I bluffed with, "I actually don't know much about the war."

She made a face. "The civil war? In Guatemala and El Salvador? Your parents never told you?"

"Maybe . . . they forgot?" Or maybe I'd shown zero interest.

"Ha! Impossible. It lasted thirty-six years."

Whaaa?

Tía spat. "There was a terrible, horrible rat of a general named Ríos Montt. He wanted to kill all the indigenous people."

I stopped picking the stone. "Indigenous? Wait. Is my dad . . . indigenous? And, and, why did this guy want to kill them?"

"Mija, listen." She gnawed at the lime wedge. There was practically only rind left.

"Sorry, Tía."

"So, Ríos Montt, he and others—mostly politicians—were afraid the indigenous people would revolt."

"Revolt?"

"Against the government."

I nodded, even though I wasn't quite following. But I wasn't about to interrupt again.

She continued. "Some had already started to do that, actually. So this estúpido decided that to stop this, he needed to get rid of the indigenous communities."

I gaped at her. "Seriously?"

Tía Laura threw the lime rind into the street. I took that as a yes.

I hadn't known *any* of this. Questions were bruising my brain. "But hang on a sec. You didn't answer my question. *Are* my parents indigenous?"

"To some extent, we all are, mija. We have indigenous blood mixed with Spanish blood."

I sat on my hands, my head heavy with all this new information.

Tía Laura went on to explain more. There was a civil war in El Salvador, too—and the United States actually supplied weapons and money to the governments that wanted to basically wipe out all the people who disagreed with them. Isn't that insane? Friggin' insane. So *that's* why my parents left, leaving everything, every*one* behind.

"I had no idea!" was all I could manage at first, as questions, so many questions, bombarded me. Then I had to ask. "Were any of our relatives killed in the war?"

Tía Laura nodded like she'd been braced for this one. "Sí, mija." She didn't add anything more. I waited, quiet, quiet.

"I'm sorry," I finally said.

"Así es," she said at last. "You can't go back in time. They were older, two uncles. And they were very involved in the revolution. That's why they were targeted. We had to hire a psychic to help us find their bodies."

"A psychic? Did it work?"

She nodded. "The searchers found a grave with six men— their hands and feet bound by rope." Now Tía was crying. But almost instantly she stopped. "Así es," she said again, her voice soft, soft.

JENNIFER DE LEON

I needed to change the subject. I needed to stop her hurt. "So, what's the government like now?"

"Pah!" She waved a hand as if smacking away a mosquito. "There are no jobs and not enough food. Schools are for the rich. So it's a cycle. You see?"

"No wonder so many people try to cross the border!"

She was nodding again. "Now you *see*."

I saw. Oh yeah, I saw. Suddenly a great big map of Latin America—Central America, South America, and the Caribbean—popped into my head, the one on the wall in Mr. Phelps's class.

It was weird, almost like the two histories—what I learned in school and what I learned about my family—were converging. But why did it all have to be so divided? Like the cafeteria at lunch, for instance. Like Westburg kids and METCO kids. Like chocolate cities and vanilla suburbs.

Then another image popped into my head—a thick white line along the border between Mexico and the United States. And another—a tall, rusted orange wall. I scootched closer to my aunt, lowered my voice so there'd be no way my brothers could hear. "But Dad is going to make it across the border, right?"

"It's not that simple, Liliana." An odd mix of sadness and pity flickered across her face.

"But—aren't you—bringing him money, so, you know, so he can pay a really good coyote guy?"

She drained the cup, gazed out at the twins. I didn't like

the look on her face. Like she was holding on to some bad news.

"What?" I asked, now clutching her arm.

"Nada," she said.

"Tía? Please. You can tell me."

My aunt looked suddenly haggard. "It's just very dangerous, Liliana. Even with a coyote. The Border Patrol . . . some are real bastards—shoot first, then ask questions."

A chill raced through me. Shoot *first*?

"I'm sorry, mija, but it's true. Crossing over . . . it's not like it was before—not that it was ever very easy, but it's just . . . much harder now. The Border Patrol hide behind bushes, analyze footprints, follow you with these special night lights and everything. You hear stories of—" She stopped short.

"I know. Kids hiding on top of trains. Starving to death, or falling asleep and getting killed by falling off. Women being raped. I know. I'm learning about it in school."

She looked surprised. "They teach you about that?"

"I just finished reading this book, *Enrique's Journey*. And there's another book, *The Distance Between Us*. It's about—"

Tía's eyes went bright. "Ahh. You really are your father's daughter."

My father's daughter. Tía couldn't possibly know how good those three words made me feel.

"Here." She reached inside her bra, took out a worn embroidered change purse, and handed me a twenty. "Go down the street and buy a couple plates of food from that Dominican restaurant. Anda."

"Thank you!" I ran down the hill. When I reached the restaurant on the corner, fried pork and arroz and plátanos and coconut mango smoothies had never smelled so fab.

19

Then they were gone. No lie, I was going to miss them. Okay, Tía Laura. Maybe I'd write about her in Creative Writing. Maybe Mrs. Grew would actually give us an assignment I could get into. When she handed back the road trip writing one, my pages were covered in her blood-red scribbles and comments, and I mean COVERED. (Like dang, doesn't she have anything better to do with her weekends than edit every single line of my essay?) At the bottom of the last page she literally wrote: *This isn't writing. I suggest you visit the Writing Center.* She didn't even have the nerve to say it to my face. Wow. *This is stream of consciousness and it must be shaped—scenes, dialogue, reflection, and more.* Okay . . . But to say it wasn't really *writing*? I sulked in the corner for the rest of the class. I even flat-out worked on my math homework, anything but pay attention to her Royal Writerliness, who was going on and on about openings—how it's effective to begin a scene with dialogue or action or a beautiful description. *Screw you.* How's that for a scene opener?

After class Rayshawn caught up with me again. "What's wrong? Let me guess: nothing." He arched an eyebrow.

"I'm not in the mood."

"She's really getting to you, huh? I told you, don't sweat her."

I don't know if I was following him or if he was following me, but we walked together down the hall.

"It's not just Mrs. Grew. I thought I did a really good job too, not for nothing. You know, I was actually the best writer at my old school."

"Really?"

"Yeah, and half of what the other kids write is so boring."

"I'm hip."

I stopped. It had been a while since I'd heard anyone say "I'm hip," and it sounded so—*my* normal. It was so easy to talk to Rayshawn. I wished it were this easy with the other METCO kids.

Rayshawn and I walk-talked all the way over to a building I'd never been to, a wing behind the natatorium (that's a fancy word for a swimming pool). The smell of chlorine brought me back to the swimming lessons I'd had at the YMCA in Hyde Park when I was little. My dad would take me on Saturday mornings. And all of a sudden I was imagining my dad swimming across the Rio Grande River, and I tripped.

Rayshawn grabbed my arm, steadied me. "You okay?"

"Yeah. I'm good."

"K . . ."

Then neither of us said anything. So we burst out laughing.

Then Rayshawn asked, "You coming to the big game Friday night?"

"Basketball?"

Rayshawn stopped walking. "You aren't seriously asking me that."

"Sorry!" I started laughing again. Yes, of course he meant basketball. He was on varsity—one of the stars. Duh!

"Lili?" I heard my name, and turned.

"Hey, Holly—"

"Hey . . ." Then Holly looked at Rayshawn like, *What are you doing walking with my best friend?* I didn't like it.

"What are you—" she and I said at the same time.

"Oh, I was just at the WC," Holly said.

"The bathroom?" I asked. "Aren't *you* British!"

Rayshawn laughed. Holly's ears turned pink. I felt so bad; I wasn't trying to make fun of her.

"Uh . . . yeah. But it also stands for 'Writing Center.'"

"You go there?" I must have sounded accusatory or surprised or judgmental or all of the above, but I couldn't help it. I didn't know Holly went to the Writing Center.

"Yeah. They literally help you with your papers and you literally get a higher grade just for going. See?" She took out a mustard-colored paper; it had a couple of signatures at the bottom. I took it from her and began to read.

"Hey," Holly interrupted. "I thought you had study hall now."

"I do." The bell rang. "Eee! I mean, I *did*."

"I'm out," Rayshawn said. "Test in bio. Wish me luck!"

"Luck!" Holly and I both called out.

As we walked back to the main building, Holly asked,

"So . . . whatsup with you and Rayshawn?"

"Nothing. Can't a girl walk down the hall with a guy?"

Holly gave me a smirk. "No. And you know it."

I smirked back. "Oh my God. It's *nothing*."

"You say so. But I wonder what Dustin thinks about your nice little walk with Rayshawn."

"So, about the Writing Center . . ."

"Smooth, Lili."

"Yeah, wasn't it?" We laughed. "I swear, it's not like that . . . with Rayshawn."

"Whatevs."

As soon as she was out of sight, I backtracked to the Writing Center to get some more info. I really was surprised that Holly used it. I guess I just didn't think kids who were already smart needed to do that. And after my last big talk with Tía Laura, I knew for sure going to the Writing Center was something my dad totally would have done. When I was signing up for a tutoring slot, I looked up to see Ivy.

"Hey," she said. No lie, I kind of held my breath. Why was I so nervous? I guess I was used to her and all the METCO kids icing me out. Well, not Rayshawn. Okay, mostly Dorito Girl.

"Hey," I said back. Clever, Lili!

But at least Ivy smiled. And when I was done writing my name on the clipboard, I passed her my pen.

20

On the real, it was crazy to picture Tía Laura and Tío R. in Guatemala, handing my father this big wad of cash. Money cobbled together from lots of IOUs. To hire a coyote. To smuggle Dad across the border. And for him to return home. To us. Saying it like that made it sound like a movie, not a *real* life. Not *my* life. But it *was* my life. I wasn't quite sure how Mom managed to gather the money, but by snatching bits and pieces of her conversations with my aunt late at night, it seems she had borrowed most from other people (mostly kind folks from church). Apparently she'd needed seven thousand dollars in total. And it had to be cash. Either way, Mom had some major IOUs to pay back.

With my aunt gone, my mom, alone all day again, was even more wigged out. She literally jumped at every noise she heard—even the toilet flushing! It was like she'd forgotten how to relax. So one day I asked her if I could use some of her CVS ExtraCare bucks for some school supplies. Instead of graph paper and highlighters, however, I returned with nail polish, polish remover, cotton balls, hand lotion, and a little brush that was supposedly for scraping the dead skin off the bottom of your feet. Kinda gross, but it was only ninety-nine cents, so. I set up a little mani-pedi station in the living room, laying a folded towel down on the rug, placing two bowls of warm water on it. In one I poured some drops of hand soap and stirred them around until they made suds.

"Hey, Mom? Can you come here a sec?"

After a minute she appeared in the living room doorway. "What's this?" She cinched her robe at the waist.

"It's for you. I'm going to give you a mani-pedi. Come sit."

Her smile was everything. "Really?"

"Yes. Come on. Sit."

"Ay, Liliana." Just like old times. Thing was, this used to be Mom's "thing." I even think she had dreams of opening her own salon one day. Eh-hem, Sylvia's Salon. I needed to finish that one. It *did* have a nice ring to it.

I think the mani-pedi helped, because that weekend Mom actually thought it would be fun if we invited Jade and her grandmother, Doña Carmen, out to eat with us at the Chinese Buffet on Route 9! Jade + Chinese food = heaven. And my brothers would be at a birthday party, so they didn't have to tag along. So on Sunday we borrowed a neighbor's car (rented, actually, by the hour), and off we went. I hadn't seen Jade in like forever. She brought Ernesto.

The whole time, Jade and her boy stole tiny kisses from one another between nibbling on fried shrimp. His skin was kind of shiny, and he smelled like cocoa butter.

"I'm going up for more egg rolls," Doña Carmen said. "Anyone else want anything from the buffet?"

"Hm? No, thank you," I said.

"Vaya, pues," Doña Carmen said, and excused herself.

Now Jade and Ernesto were eating off each other's plates. Gag me. But if Dustin were here, wouldn't we have been doing the same thing? Truth: I'd never even told Jade about Dustin. I liked having my worlds separated, like food at salad bars. Corn stays in the *corn* area, lettuce in the lettuce area.

"I'm getting more rice." Mom interrupted my Dustin daydream, shot Jade and Ernesto a look, and left the table as well. As soon as she was gone, Ernesto actually spoke to me. "Hey, Liliana," he said. "What's the deal at your new school?"

The deal? I had never literally *talked* to Ernesto before, to be perfectly honest. He was just there in the periphery—picking up or dropping off Jade, and texting her like crazy. "I mean, it's whatever."

"Lots of entitled kids there?" he pressed.

"I guess."

Jade gave me a look like, *WTF, how rude are you?*

I took a sip of tea. "Well, I mean, I don't know. It's weird. . . ."

"Well, there's a rally coming up, in JP. We're partnering with SIM. You know, the Student Immigration Movement. Some youth are going to speak out, share their stories."

Partnering? Youth? Was he kidding? He was seventeen! Wait. Maybe he was older and he'd just told Jade he was seventeen! "How old are you?" I blurted out.

"What?" he and Jade said simultaneously.

"Forget it. Yeah . . . a rally. Sounds cool. Maybe I'll check it out."

Ernesto cocked his head. "I thought you'd be more interested. You know, because of the situation with your father and everything."

The situation with my— What the hell? I shot daggers at Jade, but she was suddenly intent on picking up a kernel of fried rice with her chopsticks. She'd told him about my dad? She'd *told* him? I couldn't even sit there. I excused myself and stormed to the restroom. After washing my hands, I held them under the heat of the dryer for a long, long time, scared of what might come out of my mouth if I went back to the table. She had NO business—And that's when Jade busted in all dramatic-like.

"Hey," she said, her hands on her hips, with all kinds of attitude.

I slammed my palms on the counter.

"Don't even be like that, Liliana." She lit right in. "Ernesto and me . . . we're good. Happy. So I share stuff with him. But you seem to have a major problem with that based on your little METCO whatever program and your white-school attitude you got going on."

"What?! Whoa. Hold on a minute. This is not about *me*. *You* told him about my *father*, Jade. Really?"

She stepped closer. "See what I mean?"

"See what?"

"That. That right there. You have such a stank-ass attitude. You're all sarcastic. Is that what your new best friend

Heather or Holly or whatever-her-name-is talks like?"

I narrowed my eyes. "Oh, so *that's* what this is about. You're jealous."

"Girl, please."

"No, for real. You act like I'm the one who has changed, when YOU'VE gone from zero to a hundred with Ernesto. He's all you ever talk about, and talk to, and it's just, wow. And for real, Jade, why are you telling him *my* business? What if he tells someone? Did you even *think* about that, for one second?"

I must have hit a nerve, because she got all spooky calm, lifted her chin. "You know what? Forget you."

"Forget *you*, then." I stepped backward and bumped into the hand dryer, setting it off. I jumped a mile. A woman in a stall farted really loud. When the dryer stopped, the woman didn't. She just let it all out. And, yeah, so, we're apparently mad immature, because Jade and I started laughing. Hysterically.

"Ew. Let's get out of here," I said.

Outside the door, Jade laid a hand on my shoulder. "Liliana?"

"Yeah?"

"On the real, I'm sorry I told Ernesto. He's just into these issues and helping the community. He's not a bad guy. In fact, he's really great, actually. You gotta get to know him." Her eyes were all soft now, pleading—

"I know. I mean, I'm sorry. It's just that yeah, I'm busy at my new school and all, but you're still my best friend. I just feel like, I'm the one who goes to a school a million miles away, and yet you're the one who's never around. And you literally live next door."

Jade started laughing.

"What now?"

"Girl. You say 'literally' a lot now."

I didn't know what to say to that.

"But it's all good. I still love you," she added quick.

Just then the lady from the bathroom—you know who—came out the door. She speed-walked past us. Jade and I couldn't help it. We tried so hard to restrain our laughter that we were practically crying.

"Liliana!" My mom's voice broke our little reunion as she hustled toward us. "Where have you girls been? We thought you'd been kidnapped!"

"Okay. . . . Dramatic. Mom—"

"Let's go! We already paid the check."

"But I wasn't even done eating," I protested.

"Well, that's your fault. We have to return the car. Vámonos."

On our drive, I played around with the radio stations. But I wasn't really listening to the music as I looked out the window. The closer we got to the apartment, the more cop cars we saw. More stop signs. More drunk dudes chillin' on the corners. More tagged apartment buildings. A boy on a bike almost getting hit by a car. The man in the car yelling at the boy, "I could've fucking killed ya! Ya idiot!" I hadn't really . . . noticed this stuff before. It was like the streetlamps had been changed to a different wattage, and now, even though everything was the same as it had been before, it was cast in a different light or something. The wind picked up. And it carried smells of sewage and such funkiness. I rolled up the window, covered my mouth with my sleeve. Everything seemed . . . different.

"What are you thinking about?" my mom asked.

"Nothing," is what I said. *Everything*, is what I thought.

21

When I mentioned to Holly at lunch that my tía and tío had left, she got the same look on her face that she had when she told me she was getting her braces off. (Her teeth looked magazine-advertisement perfect, by the way.) "Now I can come over to *your* house," she said, all kinds of happy. I told her I would hang out at her house that weekend instead. I had no idea how I was going to convince my mother, but it was better than the alternative. But Holly was sooooo sick of Westburg, she said. It was . . . awkward. Corn in the corn area, remember?

Take Dustin, for example. I only ever saw him at school, and for now, that was working. I mean, what was the alternative? *He* definitely couldn't come over. But we texted all the time—not quite at Jade and Ernesto's level, but I did save some:

My Lili . . . donde estas?

Save me from bio. Dissecting cats again today. J/K. I think. . . .

Saw you writing like crazy in class just now. Whatchu writing?

On the last one—yeah, no. Corn in the corn area. Period. I wasn't ready to share ALL my stuff with Dustin yet. My writing was . . . mine. So I never responded. He didn't push. Holly, on the other hand, wouldn't let up. She was mad *persistent*. Kept asking to come over. She called a few nights later to say her parents were really on her back about college (even though we were only in tenth grade!), and she'd overheard them talking about sending her to some prep school up in Maine. What was it with Westburg people and Maine? Still, Holly was practically crying into the phone, and I felt so bad that I ended up inviting her over.

In preparation, in addition to my usual chores, I stepped it up big-time. I dusted the random collection of hair spray and mousse bottles on my bureau. I got out rags and Windex and wiped down the windows, TV screen, coffee table, lamps, everything. I made sure the trash bin in the bathroom was empty, and got rid of all the coupons and overdue notices on the refrigerator, stuffing them in a drawer. I even freakin' mopped the kitchen floor. Benjamin asked who was coming over.

"No one." If I'd told him the truth, he might have stuck a whoopee cushion under Holly when she sat down, or started a burping contest with Christopher—those boys could BURP. Luckily, turned out some special TV chef was giving a demonstration at the YMCA, and my brothers begged to go. Phew!

Saturday afternoon, exactly on time, Holly's father pulled up in his Lexus. The neighborhood kids gaped at the car, at

JENNIFER DE LEON

him, at Holly as I said a quick hello and ushered her into my building. Her father didn't leave for a long time. We could see him still parked outside through the second-floor window. Finally Holly texted him and told him to go. He did.

Even though Mom appreciated how Holly's family was my METCO host family or whatever, I got the feeling that she was looking for evidence right out of the gate that Holly was a bad influence. Did her T-shirt smell like cigarettes? Did she have swears written in marker on her bag? Did she stick her nose up at the doilies on our living room couch? No, no, and no.

Besides, Holly was totally cool and normal. Yeah, she swore like a truck driver, and no, she didn't always say the most polite things to her parents. But she was my new friend, my only real friend so far at Westburg. As we settled in the living room for what I hoped would be a two-minute conversation before Holly and I could go hang out in my room, I low-voiced to my mother in Spanish, "Just be easy on her, please."

Then I switched to English. "So, Holly, this is my mom. Mom, Holly," I said all cheery bright, like we were being recorded on camera or something.

"Hello, mija," Mom said.

I glanced at Holly. Did she know what "mija" meant? She took Spanish. Of course she did!

"Nice to meet you," my mother added. She kept smoothing her hair down. Was Mom . . . nervous? About meeting *Holly*?

"Hi," Holly said, all casual, like she was meeting another friend of mine.

Fifteen years old, and this was the first time I was bringing a friend home from school. (Jade didn't count. She was like family.) But unlike Holly, Jade called my mother "señora," and always said "excuse me" and "please" and "thank you" in every single sentence she directed toward her. It was like the law or something. You had to be super polite to adults, especially your friends' parents. My mother sort of smiled at Holly. Holly sort of smiled at my mother. Neither said anything more. Total crickets. After twenty seconds of silence, I couldn't stand it anymore.

"Hungry?" I practically shouted, and hauled Holly to the kitchen, where I grabbed a packet of Ritz crackers and two glasses, which I quickly filled with orange juice.

Holly looked around, pausing at the massive wooden utensils on the wall. "You all must make crazy house salads," she said, gesturing.

"Let's hang in my room," I suggested.

"Cool." Holly peeked into the rooms coming off the hallway. "Your apartment is so cute."

"Thanks?"

In my bedroom Holly began flipping through my journal without even asking.

"Uh—excuse you," I said, easing it out of her hands.

"You really *do* love writing," she exclaimed as she continued to poke around my room. I tried to imagine it all through her eyes. The faded pink rug my father had promised to replace the year before. The mismatched furniture—all purchased at flea markets or yard sales. A photo of Jade and me holding our fingers up in peace signs sat along the left edge of the mirror. Bottles of (dusted!) hair gel and mousse stood unevenly on the bureau. I never bought the same brands; I bought whatever was on sale. One month that meant XXX volumizing gel. Mom said it made my hair look like Diana Ross's, whoever she was. Not even my bedsheets and pillowcases matched, unlike the ones in Holly's bedroom. Everything there was part of a set, down to the sage-colored towels in Holly's own bathroom. No lie, I wished I had matching towels.

I followed Holly's gaze to the Romeo Santos poster on the wall, the drugstore perfume bottles on the bureau— some still in their original packages—and the mesh laundry bag tucked in the corner.

Then she let out a happy cry. "What are those?" She pointed at a pair of cardboard houses I had placed by the window. A little church and Lorenzo's Liquor. I stuffed a Ritz into my mouth and waited to see where she was going with this.

"Lil? What are these? Oh my God . . . I'm obsessed."

"Really?" Crumbs fell from my mouth. "Just something I like to do, you know."

"They're amazing." She bent over, checking out every detail. "Is this what you work on in art club?"

"Yeah . . . well, when I go."

"Ha."

Noticing a lime-green elastic band beside the church, Holly picked it up and put her hair in a high bun, or at least she tried to. Honestly, she was doing it all wrong. As she tried again, I noticed Mom standing quietly in the doorway. She was holding a plate of butter cookies, the kind with red fruit filling in the center. Aww.

My mother placed the plate on the bureau, wiped her hands on her gabacha. Holly dropped her arms, her red hair falling back onto her shoulders. "Oh, hi," she said quickly.

"Thanks, Mom . . . for the cookies," I said.

"Yeah," Holly added. "Muchas gracias." Points!

"De nada," Mom replied.

The room felt suddenly claustrophobic. My mom headed for the door, thank God. Then like two seconds later she turned back to ask, "Do you want anything else?"

At that *exact* moment Holly had to ask, of course, OF COURSE: "Hey, Lili, do you have any tampons?"

Mom's eyes almost popped out of her head.

"What? Oh, no. . . . I must have run out." I begged my mother with my eyes to leave, but now she was not only fixated on me, but her hands were on her hips. Not good.

I swallowed.

"You use tampons now, Liliana?"

Holly looked from me to my mother to me again. "Wait, you're not allowed to use tampons?" I wanted the floor to open. How could I explain that my mother believed that tampons were for loose girls? That if you used a tampon . . . you technically weren't a virgin anymore?

"Mom . . . ," I said, now praying she got my *not now, please* tone.

"Liliana? What if your father found out you use tonterías?"

"Wait," Holly cried out. "You have a *dad*? You've never mentioned a dad before!" She looked around like he might pop out of the closet.

What was I supposed to say? *Yeah, my dad is actually getting ready to cross the border as we speak!* Pang. In. Chest. Oh my God. I so did not want to deal with this right now.

"Answer," Mom said, her lecture voice full throttle.

Holly was probably thinking, *WTF?*

"Sorry. Sounds like maybe it's a touchy subject," Holly said. She grabbed a cookie, took a bite. "Mmm. These are delicious, Mrs. Cruz!" she gushed.

Holly was trying to smooth things over, tuck it into a folder labeled *That Was Awkward.*

And Mom was eyeing Holly, trying to decide whether she was being sincere. Then Mom eyed me, and must have decided she'd deal with me later, because "Keep the door open" was all she said before pivoting and walking down the hall. I sat down hard on the bed, my heart pounding.

Holly mouthed, *Sorry!* before reaching for another cookie. "I swear, Lili, I didn't mean to get you in trouble. I just have my period."

"I'm not in trouble," I said quickly, but we both knew the truth.

After that we watched a movie in the living room, but I was so stressed out, I couldn't tell you what it even was.

When Christopher and Benjamin came home with Mom, I heard her tell them to leave us alone. Holly's dad picked her up at five o'clock. A couple of texts and two honks let us all know he had arrived and was expecting Holly to pop out of the building and back to her world, where daughters were allowed to use tampons. I noticed that Holly had left her orange juice on the bureau in my room. Glass still full.

"What a rude girl," was the first thing my mother said as I poured the juice down the drain. "Liliana, you know we don't use those . . . things." Tampons. She couldn't even say the word. Tampons lived in the same category as face piercings—gateways to hell.

"I know, Mom," I said, shaking every last drop out of the glass.

"And she didn't even finish her orange juice," Mom said.

"Nope." That little word was all I could give in the moment. My temples throbbed.

And *that's* why I hadn't wanted Holly to come over.

As I ran the faucet to wash the glass, I heard my mother sigh, then mutter, like it was an insult, "Americana."

The glass slipped from my hand.

Yeah—Holly was American.

But wasn't I, too?

22

Yes, I am American. I mean, I was born here, hello. Even if my parents had brought me here as a baby or as a little kid, I would still consider myself American. But . . . I'm also Latina. I'm *both*. Why did that all have to be such a big deal? Besides, my dad was trying to get back to us because he wanted us to be together, in *America*. He wasn't asking *us* to move to *Guatemala*. Which he *could* have!

I wondered if he was saying good-bye to Tío and Tía right then. "Please, God, watch over him. Please," I whispered. Just your normal walking-into-school prayer, you know. On Monday, when I reached the main entrance, bam, my attention was immediately diverted by orange and black streamers that hung in spirals from the wall. A huge hand-drawn poster read: C'MON WESTBURG! LET'S KICK SOME B-BALL! Huh? Oh, right, the major game this weekend. I saw a group of cheerleaders huddled in the corner, drawing the number sixteen on each other's cheeks in lipstick. Sixteen? Chris Sweet was number sixteen. The only reason I knew that was because he wore his basketball jersey over his T-shirts like, every stinkin' day. I guess he was the captain? Center forward? Or was that only in soccer? Except for knowing that Rayshawn played, I'd pretty much get an F on a basketball basics exam if they ever gave such a thing. I made my way down the hall, taking in the posters, more streamers, balloons, pictures of the teammates all over the doors—yeah, a little extra—and looked for Rayshawn. His big ol' paper face was right beside that massive Celtic's shoe. Probably considered the place of honor!

I found Holly at her locker, nudged my shoulder into hers. "What . . . is all this?" I waved a hand toward a bouquet of balloons.

"I know. The team won on Friday. That's eight in a row—a record. Oh, by the way, does your mom, like, hate me? I got this weird vibe from her."

"What! No . . ." Um, maybe, kinda, sorta? "So. Westburg. Basketball." I was becoming a pro at changing the conversation.

"Yeah, if you couldn't tell, Westburg has a *thing* for basketball." She pulled a notebook out of her backpack and dumped it in her locker.

"I hadn't noticed."

We laughed. "And I guess Chris Sweet is going to take us to the state semifinals, something that hasn't happened in like, twenty-seven years or something. So—"

"Cool?"

Holly smirked. "Anyway, see you at lunch."

Dustin—and his smelly friend Steve—met me at my class and walked me to lunch before they headed to the locker room with the rest of the team. In the hall, as we passed the big shoe, I glanced toward Rayshawn's picture and stopped dead in my tracks. Someone had drawn a huge *X* through his face! Whaa? I looked to the other players' photos. They were fine.

"Oh shit," Dustin said, also stopping short. He looked at Steve. "You *know* what that's about."

Steve laughed. "I don't blame them, man. I'd be pissed too."

I gave Steve serious side-eye. "What's going on?"

Steve whistled at Dustin, then turned to me. "Nada. Dustin, man, coach'll be pissed if we're late." Dustin gave me a quick kiss on the cheek—had his lips even grazed my skin?—and took off with Steve.

I entered the cafeteria uneasily; I could sense the whole room buzzing. As soon as she saw me, Holly grabbed my elbow. We sat down, and she dished out the info. Apparently, just before Friday's game, to everyone's shock, the coach had replaced Chris Sweet with Rayshawn as point guard. Best as I could figure it out, Chris hadn't kept his grades up. Anyway, Chris—or some of his friends—didn't agree with the coach's decision. So someone had drawn an *X* over Rayshawn's face.

Before I could begin to wrap my brain around all of *this*, a girl from student council came up to us. "Hiiiii, ladies. So, we're having a fund-raiser today. Come over to the tables and support Westburg! Big game coming up!" As if we didn't know.

"K," Holly said in her awesome deadpan tone.

Across the room a bunch of student council kids had set up a couple of folding tables. They were piled high with sweatshirts and jackets and T-shirts, with little signs that read, SUPPORT WESTBURG HIGH! and TOGETHER WE WILL CURE CANCER! Huh?

Holly nudged me. "Let's just check out what they have." Wait? Was she still being sarcastic?

"Seriously?"

"What? It's better than doing math homework."

"You go," I said, and stayed put.

Within minutes Holly came back and showed off her new T-shirt, the letters *W-E-S-T* across her chest. She'd put it on over her other shirt.

"Let me see the back," I said.

She turned around. Sure enough, the letters *B-U-R-G* were on the back.

"That's literally so cute," I said.

"You wanna get one?" she asked.

I *could* use something new. A hoodie? "Maybe," I said. Kids crowded around the tables, taking out credit cards and debit cards, and the student council kids were swiping them into a white square on their iPhones. They looked so professional.

"Hey, Lili," one of the council kids said. "Oh my God. You would look so cute in this." She held up a Westburg hoodie. Black and orange. It *was* cute.

"How much?" I asked.

"Fifty," she said without hesitation.

I practically gagged. "Dollars?"

The girl laughed. And when she saw that I was serious, her smile fell and she added quickly, "It's for cancer research."

I dug in my jean pocket (like I had more than five bucks!) and pretended to be annoyed. "Shoot! Oh, I left my money in my other jeans. Are you guys going to be here tomorrow, too?"

"Yup." The girl moved on to someone else with a credit card.

I pulled Holly's sleeve. "I'm good. Let's go buy a Chipwich or something, my treat."

"I thought you liked the sweatshirt."

"I do, but it's crazy expensive." With Holly, I could tell the truth. Or, at least skim the top of the truth and give her the foamy layer that wasn't too complicated or bitter.

"Hey," Holly said, lowering her voice. "I can loan you the money if you want."

I sucked in my cheeks. "No thanks," I managed, walking quickly back to our table. Holly trailed me.

"Hey, Lil. It's no problem. I know you'll pay me back."

I crammed my notebook into my backpack, pretending not to hear her.

"Seriously. It's no big deal."

No big deal. What was I supposed to say to that? Fifty dollars *was* a big deal to some people. Hello . . . me. Plus, it was more than the money. But, no big deal.

"Lil? Are you mad at me or something?"

"Nope." I zipped my backpack closed.

Holly just stood there, like she genuinely didn't know what to say. Like she . . . totally didn't get it.

"Look, thanks for the offer. It's crazy nice of you. But I actually have too many sweatshirts. Anyway, I gotta go check in with Mrs. Davila. She ordered some new . . . paper, and I want to get some before it's gone. See ya," I said, and took off.

On my way out of the cafeteria, I heard the principal announce over the PA system that from now on, all posters and flyers had to be approved ahead of time by his office. Right. But the damage had already been done.

Actually, it was just beginning.

Outside homeroom the next morning, I saw Rayshawn and his METCO friends on their phones, scrolling, scrolling, looking furious. "Aw, no fucking way!" Rayshawn cried out, his voice anguished. His friends huddled around his screen.

"That's total bullshit!" another guy spat out.

"What is it?" I asked, coming close.

Rayshawn smacked his head back against his locker. Whatever it was, it was bad.

"Let me see."

His boys ducked their heads, shifting away.

"Rayshawn." Now I *had* to see.

Looking totally gutted, Rayshawn turned the screen my way. It was worse than I could have ever imagined. Someone had posted a meme on Insta—with a noose made of basketball net around Rayshawn's neck.

The person had taken down the post, but not before someone else had taken a screenshot of it and reposted it. I looked wildly up and down the hall. How could this be happening? I couldn't begin to imagine how Rayshawn must have been feeling. I reached for his arm. I wanted to say something, but there were no words. The look on his face was so hurt that my eyes filled with tears.

It wasn't till he was a few feet away that I saw Dustin walking toward me.

"We gotta do something about this," one of Rayshawn's friends was saying.

Another answered, "Damn straight."

Dustin reached for my hand. "Hey."

"Hey."

Dustin lifted his chin hello at Rayshawn and the others, but Rayshawn's face had shut down, and his hands were balled into fists. "Yo," he said, his voice hard. "You better tell your boy Chris or Steve or whatever asshole made that meme to stop this shit."

Dustin stepped back. "What shit?"

Rayshawn's friends laughed, but the sound was the opposite of joy.

Rayshawn narrowed his eyes. "Okay, have it your way. Don't say I didn't warn you."

Dustin actually smirked. "Come on, bro. What are you talking about?"

I literally winced when he said "bro." Rayshawn's jaw locked.

The bell rang. No one moved. Except for me. I grabbed Dustin's elbow. "I gotta go," I mumbled; it was the only way I could defuse the situation.

When we were far enough down the hall, I filled Dustin

in. He was as shocked as I was. "Do you think it was Steve?" I asked.

"Why do you think it was Steve?" Dustin bit the side of his thumb. "No way," he said, but not quite convincingly. Plus he wouldn't look at me. But I didn't think Dustin would lie. . . . If he *knew* it was Steve, he'd tell me. So either he really didn't know . . . or Chris Sweet had done it.

By lunch everyone had heard about the meme. Rayshawn and his friend Patrice set up a meeting with the principal, but all the principal said was that they were "looking into it." So Patrice put a strip of duct tape over his mouth to symbolize their voices being silenced, and wore it until a teacher told him to take it off or else. I usually sat with Holly for lunch but that day, I don't know, I just felt the need to stop at the METCO table. They were all in a frenzy, talking all loud, talking all over each other.

"This ain't right."

"Do they have any idea who would do this?"

"Had to be someone on the basketball team."

"Whoever did this better be expelled."

One kid sat with his head on the table while the girl beside him held his hand.

Lunches sat untouched.

"Hey," I finally said to Brianna. Her hair was up in a bun like mine. She glared like I had just interrupted a funeral service.

"What do *you* want?" she asked, all mega-attitude.

"Nothing. . . . I . . . I just wanted to say . . ."

Brianna waved me away. "Why don't you go back to your white-girl table? We're good here."

My chest tightened. "I . . . I . . ."

She sucked her teeth and added, "Gringa." I gaped at her. I wanted to scream, *But I'm in METCO too! I'm from Boston too!* But that one word—"gringa"—sapped all the energy out of me. Gringa?

"Whatever," I said, and spun away. But instead of heading to the *white-girl table*, I aimed for the art room. I wasn't hungry anyway.

24

Rayshawn wasn't in school the next day. Dang. Just as I was picturing again that meme of him, the principal announced over the PA: "Students who engage in posting racist messages online WILL be expelled. And in some cases we WILL be contacting colleges and notifying admissions counselors of hateful posts."

Well, *that* got everyone's attention. It was pretty awesome that the principal would make it a big deal. It WAS a big deal. Kids tucked their phones away as if just by holding them they would somehow be culpable. Then one guy in the row by the window mumbled, "That goes against the First Amendment, but whatever."

The girl in front of him swung around. "What?"

"You can't prevent someone from posting their ideas. Freedom of speech, anyone?"

A few people snickered. I wanted to smack the guy upside the head. But what good would that do? I'd be the one suspended, probably.

* * * *

In first period French, Madame Volpée had everyone practicing the unit vocabulary in pairs. Pastel flash cards—baby blue, powder pink, light green—supposedly helped the memorization process. My partner: Peter Rubenstein. He was a straight A+ student, and he smelled like peanut butter. He wore Vineyard Vines clothes, from his navy-blue pants to his pink button-down.

Peter had just asked me for the word for "building" when I heard the echoey scratch of the loudspeaker. "Liliana Cruz . . . to the main office. Liliana Cruz . . . to the main office."

Why does hearing your name over the PA instantly make you feel like you're busted for something? At my old school, kids would start oohing and saying things like, "Oh snap!" and "You gonna get it!" but here, in my honors French class, no one except me even looked up.

As I headed for the office, I heard other names being called—all METCO kids—yes, including Brianna. Oh man, what was *this* going to be about?

Walking by Dustin's bio class, I slowed down and peeked in. His legs extended almost past the kid in the desk in front of him, his Red Sox hat was on backward, and he was taking notes. He looked so cute. I gave a cough, hoping he'd look up. When he did, he smiled so wide that I instantly felt calmer. He gave me a *Whatsup* look. Guess he'd heard my name over the PA too. Then the teacher came over and shut the door. I could just imagine Dustin rolling his eyes.

Just past the shoe, I ran into Steve of all people.

"Hey," he said awkwardly, walking into the main office.

"Hey," I said, just as awkwardly.

At the same time we said, "What are you doing here?"

A teacher holding a clipboard and a massive bulky backpack nodded at Steve. "You ready to roll?"

Steve gave a thumbs-up, then turned to say, "Environmental Club field trip. We're going to do research at the marsh in Barnstable."

I blinked in surprise. Steve was in *Environmental* Club?

"Have fun" was all I could come up with.

As he walked off, I approached one of the secretaries and in my polite school voice said, "Good morning. I was called over the PA."

"And your name would be . . . ?"

"Oh, sorry. Lili."

She leaned forward. "And your last name? Work with me, sweetheart. I have a thousand students on my roster."

"Cruz. Liliana Cruz," I said, all nervous again.

"Oh yes. In there." The woman pointed to a door down the hall.

I hesitated just outside until a voice called, "Come in!" It was Mr. Rivera. He was smoothing a pink tie and wearing a wide smile. "Welcome, welcome! Have a seat, Liliana." He motioned toward an oval table and leather chairs, like in the boardrooms I'd seen on TV. A few other METCO kids were already there. Yep, including Brianna.

"Please. Help yourself." Mr. Rivera nodded toward a box of donuts. "There should be fifteen in total." He paused, smiled again. "Students, not donuts."

A guy in a red sweatshirt—I think his name was Isaac—spun his chair around and then leaned back. "I could get used to this," he said, propping his feet on the edge of the table.

Mr. Rivera waited another minute as more kids arrived, then said, "All right. Good morning, guys." He started loosening his tie.

We all just stared at him.

"So, you probably know why you're here."

Well, yeah. It was pretty obvious that the administration was having us meet *now* because someone had posted the meme of Rayshawn.

"This some kind of Big Brothers Big Sisters program?" the guy in the red sweatshirt asked.

Brianna raised a finger into the air. "Yo. I already did the Big Sisters program. And I didn't like it. All the lady did was take me to Chipotle twice, and for my birthday she gave me a boring-ass book and that was it. So can I leave now?"

Mr. Rivera passed the box of donuts to the guy in the red sweatshirt, told him to pass it down. "It's important to have a space to . . . talk," he said.

I was choosing a Boston cream donut when the door swung open.

"Excuse me. Sorry I'm late. I had rehearsal." Genesis. Thank God. I nodded at her, but she—ignored me. Actually, she kind of gave me a neck roll and sat down across the room, when there was a perfectly good empty seat next to me. Okaaay . . .

"So," Mr. Rivera was saying, "starting tomorrow, we'll meet each Thursday—you'll be excused from lunch. We'll talk about different topics—racism, classism, sexism, discrimination, stereotypes, and college. Perhaps we'll bring in guest speakers, do special projects. Sound good?"

"Talk about racist memes?" Ivy asked. Mic drop.

"Absolutely, yes," Mr. Rivera said.

"Will there be donuts?" another kid asked.

"You betcha," Mr. Rivera said, sounding overwhelmed.

We all signed the sheet being passed around. When the bell rang, I tried to catch Genesis, but she booked it out of the room and disappeared into the hallway. She was clearly ticked off at me. What was up with that?

I was dragging the recycling bin out to the curb just before bed when I heard yelling above me.

"I swear! It's not like that!" It was Jade!

Then, silence. I raced back upstairs to my window.

Then, a cry.

Jade began yelling again. And then more crying. Sounds of furniture being dragged around or something. I crept over to the living room window, but all I could see were shadows behind her shade. And then dark. I ran out of the apartment and raced down the stairs to find Jade at the front door of my building, one side of her face all swollen.

"Oh my God! Jade!"

She hugged me tight. I pulled her up to my apartment, so the whole building wouldn't hear Jade's business.

My mother bustled in, took one look, and ordered Jade to sit down. "I'll get you some ice, mija."

I plunked down next to Jade on the couch. "Jade . . ." I didn't know what to say. But I knew what I was thinking: *If this was Ernesto, I will legit strangle him to death.*

"It's not what you think, Liliana, so just don't." Jade glared at me.

"What? I wasn't thinking—"

"Yes, you were, and it *wasn't* Ernesto."

Okay. But if it wasn't him . . . Still, I nodded. "Okay. But. Jade. What happened?"

Jade's chin trembled, and then she just started bawling. Mom hurried back with ice wrapped in paper towels. "Here, hold this to your cheek." She sat down on Jade's other side.

"It was . . . it was my grandmother," Jade said, and began hiccup-crying. "She got all on me because a teacher called about my attendance, saying I was absent, and my grandmother decided I'd skipped school to be with Ernesto, but I swear I was just late. Yeah, I'd stopped at Dunkin', so I was late for first period and they marked me absent, but I swear I was just late. I didn't skip." Jade glanced at my mother. "I swear."

My mother nodded.

"*Anyway*, my grandmother won't believe me."

"So why didn't you just try to explain what happened?" I didn't get it.

"Girl, please." Jade rubbed the ice back and forth across her cheek. "Abuela was going ballistic. She wouldn't listen to a word I said."

Jade looked from me to my mother. "Can I stay here tonight? Just until things calm down?"

"Of course," I said, just as my mother was saying, "I don't know, Jade—"

"Mom!"

"Let me call Doña Carmen and tell her you're here and that you're okay, but, mija, tomorrow you two have to get this sorted out."

Jade nodded, tipped her head back against the couch cushion, pressed the ice against her cheek.

Mom left. I could hear her on the phone. Jade and I moved to my room. "You want some Cup O' Noodles?"

"Yeah."

I made us soup, then set one of the containers down on the rug beside Jade. She held a pillow on her lap.

"Thanks, girl."

"No problem."

My clock said it was almost midnight. I was going to be mad tired tomorrow morning. But Jade was my girl, mad tired or not.

"Liliana?"

"Yeah?"

"You still writing?"

"Yeah, why?"

"Could you, like, read me something? It'd make me, I don't know, maybe feel better?"

"For real?" I hadn't done that in so long. Come to think of it, I hadn't *written* anything in a while.

She slurped up a long curly noodle. "Yeah, for real."

"Okay." I grabbed my purple notebook. Who cared about mad tired?

"Liliana?"

I searched for what to read. "Yeah?"

"You hear from your dad lately?"

I looked up. Shook my head. "I know he's trying to come back, though." A quick prayer in my head: *Please let him be safe, God.*

"That's whatsup," Jade said, and crisscrossed her legs. "Okay, so whatcha got for me?"

I cleared my throat and began to read.

On the way to school on Thursday I sent Jade a billion texts. Mom said she was going to make breakfast for her and her grandmother at the apartment and then, you know, make Jade return home after school. I crossed my fingers, legs, and arms. I would have even crossed my toes, if I could! Just before lunch, Mom sent me a **gracias a Dios** text with a picture of Jade and her grandmother hugging. *Good work, Mom.*

At our first official METCO support group meeting or whatever it was called, we brainstormed a bunch of "issues" and "concerns": vending machines not being refilled that often, SAT prep classes on the weekends vs. weekdays, jobs.

A guy named Biodu brought up that last one. He crossed his arms and announced, "Mr. Rivera, what I *need* is money."

Others quickly nodded.

"My sister's in college, and she does this thing called work-study. And she gets *paid*. Why can't we have something like that?"

Mr. Rivera threw the question right back at us. "Why not?"

"I asked you that!"

"Biodu, if you want to start a work-study program, write up a proposal and we can look into it. Bring it to me by next Monday, and we'll put it on the agenda for our next meeting."

"For real?"

"For real."

"Word." Biodu took out a notebook and started working on it right then and there.

Then, crickets. But *then*, timidly, we brought up deeper stuff—color-blindness, insensitive teachers, Rayshawn. Apparently the district was going to give Rayshawn a home tutor while things calmed down.

There wasn't time to get into all the issues we brainstormed, at least not in one meeting, but it was a start.

By the *next* METCO meeting, miracle upon miracles, Brianna had stopped rolling her eyes at me. So, that was something. We weren't talking or anything, but at least I didn't think *DORITO GIRL* every time she walked into the room. Mr. Rivera made us partners in some activity called two truths and a lie. I learned that she played the violin and she had been in METCO since first grade. That was a long-ass time! It made me wonder how long Rayshawn had been in METCO. It was a bummer that he was missing these meetings; they weren't *so* bad. Plus, it felt weird not to have him there. So I sent him a text telling him I was thinking about him. He texted back a brown thumbs-up and a smiley face, but that was it.

Not a minute later my phone buzzed. It was Dustin. He

asked me if I wanted to come over to his house after school, and what the hell, I replied **yes**.

So a few hours later, there I was, breaking like eighteen of my mother's laws—walking with a boy, walking on a street without a sidewalk, not going where I said I was going, and oh yeah, going to a boy's *house*. Which was why I'd borrowed Holly's blue hoodie. I zipped it up to my chin, and I even wore the actual hood and tied it tight at my neck. Paranoid? Yes. It was clearly in my genes.

"So what's it like being the youngest?" I asked Dustin as we walked to his house—ten minutes away, he said.

"Not too shabby," Dustin said. "I get to do a lot more than my brothers ever did. And my oldest brother is already married. Did I tell you his wife is pregnant?" Then I swear he blushed.

"No," I said. "That's exciting."

"Yeah. I'm going to be Uncle Dustin. Anyway, I'm not just the youngest. I'm also the smartest. And the coolest."

I laughed. "It's a good thing you don't lack confidence or anything."

I tried to memorize the area as we walked by. The neighborhood didn't have blocks exactly, more like winding streets with looming trees that shaded the lawns and driveways so that it seemed later than it actually was—I was going to come back this way to catch the METCO late bus. But maybe Dustin would walk with me?

Dustin poked my arm. "Hey, can I ask you something?"

"Sure."

"Why do you look like you're in a witness protection program?"

I laughed again.

"Look at you. All I see is your face. I mean, don't get me wrong. It's a cute face. But you look like you're wanted for murder." Now he laughed. "Which would make me an accomplice."

"Oh . . . I'm just cold."

Dustin reached for my hand, pulled it out from my sweatshirt pocket. "Well, your hands are on fire. You sure you're okay?"

"Yeah. I'm good."

Dustin's phone buzzed. He looked at the screen, then put the phone back in his pocket. "Just Steve," he said, as if reading my mind.

"Hey, can I ask you something?" I asked.

"Shoot."

"Why— How come— So how long—"

"Let me guess: Why are we such good friends if he's kind of a dick?"

I almost tripped. "I didn't mean—"

Dustin laughed. "It's all good. I get it. He can be . . . obnoxious. But I've known him since preschool. Our parents basically put us together in every sport possible, since like, T-ball."

What the heck was T-ball? But before I could ask, Dustin veered up a driveway, and my mouth fell open. Daaaaang. I could barely take it all in as he was whisking me through huge double doors, past a chandeliered foyer, and straight to the living room—not beige, like Holly's, lots of blue tones instead. The furniture was all real leather—I ran my hand along the top of a chair as Dustin led me through the room. My brothers would rip that chair in a hot minute!

The wall on the far end of the room had a huge map of the United States on it. A bunch of stars marked different cities and a hand-drawn line connected the first half of them, from Massachusetts to Kansas. Dustin bounded over to it. "My brother Pete is driving cross country with his college buddies. We're mapping out his trip." He pointed to the stars, as if it wasn't self-explanatory. I stepped closer to the map. Squinted. Dad was definitely on a different kind of trip.

"Whatcha thinking about?" Dustin was so close that I could smell his soy sauce breath. He'd had lunch in the cafeteria, and they'd had Chinese. You would think the smell was gross, but . . . Okay, it was gross. But still. It was Dustin. I couldn't turn away. And then, his hand was on my waist and we were making out right there, standing there. Finally we moved to the couch, and even though I kept asking him if his mom was going to come home or something, he never answered, which I took as a no. Instead it turned out to be . . . one of his brothers who stood in the doorway and cleared his throat a few times until we noticed his presence.

"Uh—Dustin?"

I sat up real straight, tucked my hair behind my ears. Dustin hopped to his feet, stood halfway between me and a tall guy who looked like Dustin—but ten years from now.

"Oh, hey, Kev. This is Lili."

"Hey," his brother said.

"Hi," I said.

I couldn't read Dustin's brother's expression—surprised, curious, impressed—confused? His hair was so blond, it looked gray, but he was also tan, which made him look like an oxymoron, like I couldn't tell if he was young or old or what.

"Dustin . . . I just came by to . . . pick up some books." He turned to me. "I'm working on my dissertation."

"Pretty soon, we'll have to call Kevin *doctor*," Dustin told me.

"Oh, and tell Mom I'll be back this weekend to do some laundry," soon-to-be-doctor Kevin added.

"Laundry day. Yep." Dustin gave his head a shake to flick his bangs out of his eyes.

"Well, nice meeting you, Lili." Kevin smiled in my direction.

"Nice to meet you, too. Bye." A moment later we heard him leaving out the front door.

"Well, that was a little embarrassing," I admitted. Dustin stroked my cheek.

"Nah, Kev's cool." He paused for a second, then said, "He doesn't really have that much laundry, you know."

"What do you mean?"

"And he probably didn't really *have* to come here to get those books."

Now I was totally confused.

"My parents are . . . getting divorced."

Oh. Ohhhhh.

I reached for his hand. "That must be so hard."

Dustin flopped onto the couch, patting it for me to join him. "Yeah. Kev comes over all the time with these totally random excuses, to check on me like I'm a little kid or something."

"That's actually kinda sweet."

We scootched closer to one another on the couch, but making out didn't exactly seem like it was on the menu any longer. Then, in the softest voice, Dustin said, "My mom . . . she, like, had an affair or whatever."

"Seriously?"

"Yeah . . . with her boss. So cliché, right?"

"Well . . ." I didn't know what else to say.

"Only, it isn't really a cliché. I mean, her boss is a woman."

Dustin went on about his mom and her lady friend and basically everything that had happened. I listened. Rubbed his hand. He kept moving it to bite the side of his thumb. But he kept talking, kept sharing.

Then he suddenly asked, "So what about you?"

"What about me?" I said warily.

"Your family. Your parents. And your dad—you hardly ever mention him. At all, really."

"Well, my father . . . ," I began, then shifted to, "What time is it?" I took out my phone. "Oh my God. I'm going to miss the late bus if I don't leave like right this second!"

Dustin pulled me up to my feet. "I'll walk you, and you can tell me on the way."

I pressed my lips together hard. I didn't have to walk to

the bus stop by myself! But I'd have to tell him something about my dad.

Turned out, talking to Dustin about my dad was so easy, and once I started, I just couldn't stop. I told him everything, then swung back to when I was a kid—how Dad had gotten me hooked on reading.

I used to totally hate reading. Then, once, after a school book fair, I came home all annoyed. Dad asked me what was wrong. I drank juice from a small carton with the curly red straw I'd gotten from Chuck E. Cheese at a birthday party. I loved that freakin' straw. "Boring books at school," I said. "We have to pick, and they're all sooo boring!"

Dad nodded, thought for a minute, and nodded again. "Let's go. I'm taking you somewhere special." He grabbed his keys and we tiptoed out of the apartment.

I loved going into Boston with Dad. He whistled while we walked. He nodded to strangers on the street. When he saw a homeless person, he always—and I mean, *always*—gave them a dollar. A whole dollar! On the street sometimes women checked him out. Sometimes men. I mean, Dad *was* handsome. He had black hair sometimes cut close to his scalp or sometimes grown out into a long ponytail, big eyes, a wide forehead (which he said means you're smart), and dark skin like mine. And he was tallish. Too bad I didn't get that gene. Whatever. That afternoon we took the orange line train to a stop I had never been to before—Haymarket. When I asked where we were going, he kept saying it was a surprise.

After a few minutes we reached some concrete steps. Dad took them two at a time to the landing. I scrambled after him.

"What is this place?" I said, looking around. People everywhere. Tables lined up in rows, boxes and crates and stacks upon stacks of books.

"*This* is a book fair," he said. "A street book fair."

I wandered around as Dad explained that this was the best place to get books in all of Boston because (1) they were cheap (and they really were; some were only ten cents), and (2) they were used. "If you read a book you love, you want someone else to read it," he said.

That afternoon, with the sun following us around from table to table, Dad helped me pick out a whole bunch of books, including one by Sandra Cisneros. He said I was too young to read her books yet, but he would buy it for me and give it to me in a couple of years. The fact that he'd said I was too young to read it of course only made me want to read it more. Come to think of it, maybe he knew exactly what he was doing. Because that was the afternoon I became a reader, for real.

"So, your dad got you into reading *and* writing," Dustin said now.

"Yeah." I was wishing the walk back to school were longer. We were only a couple of blocks away.

"Man, that really sucks, what you all are dealing with. It's not like he did anything bad or anything!" Hearing those words from Dustin's mouth made me—all kinds of ways—relieved. I wasn't hiding anything anymore. And it really *didn't* sound all that bad: It sounded fixable because Dad wasn't a bad guy. But at the same time I also felt a little uneasy. Like, now I had to trust Dustin with that information. And I *did* trust him.

"Exactly," I said. "My dad is actually a pretty fabulous guy."

"So, wait." He stopped short. "Are you, like, undocumented too?"

"No," I said. "I was born here, remember?"

"Oh yeah." And he clasped my hand.

I thought about the two of us walking down this shaded street, together. There I was walking free in this suburban neighborhood, but where was my *dad* walking—where was he walking to, or away from? It was like the latitude and longitude of your birthplace can ultimately determine your life's borders. I know—heavy. My head literally began to hurt. I squeezed Dustin's hand tighter. And I didn't care who drove by. I held his hand the whole way back to school. Hood *down*.

And bonus—Mom didn't suspect a thing! I brought my cardboard art supplies (including some cool neon paper I'd gotten at school) to the kitchen table. I told Mom, "I need to be able to spread out." But really, being in the kitchen made it easier to perhaps maybe a little bit eavesdrop on my mom's phone conversations. How else would I find anything out now that Tía was gone? And that's exactly how I discovered that Mom was now talking to some lawyer lady about Dad's situation.

A few days later I came home to find some white

lady—the lawyer—at the kitchen table with my mother. They spoke in Spanish. Lady's Spanish was mad good. My brothers were in the living room, watching a WWE SmackDown rerun, but I made like I was cleaning my room and kept coming back into the kitchen for paper towels, for Windex. Best I could follow, Dad was now in Mexico. He had traveled from Guatemala City to Tijuana, but at the border he kept having to turn back because of spotting Border Patrol. So Mom and the lawyer lady were looking into asylum. I think. Apparently, if they could somehow prove Dad was a political refugee, then he could possibly be let back into the United States. But it wasn't exactly a good time to be seeking anything from the current presidential administration, hello.

Now Mom was shredding a napkin. "My question is, if he gets caught crossing with a coyote, can we still try the asylum route?"

The white lady's eyes, for real, were full of sympathy. "If he gets caught trying to enter the country illegally, then no, unfortunately, he won't be eligible for asylum anymore. So for today let's focus on asylum?" She pushed her hair—curly, brown, streaked with gray—away from her face. I guess she was kind of like an amnesty lawyer or whatever. She seemed kind, and super calm. Not like Mom, who was totally mangling that napkin. The ripping sound alone was making my shoulders tense up.

"So, then, how long will *this* process take?" Mom asked.

"Well, it really depends."

On what? How long could it possibly take? Would Mom

kill me if I asked? More paper towels in my hand, I now pretended to look for something in the refrigerator, settled on orange juice, and took my time pouring it.

"Sylvia," the lawyer continued, intent. "Crossing is extremely dangerous . . . now more than ever. Yes, seeking asylum might take longer—a good deal longer. But that's the reality for a safer way in."

My mother shot me a *Get out of the kitchen* look, so I hightailed it back to my room, thinking the lady was right. Even I knew that lawyers took mad long to do anything. Take this lady, for example. She sat at the table with Mom for, like, ever. I could still hear them as I tried to focus on my homework, all the words distracting me: "immigration," "amnesty," "refugee," "human rights," "Ronald Reagan." What did Ronald Reagan have to do with anything? Wasn't he president like a hundred years ago? And every time the white lady lawyer said my father's name, it really bugged me, like she knew him, like she knew what *he* thought. She didn't know my dad. I wished she would just stop. I mean, unless she was actually going to help. But what if she only made it worse? Though she *had* smiled at me when I went into the kitchen. Maybe she really was trying to help. She didn't look that rich, the way her socks bunched at her ankles. It was trippy to hear really good Spanish coming from her, just like it was weird to hear English coming from my mom whenever we were in public. Man, I was hyper. As I went to brush my teeth, I heard Mom saying, "It's dangerous no matter what . . . but we have to try."

Try? The word echoed in my head. *Try* meant with the coyote.

In *Enrique's Journey* there'd been a part that said that some coyotes just take a person's money and then kill the person and vanish. There were so many men and women and children—entire families—trying to cross the US-Mexico border, like every minute. And now, right *now*, for real, for real, so was my father. What if . . . What if he ended up like all those others who didn't make it? I couldn't get my brain to stop pushing at these darkest places. What if the coyote just took his money and abandoned him in the desert to die of thirst? Or, what if Dad was caught by Border Patrol? What would *they* do with him?

My mood seemed to match the rides to and from school, which only got darker, colder. Christmas lights and ornaments popped up on nearly every house in Westburg. These suburban folks love their Christmas lights—some strung lights around their entire house! All chic white, of course. Except one house that—no joke—wrapped their house in Westburg High colors! They reminded me of that morning when the school was all dolled up in streamers and balloons. Got me thinking about Rayshawn. How long was he going to stay out of school? I'm sure the basketball team missed his skills on the court, too. They still didn't know who'd posted the meme. I sent him another text. **Miss Westburg?** He replied quick: **Nah.**

Luckily, at least things with Jade and her grandmother had calmed down. Apparently Ernesto slipped an actual handwritten letter of apology for making Jade late to her grandmother underneath the door to their apartment. Turns out Jade's grandmother really liked that. Found it old-fashioned and classy. So she let Jade invite him over for dinner, and that was that. He even started helping Jade's grandmother, fixed the leak in the bathroom sink that had been annoying her for a month. So, as Jade would say, it was *fly*.

I got into hyper-focus mode at our next METCO meeting. I was like, I don't know, looking for any kernel of hope. I wondered what an ulcer felt like. I knew worrying could cause one. And Dad wouldn't want that. But this meeting—yeah, Dad would be all over it. He'd like Mr. Rivera's enthusiasm, the way he talked fast when he got excited about something, or slapped the table with his palm. He was into it, for sure. *Okay, Dad. I'll be into it too.*

"Listen up, people," Mr. Rivera said, yep, slapping that table. "We're going to dive right in, pick up on our discussion from last week. Did everyone do the reading?" I had. I mean, I had skimmed it while I'd been talking to Holly on the phone last night.

"Anyone at all?" Mr. Rivera pressed when no one responded.

We all swung around in our leather chairs. Genesis hadn't shown up. In fact, I hadn't seen her in a minute.

"All right. Well." Mr. Rivera sounded deflated. He didn't seem to have a plan B.

Brianna must have taken pity, because she blurted

out, "I did." The signature bun perched on top of her head wobbled.

"Wonderful! Brianna! Yes. Please tell us what you thought." He looked like he was going to cry with happiness.

The article had been about the Little Rock Nine, a group of nine Black students who had enrolled in Central High School in Little Rock, Arkansas, in 1957. I guess at first, the governor had prevented them from entering the white school. But then President Eisenhower had said yeah, those students could attend that school. The article gave background information on *Brown v. Board of Education* and the Supreme Court, and there was a whole sidebar on the NAACP (the National Association for the Advancement of Colored People). I got why Mr. Rivera was having us read it. Okay, so I'd done more than skim the article. Still, this wasn't the 1950s.

Brianna leaned back in her chair. "I can be honest, right?"

"Absolutely!" Mr. Rivera was nodding all enthusiastically. He really needed to tone it down. If he wanted the students to talk, he'd better just, yeah, tone it down. That would be my advice, anyway.

"It's ridiculous," she said, flat. I felt totally bad for Mr. Rivera!

His face fell. "Ridiculous?"

"Literally nothing has changed."

"Hmm. Nothing has changed." Mr. Rivera adjusted his tie. Little globes.

"Mister! Are you gonna repeat everything I say?"

Now the tips of Mr. Rivera's ears turned pink.

"She means the article only proves that like, segregation is the same today," a guy named Anthony said. He had a shaved head and kept "drawing" on the table with an eraser, then wiping away what he'd drawn. Little pink pieces of eraser piled up in front of him.

"Care to expand on that?" Mr. Rivera asked, his hopeful look blooming again.

Brianna went off. "Sixty years later, and the fact is, white kids still go to white schools and Black kids go to Black schools. I mean, except us. But like, there has to be a *program* for it."

Three people nodded. Including me.

"All right, all right." Mr. Rivera stood up, pushed a finger between two slats in the blind and stared out at the parking lot. When he turned back around, he looked kind of sad, actually. Then he took off his glasses and wiped the lenses with his handkerchief for what felt like forever. "Do you all know why you're here?" he asked at last, folding the handkerchief back up.

I could feel a speech coming on.

"At this school, I mean?" he asked.

"Yes," Marquis said, his voice all defiant. "I know why they *want* some of us here, and that's to win basketball games. Don't even pretend it's not like that either."

I gaped at him. O.M.G. I hadn't even thought of *that*. *Were* some METCO kids chosen because they had game?

I glanced around. Lots of heads were nodding. Damn.

"I'm sick of this stupid school," Ivy said, interrupting my growing outrage. "On dogs. I'm sick of dumb people asking me all kinds of dumb questions. This girl actually asked me today in bio—we're learning about DNA and inherited traits and whatever—'Why do you look Asian if you're Latina?'"

"Interesting," Mr. Rivera said, fully back to all eager. It was like he had only one station on his emotional radio or something.

"Nah, for real. What Marquis said is kinda right," Biodu cut in. "I'm hip. Why don't they bus white kids to *Boston*?"

"Because!" Marquis pretend shot a basketball. "They won't win basketball games!" He laughed at his own joke, but it was like a dam had broken, cuz then the comments just sort of . . . took over.

"Last week a teacher accused me of copying another girl's homework when that girl had copied MINE. Why did she just assume that *I* was the one copying?" Jo-Jo said.

We moaned.

"I got one," Biodu said. "White boys using the word 'nigga.' Like, that ain't your word, yo."

More moans.

"Also," a girl named Patricia chimed in. First time I ever heard *her* speak.

"Yes, Patricia?" Mr. Rivera asked.

"I'm sick of people saying I'm *Spanish*. Like, whatsup with all the corner stores and restaurants in Hyde Park and Roslindale advertising *Spanish food* and whatever?" she said. "We're not Spanish!"

"Hold up. Just, hold up a second. What you mean?" Marquis looked all kinds of puzzled. "Yeah, you are Spanish. And I'm Black."

Some people laughed. But not Mr. Rivera. "You bring up a great point, Patricia. Many Latinos *speak* Spanish, but that doesn't mean we *are* Spanish." Now a bunch of us looked all kinds of puzzled, me included. Mr. Rivera noticed. "Those of you who've been paying attention in history class already know this, but it's important. The Spanish conquistadors bombarded most of Latin America at various points in history. They destroyed entire civilizations."

"Dang," Brianna said.

"Dang indeed." Mr. Rivera adjusted his already-adjusted tie. "When they came over, they brought their language: Spanish. But that doesn't mean that everyone in Latin America suddenly *became* Spanish. They had their own cultures and traditions and everything already in place."

Made sense.

"And another thing—the term 'Latinx.' Use it more. It's meant to be inclusive."

"Well," Brianna said in her flat end-of-discussion way, "I don't know if I like it . . . yet." I was glad she said that, because I admit, I wasn't 100 percent sold on it either. "What's the *x* for anyway?" she asked.

"Like I said, it's meant to be inclusive of all people of Latin American origin or descent, no matter what gender."

Brianna propped a foot on the edge of the table. "Okay. I can live with that."

"Ha!" Then Mr. Rivera started explaining about how this term was an attempt to go against that old mentality of Spanish-language words having a gender—masculine or feminine. He was clearly going off on a little tangent, but it was interesting. To be honest, I'd never actually known that when I said "Spanish" for someone whose heritage was Dominican, Puerto Rican, Guatemalan . . . that I was wrong. I mean, all the restaurant and bodega and corner store signs in my neighborhood advertised "Spanish" food, so I never thought twice about it. In my old school, most people just said "Spanish" for anyone who spoke Spanish, regardless of where their ancestors were from. It was as if he could see the wheels turning in my brain, because Mr. Rivera looked directly at me.

"What about you, Miss Cruz? As our newest student, what has your experience here been like—in terms of race and class?"

I raised an eyebrow. "Well, to be honest . . ." I had a lot to say, and yet, what was the point? I thought of the cafeteria, how it was divided by groups. No one mixed. Same with a lot of my classes.

"Yes?" Mr. Rivera encouraged, like he could see inside my waffling mind.

So I let it out. "I guess I'm just . . . surprised that there isn't more interaction between groups here, you know?" I thought back to my first day, spotting the huddle of METCO kids on the bleachers among the sea of white kids. Then, lunch. Same deal. I went on, "I mean, it's one thing to have diversity or whatever, but if people from different backgrounds aren't actually interacting, then isn't that just like segregation all over again? Like, have you ever checked out the cafeteria at lunch?"

Marquis squinted at me. "You know what?"

I looked at him uneasily.

"That's true," he said. To my surprise, everyone began nodding. And I breathed again.

"All right," Mr. Rivera said. "What Lili brings up is important. Why do you all think the cafeteria is, as she says, segregated?"

Mr. Rivera paced around the room for a long minute as no one answered. Then he clapped his hands together. I noticed he did that whenever he was about to tell us something big. Sure enough, he began. "It's fortuitous that Liliana—sorry, Lili—brought up bringing different groups together today, because, in fact, the administration wants us all to do exactly that—to plan an assembly. An assembly of hope."

"Huh?" I hadn't meant to say it aloud; Brianna actually laughed, and not in a mean way.

"An assembly where different student groups will give presentations about equality and empathy."

He was kidding, right? An *assembly*? Like that was going to do anything. Plus, can you spell "dorky"?

Mr. Rivera ignored the chorus of moans and groans. "We, as in the administration and teachers, want you all to present together, on anything related to METCO. Something you want to say, do, change—really, it's in your hands. We've got a few weeks to pull it together—it'll be right before winter break."

"Wait," I said. "Only the METCO kids? Why don't *other kids* have to do presentations? See, right there! Segregation again! Why do we have to school all the white kids?"

"Yeah!" Brianna added, her voice loud, mad.

"Who says you are?" Mr. Rivera asked.

"Oh, come on," I said.

"Okay, focus, guys, focus. This is a great opportunity. People can't know things they don't know. So, you may call it 'schooling,' but I call it a great opportunity. Let's own it. And discuss what it is you all could do."

"Can we have a bikini contest?" Marquis asked.

Mr. Rivera didn't miss a beat. "Well, that depends, Marquis. Are you going to wear one?"

"Hell naw!"

Everyone started hooting "Marquis! Marquis!" until the bell rang. I thought Mr. Rivera would be all mad, but he was watching us, this goofy smile on his face. Like a dad.

On my way out of the meeting, Dustin sent a text. **Walk u to art after school?** I wrote back: ☺. Then, in the hall, I spotted him. No, not Dustin. Rayshawn! He was back! Getting fist bumps from every direction. One girl asked if she could give him a hug. Of course he said yes. He was in midhug when he caught my eye. I raised my chin ever so slightly, and he returned the gesture. For real: I had really missed him.

*   *   *   *

The countdown until winter break began, and the school totally got its Christmas on—and Hanukkah, and Kwanzaa. All kinds of decorations filled the lobby; a regular UN of festive. But, yeah, festive. And yeah, we needed an idea for our assembly presentation ASAP. I skipped my lunches with Holly to brainstorm in Mr. Rivera's office: a project on busing, a PowerPoint on the history of METCO, a panel of METCO alumni. No, no, no. It wasn't that those ideas were bad, but they were all kind of . . . safe. Kind of—dull, dull, dull. I wanted to do something that had energy, that would actually put people on the spot, people who weren't all that used to being on the spot. Like, wake them up, not put them to sleep. What that was, I had no idea. *Yet.*

One day as I was rushing toward Mr. Rivera's office, Holly caught my arm. "Hey, stranger," she said with her bright grin.

"Hey." I gave her a hug. It felt like I hadn't seen her in forever. I sort of hadn't.

"Where are you headed?" she asked. I knew she knew the answer. I'd already told her about the METCO meetings.

"Yo, Lili!" Brianna called from the stairwell. Yeah, we talked now. We weren't going to get matching nose rings or whatever, but we were cool. I *know.* Stranger things have happened, right?

I looked to Holly. "Hey, we're still working on that assembly stuff I told you about. Call you later?" Holly looked hurt. I could see it in her eyes. I felt so bad, but I really had to go. I shoved the feeling down as I caught up with Brianna.

"Okaaaay," I heard Holly say, and I felt even worse.

* * * *

Mr. Rivera told us he'd been talking to Mrs. Davila about the assembly, and she had some ideas, so we were taking a "field trip" to the art department. There, she had laid out a half-dozen posters she'd printed out. One, in black-and-white, was of a civil rights activist named Audre Lorde raising her hands in the air. The quote above her read: "Without community, there is no liberation." Beside that poster were ones of Dolores Huerta, Martin Luther King Jr., and Cesar Chavez. That last one read: "Preservation of one's own culture does not require contempt or disrespect for other cultures."

I paused, read it over again. I thought of the meme about Rayshawn. How Genesis's teacher hinted that Gen might need a scholarship. Then, truth, I thought about how I had judged Westburg kids before even coming to this school. I'd judged . . . Holly . . . before I'd even met her! I looked back at the first poster, an idea brewing. *Community. Culture.* But how could we get people to, you know, talk? That's what METCO was ultimately trying to do—integrate. Yeah, I'd read the pamphlet, remember? But was that really possible?

I glanced at the clock. Our time was almost up. "I had a thought," I called out. "What if we run a slideshow of posters and quotes, and pass around microphones so people can respond?"

Brianna pursed her lips, thinking. "Hmm." Then she nodded. "Not bad. Lay in some music in the background, too."

"I'm cool with that," Ivy said.

"I'll take pictures of these, and I bet we can find lots

more online," Brianna said. As she pulled out her phone, I sent a Snapchat photo of our art room to Jade. She would kill for a space like this. She immediately pinged me back. **Girl. I'd go to school on the WEEKEND if our art room looked like that.**

Not that Jade let anything keep her from painting. Just the week before, she'd bought paintbrushes from the Dollar Store to paint a mural in her bedroom. It was cool. At Jade's school you couldn't exactly borrow paint supplies. And—whoa—I'd just thought of my old school as *Jade's* . . . not mine.

As I reached the door, I paused. I could go do math homework, or I could channel my best friend. So I swiveled. In the opposite direction. The opposite direction being the direction of the Writing Center. Signing in at the front desk, I could feel someone watching me. I finished putting in the date and time and looked up.

"Hello, Lili. I'm surprised to see you here." Mrs. Grew! She looked like she was on her way out.

Wait—was that an insult? I studied her face while saying, "Oh, yeah . . . I decided to check out the Writing Center after all. And you said we could rewrite one assignment for a better grade."

"And you're smart to take advantage of the opportunity," she said with a grin.

"Yup."

She grinned again. But it wasn't sarcastic. She looked maybe something like happy or proud or just . . . satisfied.

"Well, enjoy!" she said. "I look forward to reading your rewrite." And she swept out the door.

I settled into a cubicle and pulled out my pages about the road trip. Almost immediately, a teacher called my name from the sign-up on the clipboard.

"Oh, hi. I'm Lili," I said, picking up my essay and walking over.

"Great to meet you. I'm Mr. Hall and I teach senior seminar. Let's sit over here and get started." He looked younger than a lot of other teachers. His hair looked wind-swept, and with his ruddy complexion he made you think he'd just stepped off a sailboat. But he smiled with his eyes, and he wore an old-school pocket protector, which made me like him, actually.

We sat at a round wooden table. I held out my essay and braced myself as he read, waiting for him to shake his head and say, "Tsk-tsk." I could tell he was speed-reading by the way his eyes darted across the paper. "Ha," he said at one point. I just sat on my hands, feeling all kinds of nervous.

Then he passed back the paper. "This sounds like a really fabulous trip."

"Thanks?" I laid the essay on the table and used the side of my hand to iron out the wrinkles.

"Oh, we won't need that anymore," Mr. Hall said.

"We won't?" Wow, it was that bad?

"No." He reached over for a blank piece of printer paper, laid it down horizontally, and drew a line across the middle. "Tell me about your trip again, from beginning to end."

What? But I did. As I talked, he wrote. He filled out a timeline with basic events.

"Okay, now this is what we call the front story. The main events. But let's figure out the best order in which to tell this amazing story of yours."

Huh. It had never occurred to me that I didn't have to stay in chronological order. We reordered the parts of my trip, starting with the most interesting moment (when we ran out of gas on the highway in the middle of a rainstorm in Tennessee) and filled in the timeline from there.

The bell rang, and man, I wished I'd had a double block so we could keep working. I wanted to hug Mr. Hall, but that would probably have been weird. I rushed to my next class, making a mental note to take Mr. Hall's seminar my senior year.

Because the assembly had been scheduled for the Wednesday before winter break—to "finish the year right" the principal had said—the Saturday before, Brianna and I met up at the Boston Public Library to do more research. I dragged Jade with me. We sat in the back by the space heater, sneak-sipping AriZona iced teas because the librarians were mad strict.

While we hunted for more quotes, Biodu and Marquis and—yeah!—Rayshawn and some of the other guys looked up images of walls throughout history at Biodu's house. We shared them all on one Google Doc. I found a really cool book called *This Bridge Called My Back*—maybe my next miniature would be a bridge!—and even though we were supposed to be looking for material for the METCO presentation, I copied down a few quotes for myself, too. They gave me an idea for a poem.

The guys were finding tons of stuff. There were lots of other major walls in history—who knew? Greece's wall along the Turkish border, Hungary's wall along the Serbian border, and, of course, the Great Wall of China. I tried not to think of

Dad, whether he was studying some wall right now, trying to figure out how to scale it. There'd been no news in three and a half weeks. Mom was now in permanent freak-out mode, like, back to sorting socks and underwear by color. She set up the spices in alphabetical order! And yelled at Christopher when he put back the cinnamon *after* the coriander! And why *wouldn't* she be losing it? At least I had school to distract me. Dustin. But Mom? She didn't even get that housekeeping job.

"You all here?" Jade asked. I must have been staring off into space.

"Yeah."

She pursed her lips, didn't believe me. But she also knew when not to push.

"Yo, Lili," Brianna said. "I found another great quote."

"Awesome. Add it to the Google Doc."

I went back to reading. Jeez! "Did you all know that the US-Mexico border cuts some communities like, in half? So they have to have their papers with them all the time if they just want to, say, go to the grocery store across town? Does that even make sense?"

"Hmm," Brianna said as she was cutting and pasting; I wasn't sure if she was responding to me or it.

"And, not for nothing," I went on, "but when the US government built a wall between San Diego and Tijuana, people just found other ways to cross into the US."

Brianna closed her laptop. Jade put down her charcoal pencil. She'd been shading in the Afro of a girl speaking into a microphone in her sketchbook.

"And get this." I couldn't stop. "At one point the government spent twelve billion dollars on constructing some kind of fancy lighting to detect people crossing the border. That's insane! Can you imagine if they'd used that money to, like, build better schools in Central America or Mexico instead?"

At this point Brianna and Jade were grinning at me like proud parents.

"What!"

Jade laughed. "You're really into this project, Lili. That's whatsup."

"Right?" Brianna added. Then she looked conspiratorially at Jade. "Yo. So you should lead the presentation, then."

"What! Me? Hell, no. Thanks, but no thanks."

Jade and Brianna raised their eyebrows at each other. I had a feeling this conversation was going to crop up again.

Just as we were packing up—the library was about to close for some special event for staff—a lady with hot-pink spiked hair came up to us.

"Hello, ladies," she said. "I'm Miss Amber. I'd like to invite you to a creative writing class we're having around the corner."

"A *what*?" Jade blurted out. I couldn't help it, that made me laugh. Brianna too.

The lady didn't flinch. She smiled all bright and just charged on. "A creative writing class. It's at a place called 826. Here." She handed us some orange flyers. "It starts in half an hour. I'd love to see you there."

I glanced at the flyer to be polite. "Hmm. How much

does it cost?" I asked. Jade nodded in that knowing-best-friend way.

"It's free!" Miss Amber said, all happy.

"Thanks, but I can't go," Brianna said. "My dad is picking me up in ten minutes, and he said if I'm not outside and ready, he'll leave me here. And he would, too!"

We started laughing again. I hoped Miss Amber didn't think we were being mad rude. Then Jade said, "Liliana will go."

"Jade!" I yelped.

"Yeah, she'll go right after we finish up here. Thank you." Jade took a few more flyers. Miss Amber was now smiling like a crazy lady.

"Great! I'll see you in a bit, then. Liliana, right?"

"Right."

She smiled and walked over to some kids who were watching YouTube on the desktop computers.

"*Jade!*" I growled, giving her a kick under the table. "Thanks a lot. Now I *have* to go to this thing." I shook the flyer.

Brianna shook her head. "You don't have to do nothin'. You don't know that lady."

Jade sucked her teeth. "Liliana. Don't even be like that. You know you love to write. And that English teacher has been doggin' you—so go see what's up! For real. Just go."

"Fine. If you go with me." I crossed my arms, calling her bluff.

"Fine," she mocked. "If *you* go with *me*." She called mine. Done.

*   *   *   *

JENNIFER DE LEON

Jade did go with me, as in, she walked me to the front entrance of the building, coats on because the wind was picking up, but then she left to go meet up with Ernesto. I actually didn't mind. Inside 826 (a strange name for a writing center, right?) one of the walls was painted dark orange, and there were like ten ceiling-high bookshelves. I sat down at one of six wide wooden tables. About eight other people, all ages, were scattered among the tables. In the middle of each sat a thick stack of plain white paper and a glass jar full of pencils and—yes!—gel pens in all kinds of colors. Cool. Some adults wearing these long green lab coats were in the back, tutors I figured, Miss Amber among them. I guess they did some wacky stuff here at 826, like, on purpose. I picked out a bright purple pencil, already sharpened.

The doorbell buzzed, and a group of kids jostled in, laughing and yelling together. Ten seconds later another girl burst into the room, holding a massive iced coffee from Dunkin. "Yo, don't be starting without me!" She raised her cup in the air and rattled the ice cubes. Her nose ring glinted.

Miss Amber took a seat at the head of one of the tables. There were about twelve of us altogether. Then she beamed at me. "I'm glad you made it."

"You heard me, Miss Amber?" the girl with the iced coffee yelled, hustling over.

"I heard you, Keisha. We would never dream of starting without you."

"That's whatsup." Keisha and her entourage sat down.

Miss Amber had us fill out name tags, then go around

the room and introduce ourselves—all girls except one Black dude with a Mohawk and earring—and tell where we went to school. Mostly the kids went to Boston Public, a couple of charter schools, all in high school. When it was my turn, I said, "I'm in the METCO program at this fancy-ass high school like an hour away, but it's not so bad." We also had to name what our favorite cereal was . . . an icebreaker or whatever. A couple of people gave me the chin up when I said Froot Loops.

After Mohawk-guy said Shredded Wheat—whaaaa?—Miss Amber said "All right. Let's start with a warm-up exercise." My first thought was, *Ugh, exercise. Just what Mrs. Grew would say. Dang.* I hoped this writing prompt would be better than the ones at school. Then Miss Amber said, "We're going to write a *six-word autobiography.*"

A six-word *what*?

"Here's an example!" she said, cheery as all get-out. Supposedly Ernest Hemingway had written a six-word story, like a thousand years before. Miss Amber had memorized it: *For sale: baby shoes, never worn.* Then she explained what the words meant. The baby hadn't survived, and so that's why the parents had to sell the baby shoes. Get it? Never worn. I know.

We started to write. Well, by "we" I mean everyone but me. I guess thinking about the baby shoes made me think about the baby's parents, all sad, like deflated or something. Then I pictured Dad, which led me down a whole other trail of thoughts. Miss Amber roamed from person to person, then paused at me. Or at my empty paper. But she didn't do the squat-by-my-side thing, or the try-your-best teacher thing. To my surprise, she said, "Sometimes, staring into space helps." Huh? "Don't think about it too much. Stare. Daydream. Wonder." Double huh? "Okay. Maybe instead of objects, your six words can be emotions, hobbies, or even words in another language, or in the form of a question. What questions do you have about the world? Remember: no more than six words. You got this."

So I did what she said—stared, dreamed, wondered. I thought of the question Steve asked me that day at the fire drill: *Where are you from-from?* Truth, when I think about where I'm from, I feel proud, like yeah, I'm from Boston. But then, well, I'm Latina, and my parents were born in Central America, and I'm from "JP" or "the city." What people like Steve were really doing was not asking a question but making a statement: *You must not be from here.* So for my six-word autobiography, I wrote: *Don't ask me where I'm from.* Yeah. And when Miss Amber asked us to share, for once I didn't hesitate. I read it aloud: "Don't ask me where I'm from."

Silence. Head nods. Me, exhaling. I felt lighter just having said it.

"Liliana, thanks for getting us started. Can you tell us more about why you chose those particular six words?" Miss Amber encouraged.

"Well . . ." I refocused. "I'm sick of people asking me where I am from. No—where I am '*from*-from.' I am sick of people assuming I wasn't born in this country or that I don't speak English or that I eat rice and beans every night for dinner."

Two girls laughed. But in an *I got you* way.

I felt lighter and lighter. And I couldn't stop. I told them about the meme of Rayshawn with a noose made of basketball net, and how there was like, no diversity at my school.

"What town is your school in?" Miss Amber asked.

"Westburg."

Her eyes went all bright. "Wait! Do you know Mrs. Grew?"

Whaaaaa? "Um, yeah. She's one of my teachers."

"Get out! I know her from graduate school. She was a mentor teacher in my program. She gave a presentation once on how she'd organized a GoFundMe page where her class actually raised enough money to go to Washington, DC, on April vacation that year. I was so impressed."

My mind = berserk. "For real? You actually know *Mrs. Grew*?"

"Yeah. She's a really fabulous teacher."

Mrs. Grew?

"All right," Miss Amber was saying. "I didn't mean to get us off track. That's a fantastic six-word autobiography, Liliana. *So* telling. Okay, who wants to go next?"

A girl named Gabriela read hers aloud: "No, I do not eat dogs." We were dying! Another girl, named Christina, read: "Write poems, eat, sleep, then repeat." Yeah, this 826 place . . . it was different. . . . Different was good. Though I could *not* believe that Miss Amber and Mrs. Grew knew each other.

29

For homework in Mr. Phelps's class we'd read an article on the subject of intersecting languages in the modern world. Now he was asking what we thought about a multilingual society, what the benefits and drawbacks of it were for any nation. As usual, he glanced meaningfully at me. As usual, my heart was beating fast. But this time it wasn't because I didn't want to share; it was because I *did*. But . . . I didn't raise my hand just yet. One girl, Erin—also the class president—did, though. "Mr. Phelps, seriously."

"Is that a comment, Erin?"

"I'm just saying, this is America and all, and we speak English. So anyone who comes to this country should learn English. I mean, it's not a crazy idea. That's our language. Like, if I went to Russia, I'd be expected to speak Russian, right? I wouldn't expect Russians to all learn English because *I* was there."

I kicked at my chair leg. *Here we freakin' go again.*

Erin adjusted her hair band. She must have really loved those things; she wore a different color, like, every day. Today's was lavender. And she still had a tan left over from wherever her family had gone for Thanksgiving. Who goes away for Thanksgiving? Isn't the whole point to stuff yourself with turkey and mashed potatoes and pie and wear sweaters and watch movies with your cousins? That's what we did every year—this year *without* Dad. No one even mentioned him the entire day. Mom worked that morning, helping a family in Brookline cook and clean for their guests, then came home super exhausted, and we ate stuffing and mashed potatoes and pie (which the boys made)—and waited for the turkey to finish roasting till midnight because, yeah, we'd forgotten to put it in the oven early enough.

Now Erin squared her shoulders, not done. "I'm just saying that it's one thing if you *want* to speak more than one language, but shouldn't everyone be *expected* to speak English in the US?"

A guy named Andrew called out, "You're just pissed because you probably suck at foreign languages. Take Spanish with Señorita Kim. She's so easy. She plays movies and soap operas or whatever, like every day."

A couple of kids laughed. I kept kicking at my chair leg.

Erin looked Andrew square in the eye. "Whatever."

This girl named Sarah chimed in. She had gorgeous hair, like down to her butt. I think she was growing it out to donate to cancer or something. "You know, Erin has a point. When my family and I went on safari in Zimbabwe and Kenya last year, we had to learn like ten words in Shona and another ten in Swahili."

"Oh my God," a guy in the back muttered. "That must have been exhausting."

I laughed. I couldn't help it.

Mistake. Phelps pounced.

"Miss Cruz? Do you have something to contribute to the discussion?"

I took my hands out of my pockets. Something to contribute? Yes. But I knew that if I spoke up, I'd have like forty eyes on me, like I was the representative of all Spanish-speaking people in the friggin' universe. So I shook my head. Pass.

Mr. Phelps looked disappointed. "Anyone else?" he asked.

"You know what I hate?" Erin's BFF Kate called out.

"What's that?" Mr. Phelps sat back on his stool.

"How Spanish is taking over TV."

Now Mr. Phelps folded his arms. "I'm not following."

Kate looked exasperated. "You know, how sometimes there are lines or jokes that are in Spanish in shows, and I'm expected to understand them. Without subtitles!"

"Yeah." "Uh-huh." "Yup." "Oh yeah." So many kids agreed with her! I couldn't believe it.

Erin's hand shot back up.

Mr. Phelps eyed the clock. "Yes?"

"It happens in music, too. Like, every time I stream music, there's always something with lyrics in Spanish. 'Despacito,' anyone? It's so annoying."

My left knee started bouncing. What, were we an inconvenience? *Annoying?* I couldn't take it anymore.

"So, um, excuse me."

Boom. Forty eyes on me. Called it!

"Miss Cruz?"

I cleared my throat. "Yeah, so, are you all even *aware* that, I mean, the word 'Florida' means 'flowery' in Spanish? And that 'Colorado' means 'red' or 'red-colored'? These words are in *Spanish* because the *Spanish* were actually here *before* the English. I'm just saying." The last part I had read about in our textbook, so I kind of thought I deserved extra credit, no lie.

Dead silence. I could hear the clock ticking on the wall. Then one kid in the front row said, "I'm hip." I almost slid out of my chair. It was the Asian kid. Cambodian? Whoa.

"Thank you, Miss Cruz," Mr. Phelps was saying. "You raise an excellent point—"

Then I remembered something else, and out came "Yeah, and the border of Mexico and the United States used to be different before. Like, Mexico actually included the states of Arizona and New Mexico and parts of Texas and California." I'd read *that* in one of the books from Mr. Phelps's shelf. Actually, I should remember to use that info for a slide for the assembly.

Mr. Phelps nodded. This time, I didn't care how many eyes were on me. I really didn't. But then Erin said, all snippy, "Yeah, well, that's not the case now."

"*Well,*" I jumped on this (with a capital *A* attitude, I'll admit). "I'm just saying that yeah, you may feel annoyed having to press one for English or whatever. But imagine how annoyed you'd be if someone came and kicked you off your own land and told you that your language, food, culture, *everything*, was wrong. And you had to change it. Or die. *That's* messed up, right? *That's* annoying, right?"

The class blew up.

"Oh . . ."

"Boom . . ."

"She told you, Erin!"

I couldn't tell what Erin was thinking. She began reapplying lip balm in slow motion. But then all of a sudden she stood and ran out of the classroom. Her face looked on the verge of crumpling.

Mr. Phelps hopped off the stool. "All right. Everyone, take out your notebooks. Write a paragraph reflection. I'll be right back."

Here's what I wrote:

> *Oh, great. Now I am going to be labeled the angry Latina who told off the blond white girl. See, this is why I never say anything in class.*

A few minutes later Erin and Mr. Phelps came back into the room. Erin's face was beet red. She snatched up her backpack and left the room once more. A couple of kids gave me dirty looks. But I hadn't said anything that was that bad, or untrue. And you know what, I'd had enough. *Enough.* "Mr. Phelps?"

"Yes, Lili?"

"Can I get the bathroom pass?"

"Yes, sure. Go," he said distractedly.

Part of me wanted to run to the nearest bathroom stall and cry. Another part of me just wanted to pretend to be sick and take a nap in the nurse's room. But then I had a better idea. I dug into my backpack and wrote out a fake pass for Dustin using my most convincing teacher handwriting— the messier, the better. I crumpled up the paper a little (to make it look more authentic), then walked to the math wing, pretty sure Dustin was in algebra. I felt almost light-headed as I stepped into the doorway. The teacher was writing out some scary-hard-looking equation.

And—damn. Steve was in this class too. He saw me first and began to cough real loudly. The teacher looked over at me. "Yes?"

"Oh. Hi. The, um, librarian needs to see Dustin." I lifted the pass, but the math teacher simply waved a green Expo marker in the air and returned to the problem on the board.

Dustin's eyes bulged, but his expression stayed cool. He strode past the rows of students and ignored Steve's cough-ing, which at this point sounded like a case of TB. For sure I thought the teacher would catch on, see that there was no real need for him in the library, that this was totally cause for detention, but no. She was already on to the next equation.

In the hall Dustin grabbed my wrist. "So . . . what's up?"

I couldn't form the words.

"Lili?"

"I—" My voice caught.

"Wait. Come on," he said, and led me down the hallway, toward the door to the basement. When we turned the corner, I bumped into Genesis. She dropped her book.

"Hey, girl," I said, bending over to help her pick it up. But—so bizarre—she just scooped it up and kept walking. Like, flat-out ignored me.

Dustin, gnawing his thumbnail, glanced toward the door. Whatever. I'd catch up with Genesis later. Right then, I needed to talk to Dustin.

After climbing over a set of hurdles and some random cones, we found our space from last time in the basement. I leaned against his chest, and suddenly shivered, goose bumps sprouting on my arms.

"Hey," Dustin said. "You okay?"

"Yeah." I crossed my arms.

He took off his Westburg sweatshirt. "Here."

I inhaled his sweatshirt's scent and put it on. It was too big, but it was perfect. "Thanks."

Then Dustin dipped his head and kissed me. His lips on my lips. Again and again. I felt like we were deep underwater, the rest of the world muted and far away. Then he wrapped his arms around me and lifted me about a foot off the ground, and I let out a little scream. I wasn't used to people, um, picking me up. I slapped my hand over my mouth. "Sorry," I whispered. "Do you think someone heard?"

"No. We better be quieter, though."

He pulled me even closer. Not close enough. I burrowed my face into his neck.

"Lili? What's going on?"

I wasn't crying, but I was struggling not to. "It's a long story."

"So tell me. You got me out of a wildly fascinating algebra class, after all."

I laughed—thanks to Dustin for that—then told him everything that had happened, how Erin had come back all hurt like I had *assaulted* her or something.

"Forget about her," Dustin said. "She's so sensitive. She's probably just mad that someone finally called her out on her shit."

"Maybe." I rested my head on his chest.

"Hey," he said, his voice cracking a little. "How well do you know Gen?"

"Who?"

"Gen."

Maybe because I still felt like I was underwater, it took me a second to make sense of what he was saying. "Oh . . . Genesis Peña? She's my METCO buddy. Do you know her?"

At that moment his phone buzzed from inside his jeans pocket. He ignored it, and we kissed some more. After a minute his phone buzzed again.

I pulled away. "Do you need to check that or something?"

"Nope."

When his phone buzzed a third time, I knew something was up.

"Fine," he said with a sigh. Then he read his texts and started to frown.

"Who is it?"

"Steve," he muttered, still reading. Then his expression changed, and I swear I felt him ever so slightly nudge me away. "Lili? What *exactly* did you say to Erin?"

Soooo. Apparently Erin had texted Steve after our little discussion in history class. She'd told Steve that I "attacked" her. Dustin showed me the texts, and I dropped the phone on his foot. He scooped it back up. "No big deal. Steve just wants to know what really happened. I'll tell him your side of the story."

"My *side* of the story?" Now I drew away.

"You know what I mean. Look, let's just forget about it." He reached for my waist, but I drew back even further.

"Lil?"

"Look, I gotta go."

His eyes looked hurt. "Where are you going?"

"I'll text you." I gave him a kiss on the cheek, then maneuvered my way through the maze of basketballs and field hockey sticks just as the bell rang. I ran so fast up the stairs that my quads burned. Back in the hallway, people stared. Or was I imagining this? I spotted Rayshawn closing his locker. I decided to stop and say hey instead of just waving. He looked surprised to see me, but in a good way.

"Whatsup?"

"Nothing," I said, trying to steady my breath.

"Yo," he said, but his happy look turned to one of concern. "You okay?"

"Yeah," I said. "Are *you* okay?"

"I am now. I heard Chris Sweet transferred to some private school. I guess his parents were flipping out because of his grades."

"Huh."

"Right? Doesn't matter anyway. *I'm* still playing ball. My moms didn't want me to miss more school, either. She thinks the tutor wasn't really doing much. I mean, he wasn't."

"So did they find out who did it? Made the meme?"

"Nah. But I'm glad Chris left. Now I don't get dirty looks for taking his spot on the court."

"Yeah, whatever." I tightened my top bun.

"Yo, Lili, you *sure* you're good? You seem . . . off."

I didn't want to get into it, what had happened with Erin in Mr. Phelps's class. Not now, anyway. So I let out a long breath. "I'm good. Listen, I'll catch ya later."

"Okay . . ." I could feel him watching me as I speed-walked down the hall to return Mr. Phelps's bathroom pass.

On the way, I spotted Genesis standing outside the guidance office. I called out to her. She didn't hear me, so I walked closer.

"Genesis!" I attracted glares from two girls at their lockers.

I was standing directly in front of her, and still, nothing. "Yo, are you okay?"

Her eyes narrowed into an angry squint, her face set like stone. "I didn't get into Yale," she spat out.

"Oh . . ." That had to suck.

"I mean, I was deferred, but whatever. I didn't get *in*."

I leaned forward to hug her, but she put up her palm.

"Don't do that," she said.

"Genesis . . ."

"Don't act like we're all friends, girl. I'm just your METCO buddy."

"Come on, Gen," I said. "We're . . . friends."

Genesis didn't answer, just pointed to the bulletin board. Pink, green, blue, and yellow flyers advertising various SAT prep classes and extracurricular clubs hung at odd angles. "This is all BULLSHIT!" she exploded. "I mean, I joined practically every club in this freakin' school for the last four years and kept a 3.9 GPA and speak three languages and volunteer at an animal shelter and at a bilingual preschool and act in the school plays, and all for what? I mean, you think I really wanted to play a bratty daughter in *The Emperor's New Clothes*? I like being onstage and all. Don't get it twisted. But it was just one more thing. You know? And all for squat."

I scrambled for the right thing to say. "Look, maybe the person reading your application was just . . . just in a bad mood or something. You can still get in! You just said you were deferred, right?"

"Yeah, right." She clutched her books against her chest. "Funny that *you're* giving me advice, Liliana, when clearly you don't listen to mine."

I took a step back. "What do you mean?"

Now she smirked. "Don't act so stupid."

"I'm not stupid." But—what was she implying?

"No?" Genesis asked. "Then why are you hanging out with Dustin Walker? Sneaking off to the basement like some skank? I told you to stay away from the white boys. But you didn't listen."

"Whoa. Who you calling a skank?" I had never been in a physical fight before, not even with my brothers, and yet I felt myself ready to smack Genesis across her smug straight-A face.

The smug stayed, because she went on. "You. You think you're the first girl Dustin's brought down there? Correction—the first METCO girl he's brought down there? Pa-lease."

I'd never really thought about that, but—so what? Dustin probably had a few girlfriends before me.

"No . . . ," I managed to say. "But that's his business. And why do you care anyway?"

She fake laughed, and that was it. I shoved her so hard that she fell back on her butt, her books landing everywhere. Truth, she looked stunned, her mouth hanging open and all. I left her and her attitude there on the floor, and as I walked away, I gave the girls at their lockers a look like, *Don't even think about saying something*. I ran the bathroom pass to Mr. Phelps, grabbed my backpack, then headed for my bus.

But I couldn't stop thinking about what Genesis had said about Dustin.

I texted him. Nada. So I called him. He didn't pick up! Something was going on. Then I remembered—he had an away game for his indoor soccer team. One of these buses had to be his team's. The buses' brake lights glowed red in the gray. I didn't have much time. I ran to the end of the bus line. There he was—about to get on!

"Hey, Dustin," I said, out of breath. The bus engine revved up, so I spoke louder. "Hey!"

"Oh—hey," he said. He glanced back at the other guys waiting to get on behind him.

"Did you get my text? And I tried to call you like a minute ago. . . ."

"What? Oh, no, didn't see it. Whatsup?" And all of a sudden I wasn't sure if I believed him.

"Nothing really. I just had a question about Genesis."

"Now? I'm about to go to a game!" But he moved away from the other guys, let them get on the bus.

"Yeah. She was acting kind of strange today, and, well, how do you know her again?"

"Me?" Dustin stepped further away from the door.

Okay, now I *knew* something was up. And I bet I knew—duh!—what it was! "Did you two . . . used to go out or something?"

"Me, with Genesis? Oh, like, not really."

I gaped at him. "What does that mean? 'Not really'?"

The coach blew his whistle and yelled, "Hurry up, ladies!" to the guys who were still pushing their way onto the bus. No one laughed. Especially not me.

"So did you or didn't you?" I pressed, almost yelling to be heard over the engine. Dustin shifted from one foot to the other, looking everywhere except at me. His idiot friend

Steve came up and slapped him on the back of his head. Oh, great. Steve. Erin's manager, apparently. "Yo, buddy. We gotta go," he said.

I gave him the side-eye. He glared at me and then said to Dustin, "Stop talking to Dora the Explorer and get on the fuckin' bus, dude."

I did a double take. "Excuse me?"

"Forget it," Dustin said quickly, shoving Steve toward the bus. "Dude, just go."

Steve laughed and jumped onto the bus. I stared after him. Wow. Okay, dude needs to like, go to the marsh or whatever, and stay there. Did he really just call me— "Did you hear what he just said?" I fumed to Dustin.

Dustin grabbed my hand. "He's an asshole. Listen, can we talk later?" He glanced at the bus. "It's just—the bus is—"

"No," I cut him off, pulling my hand away.

"What?"

Now I was the one glaring. "You're just going to let Steve say that to me?"

"He didn't really mean . . . I mean, c'mon . . . It's not that big a deal, Lili." He reached for my hand again—I swung it out of his reach.

"Not that big a deal? Are you serious?"

Steve pulled down a window and yelled, "¡Vámonos, muchacho!"

A roar of laughter followed. I wanted to vaporize. "Great taste in friends, Dustin," I said, and turned away, toward my own bus, toward a different part of the world.

* * * *

On the ride home, my hands were trembling as I sent Genesis a text.

Me: **Genesis? U there?**

Genesis:

Me: **I'm sorry**

Genesis:

Me: **what happened w/Dustin 4 real?**

Genesis:

Me:

Then finally, Genesis: **u don't even know**

Me: **?**

Genesis: **call u in 5**

To be honest, I didn't really want to hear about Dustin and her, you know, together, so I was dreading her call. Plus, I had basically knocked her onto her butt. So when my phone rang, I hovered my finger over the red button, but in the end I hit the green one. We both said "Sorry" simultaneously.

Then Genesis told me everything. Including how Dustin and she used to date and how he tried to deny it when his "real" girlfriend—some girl who was at some boarding school—accused him of cheating. Apparently it had been a *thing* and everyone had taken sides—METCO kids included—until it had become yesterday's news. Of course I instantly wondered if he still had this boarding-school girlfriend.

"Dustin and I haven't said a word since," Genesis explained.

"So, let's just say I'm good with white boys. Like, no más. Feel me?"

Truth, I felt like I'd been sucker punched. Yet I was weirdly relieved, too. It all made sense. Ever since that day when Genesis had first seen me going to the basement with Dustin, she'd been acting all nutso.

"I guess I thought you already knew," Genesis was saying now. "Everyone else does." I couldn't believe how matter-of-fact she sounded.

"But what about Yale?" I asked her.

"What *about* Yale?"

"Don't you think there'll be a whole lotta white boys at Yale?"

"Ha. Well, I got deferred, remember?"

"Like I said earlier, you'll get in. You'll see. So be positive!"

"Or what?"

"Or . . . I'll send Steve after you."

"Ew!"

And we started laughing.

For the rest of the bus ride I tried to make sense of it all. Dustin and Genesis . . . huh. Then Dustin and me. So did he have a *thing* for *exotic* METCO girls or something? What the freak? Did he like me for me, or just because I fit his *type*? Or—did he think he would get further with Latinas or something? Genesis wasn't good enough to be his real girlfriend, so he'd had her as his little B-side hookup? Was that was *I* was? My stomach hurt. The worst part was that he hadn't stuck up for me. Cuz truth, I really liked him. But truth, I wasn't worth sticking up for. I hugged my knees, trying not to cry. I felt like total crap. And I knew what I needed to do next.

After dinner, I called him. Dustin. And he picked up. I had taken my phone outside and sat on the stoop despite it being like a hundred degrees below zero out. Or felt like it. "So, here's the thing, Dustin," I said, setting my shoulders even though obviously he couldn't even see me. "I just don't get how you could, like, stand back while Steve acted mad racist."

"Lil—"

"No. For real, how could you just . . . do *nothing*? I mean, it wasn't some random person. . . . It was *me*." My throat caught. *Don't you dare cry. Don't you dare cry.*

"It really wasn't like that. I . . . I don't know how to explain it."

"So why don't you try? And while you're at it, why didn't you tell me about you and Genesis?"

He stayed quiet.

"Is it true? *Did* you have a girlfriend at boarding school while you were with Genesis?"

This time I could hear his breath, then a long sigh.

"I'll take that as a yes." When he said nothing, I said, "Back to Steve, though. . . . You don't care, huh?"

"I—"

"You don't care enough to say anything."

He stayed quiet.

I squeezed my eyes shut. There was no going back.

I didn't want to go back. "Okay, so I guess this is it."

"So . . . see you around, then," Dustin said crazy-fast, and hung up.

Wow. Just like that. We were done. I leaned into the side railing and let myself cry. When I noticed a lady walking her white poodle, heading my way, I wiped my eyes and slipped back inside.

I was so angry. And I was so stinkin' sad. I couldn't stop thinking about Dustin all night. I pictured us snuggled up on the top bleacher at lunch, then walking to his house from school that day (when I wore my hoodie like I was in a witness-protection program—ha), and all the times he'd met me at my locker, how my whole body smiled when I first spotted him. And his smell. That shampoo-ChapStick combo. I curled into bed. This. Sucked.

Turns out, I didn't know how bad suck could suck. Because after a lot of *poor pitiful me* crying, I started scrolling through Twitter, trying to distract myself, and I saw that Steve had posted some ignorant tweet about how **SOME people** don't know what the fuck they're talking about and they should **SHUT UP** and **GO BACK WHERE THEY CAME FROM**. I seriously almost rolled off my mattress. It was shared ninety-seven times! And it was as if Steve's comment lit a match. Another kid started posting links to articles and posters supporting white nationalist propaganda. I couldn't believe what I was reading, and I couldn't stop reading, and my stomach wouldn't stop clenching.

For the rest of the night all I did was text. From the safety of my bed, I texted Holly, Jade, Brianna, Rayshawn, Genesis. Other METCO kids. My thumbs were aching; I kept going. Who I did NOT text: Dustin.

Then, sometime late late that night, some anonymous person posted a meme. Of me. On Instagram.

Of *me*.

Holly alerted me to it first, texting just before dawn, before I was even out of bed yet: **Lili. OMG. Sorry to share but WTF??** and a link. After a moment's hesitation—did I really want to see this?—I tapped the link. And there it was. My face, my *face*, was photoshopped onto a piñata, and at the top of the screen was the word "wetback." It took all my self-control not to throw the phone across my room.

Seven thousand thoughts collided in my brain. *Who did this? Is this for real?* Did people really think I was a wetback? A *wetback*? That I'd, like . . . swum across the Rio Grande to get to the United States, cuz hello, that's what "wetback" means. Seriously? Aside from the term being derogatory, so what if I *had*? And—and—so what if my *dad* had? I thought furiously. Who the fuck would have done this? And really—a piñata? No one knew about my dad except Jade, Ernesto— and Dustin! Dustin! That asshole! But would he really go *this* far? Because I'd broken up with him? Seriously?

I had to put my phone down because my hands were literally shaking. Dustin! My heart was hammering. I opened my bedroom window, desperate for air. Was this a panic attack? The logical part of my brain was thinking: *I know Dustin. He wouldn't be that much of an ass. He couldn't be.* But he was the only person at Westburg who knew!

Then my brain landed on: Everyone would see this meme. What if my *parents* saw? They never would, but my brain was clearly out of my control. I couldn't stop picking up the phone again, looking again. There was bile in my throat. I had to calm down. I took deep breaths. I remembered my mother opening and closing her fists, and tried that. I clenched my fists so hard, they hurt. And that hurt shifted something—because suddenly I had a single calm thought. Which led me to a very calm decision. I took a screenshot of the meme and sent it to Mr. Rivera. He emailed me back immediately. I was to come straight to his office when I got to school. Then I texted Jade. She replied with a meme of a woman covering her mouth in slow motion.

The walk from the bus into school felt like a marathon. I didn't look up once. I could sense people eyeing me. It helped that I was bundled up in a coat and scarf and hat. Not that anyone at Westburg even wore winter coats. I'm hip. Even though they probably had thousand-dollar goose-down parkas at home, they didn't wear them to school—I'm guessing because they went directly from cars with heated leather seats into warm buildings, and back. No waiting for the T or the bus in single-digit weather. But *that* was a whole other thing. Sometimes I wished my brain could just focus.

Minutes later, I was sitting on the small couch in Mr. Rivera's office. He had already shared the meme with the administration, and he said a formal report would be written up, not that that meant anything immediately. But he told me I didn't have to go to first period if I didn't want to, wrote me a pass, said to just stay put, and then he got busy talking to other administrators and filling out paperwork.

I couldn't face going to class yet, anyway. But I was too fired up to sit there doing nothing. Yeah. Fired up. I wished I hadn't already done all my homework. I wished I'd brought my notebook, *anything* for a distraction. Damn. Even working on that METCO presentation would be better than just sitting there. My leg was bouncing like I'd downed five cups of coffee. Like every neuron in my body had gone electric. Yeah, fired up. And that's when it struck me—the METCO project. Oh yeah. Yes! *Let those administrators do their paperwork for the next decade. Liliana, you stay* chill. The METCO kids and I—we'd show those racist fools at the assembly. But until then, I was going to suck it up and go to class. And more importantly, find Dustin. He and I needed another talk. Big-time.

Before geometry I spotted him at the end of the hall, but he stepped inside the nearest classroom. Had he seen me? Was he avoiding me? What a wimp. Whatever. I'd find him later.

At lunch I sat with the METCO kids. Yep. It took a mad

racist meme, but they waved me over to sit with them at last. I caught Holly's eye at our regular table, and she *totally* got it, gave me a *Go over there, girl* head nod. They were all as amped up as I was at the other table, their voices loud, hard.

Brianna grabbed my arm. "I just can't believe this shit. No—I *can*."

"You know what? Fuck them!" Marquis fumed, his mouth full of food. He practically started choking.

"Don't die on us, Marquis," I said. Everyone managed a laugh.

"Yo." He coughed hard, cleared his throat. "I'm hip. People should just be happy I didn't start posting stuff in response to 'Go back.' Listen, I could have written some stuff." He paused. "But *I'd* be kicked out of school in a *second*."

Brianna crunched hard on a carrot. "They can't do that to you and not what's-his-face."

"Steve," I offered. "You mean Steve." I'd been thinking about what he'd written—he was super careful, actually. Saying "some people" and "go back" online weren't exactly things you could get suspended for, and he knew it.

"Whatever that fool's name is. Wasn't he the one on teen *Jeopardy!*? Anyway, doesn't matter. I don't care what show he was on, he's mad ignorant." Marquis took a big bite of his hamburger.

"For real, though, how could they make that meme of you on a piñata—" Brianna couldn't even finish her sentence. "I would be going ballistic."

"I am!" I said.

"No. Like, I'd grab whoever did that and just—" She made a fist.

Dustin. I pictured his face, his bangs in his eyes. Ugh. I'd gone over this a million times, so much that I could actually feel my brain pulsing. No one else here knew about my dad.

Then, get this: Dustin actually walked over to my table. For a second, I thought I was imagining it.

"Hey," he said, looking mad awkward. "Can we talk?"

"Actually, I need to talk to *you*," I said, willing calm into my voice.

As his friends two tables over stifled laughs and coughs, I snatched the closest carton of milk and lifted it in the air. So much for calm.

"Lili!" he yelped.

I was seriously about to pour it over his head. "How could you, Dustin?"

"What are you doing?"

"You know *exactly* what I'm talking about." My calm had fled, and I'd switched to trying not to cry. His friends were now flat-out howling.

"Know *what*?" he asked.

"God! At least have the cojones to admit it—the meme? Of *me*?"

"Have the *what*?"

"BALLS!" I yelled. One tilt of my hand, and the contents of the carton would be all over his head.

"Whoa, calm down!" he said, reaching up to take the carton from my hand. He placed it back on the table.

"I didn't, Lili. It wasn't me, I swear. That's what I came here to say. I knew you would think it was me." His face was dead serious as he leaned in and whispered, "I would never do that to you. *Never*. You know me better than that."

I gave him some real side-eye and sat back down.

"Lili!" He started to say something else, but he hesitated.

"Wait." I pivoted. "*You* know who did it."

"Shit." Dustin looked back at his table. "Over here," he said, waving me over to the windows.

"It was Steve, wasn't it?" I asked. Of course! I couldn't even bring myself to look at his table. If I met eyes with him, I would officially lose it.

"Lili, I swear, I never told him. I knew you were going to think that, too. But he doesn't know about your father—"

"Oh, okay! I'm really supposed to believe that." The bile rose up in my throat once more. "So . . . how then? How did he find out?"

"I don't know. He was just being a jerk, I guess. He's always making memes. But I swear to you—"

I was only half listening, because I was thinking back . . . back to the times when Steve had acted totally jealous every time Dustin hung out with me instead of him. Like I was taking his best friend away. Wow. Maybe Dustin *was* telling the truth. Because deep down, did I *really* believe that Dustin would do something as awful as tell Steve about my dad? Steve must have been *really* pissed about the whole Erin drama in Mr. Phelps's class too. . . . Yeah, it all made sense. And—is this pathetic?—I actually felt a little bit better—that it *wasn't* Dustin. But that only lasted for a second, because then I realized that Dustin was *still* friends with Steve even after he'd made the meme. Had Dustin just let it slide? I glanced over. Dustin was gnawing his thumbnail so hard, I thought he might bite off his entire thumb. Let me guess— he hadn't said squat.

"Whatever, Dustin," I said, and walked away.

Despite the fact that half the cafeteria was probably watching, I didn't care. I couldn't even figure out how I felt about *anything* because it was like I was feeling *everything*. Confused, pissed, relieved, embarrassed, sad. Dustin *so* wasn't the person I'd thought he was! And that sucked in a major way.

As I sat down, hard, I could see Holly three tables over. She was on her phone. Her new thing was an SAT vocab app; she was obsessed. I stood back up and tossed my lunch into the trash can.

I caught Brianna's eye. "Later," I said.

"You bet."

I walked toward Holly. "Hey," I said. "Mind if I interrupt your SAT vocab app for a minute?"

She looked up. "Fuck yeah," she said. "I hate this bullshit. I hate tests. I hate it all. But how are *you*?"

I came home to find Mom sitting at the kitchen table, her head in her hands. I raced over, dropped to my knees. "Mom! What's wrong? Is it Dad?"

"No, mija," she said, her voice so deflated, eerie almost.

"What is it, then?"

"The school called."

Oh. *Oh.*

"Liliana . . ." She hesitated. Then, like someone had lit a match inside her, she bolted up. "Liliana, I've been sitting here thinking, Could my daughter really be this irresponsible? Could she *really not understand the situation we are in*?"

"Mom, wait—"

"No! *You* wait. You listen. Liliana, the school counselor told me about the picture of your face on a piñata, con esa palabra, 'wetback.' My first thought was, who would do that to my DAUGHTER? And as I sat here, getting angrier and angrier, I started wondering *how* someone would *know* to do that— So how would they *know* that? Pues, you're not one, but I'm just trying to think about how they would make that connection. They must know about your father and me, then. Right? How? Any ideas?" She was on fire.

"Mom—"

"So who did you tell? That Holly girl?"

"No!"

"What were you thinking! What if someone over there had called ICE? Can you . . . Did you even . . . If ICE found out . . ." She couldn't finish a single sentence, she was so mad.

"Mom, no one is going to do that!" I couldn't even bring myself to say "ICE."

Her eyes bulged. "You. Don't. Know. That!"

Maybe she was right. Oh . . . no. But, no. "Mom, it was just some stupid kid who was being racist because you and Dad are from Central America. That's all."

"That's all," Mom repeated. She massaged the gold cross on her neck. "Mija, I've been thinking," she said at last. "Maybe you shouldn't go to that school anymore. . . . If you don't feel safe . . . If someone goes and tells . . ." Again with the unfinished sentences.

"No," I said, my voice all deep like I was the parent. "I'm not going anywhere. I'm not letting some ignorant people say where I go or don't go."

For a split second she looked at me, wondering if maybe I was talking about *her*. Which wasn't what I meant at all!

"Mom. No one knows anything specific. I'm fine. We're fine. Nothing is going to happen." That's what I was saying. In my head, I was praying that Dustin had actually told the truth at lunch earlier, that Steve didn't actually know about my dad or my family. He'd just hit a nerve. . . . Yeah, hit it with a sledgehammer.

Mom's eyes glassed. She reached for me, and I sat on her lap even though we were the same size now. I can't remember the last time I'd done that.

Next, she dropped this news on me: we were going to spend Christmas with my aunt in Lynn this year. For the first time in the history of my life, I *didn't* want Christmas break to come. Ugh. Usually it was like my favorite time of the year. But with everything at school—plus, hello, the assembly that was happening in like three seconds, not to mention Dad not being here . . . The holidays—and our Christmas tree—well, they sucked. "Sucked" was clearly my word of the month. In fact, we'd only put up a small plastic tree in the living room, the one that usually went on the counter in the kitchen. We didn't bother lugging up the big one stored in the basement. So, yeah, we'd still be staying up until midnight and eating tamales and opening presents on Christmas Eve, but this time we'd be using sleeping bags at my aunt's. Double ugh.

So I took my phone to the living room and stretched out on the couch, the red and green Christmas lights on the fake tree blinking beside me. I tried to focus on the Google Doc on my Chromebook (thank you, Westburg). Today was so crazy that I'd nearly forgotten that the assembly was tomorrow! Yeah, tomorrow. I stared at the screen, reading the same stuff over and over, and then I must have fallen asleep. Mom tapped me on the arm and told me to go to bed if I was so tired. "You'll sleep better there," she said. "C'mon. I'll be back in a bit. Going to get the boys." But it was way too early to go to sleep for the night. And I hadn't even eaten dinner. Just then my phone dinged. Dustin.

Dustin had sent a text. But it wasn't the kind I'd been expecting. You know, another apology or something. Instead he simply wrote: **hey, can u leave my sweatshirt in my locker? thx.**

Suddenly I was wide awake. I admit—that stung. Like he was erasing me, deleting me. His sweatshirt? Really? I had it stuffed underneath my bed so Mom wouldn't find it. Now I'd have to dig it out. And smell Dustin all over it. There was the sting again.

I didn't write back.

My stomach gave a growl, matching my mood. He'd moved on. So would *I*. Aside from being pissed, I was hungry. So I decided to try to make rice again. Only this time, I used a pinch of salt—which I measured in a spoon first, instead of pouring straight from the container—and set the timer on my phone. I really wanted dinner to be all set before Mom and the boys got home, but that didn't happen. My brothers burst through the door, slammed down their backpacks, and headed straight to the bathroom.

"Hello?" I called. The toilet flushed.

Benjamin peeked into the kitchen. He still had his coat

on and was sprinkled with snow. "Oh no! Liliana is cooking again. Please don't burn down the apartment this time!"

"Very funny."

But instead of continuing to bust on me, Benjamin came back into the kitchen. "Need help?" His voice was surprisingly void of sarcasm.

"Really?"

"Yeah. Move it." He dug in the refrigerator and pulled out some hot dogs. "Here. Cut these up into quarter-inch chunks."

I did.

Next he microwaved some frozen peas and corn, added those to the rice in the pot. Then he sprinkled in a bit of Sazón seasoning, the one in the orange envelopes that Mom kept in the cupboard between the salt and the thyme.

"Thanks," I said to my brother the chef.

"No prob. Just keep it on low heat for like ten minutes, and you're good."

"You're really learning a lot in that Kids' Chef Club, huh?"

"Yeah. When Dad gets back, he won't even believe it."

We locked eyes. *That's right, Little Brother,* mine said. His look was more guarded, but I could see the tiniest flicker of hope. Then he crowed, "I got skills!" and hightailed it to his room.

Anyway, hello, I had made dinner! Well, *we* had made dinner. That wasn't mac and cheese! And I hadn't set off the smoke detector! Man, Benjamin was right. When Dad got back and saw the boys being all Top Chefs, it was going to blow his mind. In the meantime, I sent Jade a quick text and a picture of the meal. She gave me a thumbs-up and said to save her some.

As wiped as I'd been earlier, when I finally got into bed, I couldn't sleep. I tried to think through plans for the presentation, but, truth, I kept checking my phone, waiting for another text from Dustin. Something. But, nada. Pathetic! I *know*. But there it is. I went from mad to sad and back again every two minutes. Were we that disposable? Didn't he have any feelings at all? I needed to get a grip. So I sent texts to METCO friends. Never thought I'd say that! Brianna sent me some funny-as-hell breakup GIFs—including one of a girl on a couch hitting the remote at the TV, and the caption *You canceled*. Yeah, I laughed.

So—I couldn't focus on our presentation last night, but it was the first thing I thought of when I woke up. I'm not saying I was TOTALLY nervous, but I changed my shirt six times before I headed out for the bus, and then, yeah, for real, I ran back inside one last time and put back on the very first shirt, a pinkish-purple one, that I'd started with. At school, first thing, I bombed over to Mr. Rivera's office. I guess I was kinda looking for a little final inspiration. A mini pep talk. On my way, a girl I knew from French class, Rosie—who had freckles all over her face, even on her ears—stopped me in the hall. "Hey," she said. "So . . . um . . . I just wanna say it really sucks, what they posted of you. Some people are just ignorant assholes."

It took me a second to register what she was saying.

The meme. She had seen it. Of course she'd seen it. Seemed everyone had.

"Oh . . . thanks." I smiled and kept moving. Yeah, some people *could* be ignorant assholes. But it was good to know she wasn't one of them.

Mr. Rivera wasn't in his office, so I poked around his bookshelf while I waited. One had kids that looked like METCO kids on the spine. I pried it out and leafed through it—and, no way, but, WAY—it had activities intended to help groups do exactly what we were trying to do with the assembly. I scanned the pages until one stopped me in my tracks. It was a perfect idea. I'd just need to tweak it a little. I could feel myself getting fired up again, like at the library the other week. I was lasering in on this one thing—the assembly.

Right after lunch, our METCO group had one last meeting to run through everything. By now, I was amped—in the best way. I came up with a crazy idea that might be—might be . . .

"I don't know, y'all," Ivy was saying as I rushed in, which totally derailed my thoughts. She was biting her red, chipped nails.

"You don't know what?" Mr. Rivera asked, brow furrowing.

"It just seems like . . . Like, what's the point? No one's going to take us seriously anyway."

"Facts, bro," Marquis said.

"Facts!" Rayshawn echoed. Others nodded.

"Except for," Marquis quickly added, "we *did* do a lot of work. And we *did* help you find pictures of famous walls in history." He made a mic-drop motion with his hand. "*And* not for nothing, on the Google Doc, I edited the captions you wrote. I'm just sayin', so . . ."

"Yeah, but that was *after* we'd found quotes," Ivy said. "And not for nothing, if you added the pictures, then you should have written the captions in the first place. We only did it because y'all had left that part blank."

"True," I said.

"Yeah, but y'all had them in no real order," Marquis hit back.

"And don't forget—I hooked up all the sound equipment with that IT dude," Biodu added.

"Also true," I said.

Marquis raised his voice. "*Aaaaand* some of the captions were in full sentences when others were just like, notes with no punctuation."

"He said 'punctuation'!" Brianna exclaimed.

Ivy cracked a smile. "I'm hip. It was a lot of work. And on the real, I learned some stuff. But what if they just laugh us off the stage?"

I swallowed hard. What was up? We had to do this. All of us. Ivy included. Cold feet? Okay, I got it. But . . . I was more and more convinced that if we didn't say anything, then *nothing* would change. If we didn't try to change it, we'd . . . we'd kinda be saying we didn't matter, even to ourselves! Mr. Rivera was pacing the room; even he looked a little anxious.

But no way. The least I could do—the least *we* could do—was step up to a bunch of ignorant students who thought memes like the ones Rayshawn and I got were *funny*. And, why *not* try to connect with the other kids—like Rosie!—who probably had nothing to do with that garbage and thought it was just as stupid. And . . . not for nothing, we *had* to do the assembly. We were just showing our weakness if we didn't. All this I wanted to say to my METCO people, but all I could manage to get out was, "Guys. We got this." Eloquent, right?

Ivy loosened her top bun. A few thick seconds of silence passed—and I really wasn't sure which direction we'd go.

Then: "Aite," from Biodu.

"Aite," from Marquis. "I mean, like I said. It *was* some work. So we might as well go through with it."

"Aite," from Brianna.

And finally, "Aite," from Ivy, and the others.

Phew! "So—this is totally last minute, but I have a new idea that could be cool for after the slideshow." I held out the book. Mr. Rivera raised an eyebrow to say, *Oh, I see you helped yourself to my little library.* But in a good way.

So I went on, opening to the Post-it page. "This seems really cool. We call up groups by race and ethnicity and then we ask them all three questions: 'What is it that you want us to know about you in terms of race and culture? What is it that you never want to hear again? How can we be allies and assist you?' Soooo, what do you think?"

The room was quiet for like three fat seconds, and then Marquis said, "That's dope."

"Yeah, it's, like, universal and personal, at the same time," Rayshawn added.

And I swear, we all exhaled. The missing piece! Until Mr. Rivera asked, "There's one last thing left to figure out. Who will emcee?"

Everyone looked at ME.

I shook my head fast, hard.

Brianna leaned forward. "Why *not*, Lili?" Dorito Girl—my cheerleader?

"Talking in public, in an auditorium—it's not my—Just, no."

"Look, you said it before. We got this," Rayshawn propped. "Means *you*, too, got this."

"Truth." Marquis smirked.

Truth. Getting the truth out there. I took a deep breath. Truth, my dad had offered to work for free as a janitor so I could go to a good school. Truth, my mom had cleaned other people's toilets so I could grow up in this country. Truth, my parents had learned English *and still* taught us *both* languages. Truth, I was scared as shit. But I had this.

And in what seemed like a blink, the assembly was starting. It ended up having a whack name—"Westburg High for Diversity"—because that's all the administration would approve. Inside the packed auditorium a guy sitting a row ahead of me took a piece of notebook paper and rolled it like a blunt. The kid next to him cracked up. Meanwhile, we played the slideshow with quotes and pictures of famous civil rights leaders and photos of the walls while everyone settled into their seats.

After the last slide, the principal said a few words about the "disappointing online activity of late," and the school chorus sang a few songs—the national anthem and "I See the Light." The dean talked about our school moving on from these "episodes" to better race relations. He also read some official blah blah blah about how "The Westburg School District is dedicated to a policy of nondiscrimination and to the provision of equity in its educational programs, services, and activities for all students and employees." The dean droned on and on. The assembly—a few songs, a boringville speech. Even *I* could do better than that. I *could*. I *had* to!

And finally it was our turn. The audience went silent, spooky silent, as Rayshawn, Anthony, Brianna, all of us walked onstage. I veered, mouth suddenly like the Sahara, to the podium. Adjusting the microphone, I tapped on it three times—why do people even do that?—cleared my throat. I could see Dustin out in the audience—he was with some of his buddies—but I didn't see Steve. I forced myself to stop looking at him and caught Holly's gaze. She gave me a thumbs-up and looked so mama-bear proud I almost laughed.

"Good afternoon, Westburg," I said, not loud enough. I pulled the mic closer, the flare of confidence of a few moments ago withering. I *wasn't* sure I could do this. I stood, blinking, clutching the mic. Then this voice, this voice in my head full of attitude kicked in: *You know what's hard? Your dad trying to cross the Mexican border, being turned back again and again, just to get back to* you *and your mom and your brothers. That's* hard, *girl. Your mom holding it down while working to get him home. That's* hard. *This* is *a cakewalk. Time to man up. No—girl up. Time to do this.*

Holly must have sensed that I needed a boost, because she started clapping. A few others joined her—Peter from my French class, and Paula from Creative Writing. I gave a nod, and I did this thing.

"My name is Lili—Liliana Cruz." The microphone screeched, and I gave it a flick. "So, some of you may know us up here as 'the METCO kids,' but today we wanted to share some things you may not know. Today, rather than show you all some lame-ass— Sorry!"

Students laughed. A few teachers scowled, but a few laughed, too.

I can do this.

I went on.

"Okay, so. With, you know, all that's happened recently ONLINE"—I coughed, deliberately—"there's a lot of tension out there, and in *here*—in this school. Just this week—" I hesitated, feeling heat flaming my cheeks. "Someone posted a meme of my head on a piñata with the word 'wetback' above it." There were mad gasps. Wait—some people *didn't* know? One teacher in the aisle covered her mouth. I went on. "But rather than show you all a boring presentation with statistics or whatever, we thought it'd be more interesting to share some things about us that you might not know. That's all. But we hope it's enough to get us all thinking and talking in a real way. And when we're done, we'd like to invite some of *you* to come up onstage and speak for *yourselves*."

And . . . I couldn't believe it—people clapped. Not just Holly but, like, lots of people. I saw Holly's friend Lauren. She had a look of chagrin on her face and even gave me a little wave.

Focus, Liliana! "Okay, I'll hand it over to Mr. Rivera now," I said, and passed him the mic.

Mr. Rivera faced us fifteen METCO students. "If you identify as Black, please step forward," he called out. Like in a game of Mother May I, ten kids moved forward.

"Thank you. Now I am going to ask you three questions. Please answer honestly. First question: What is it that you want us to know about you in terms of race and culture?"

Oh man, I hoped this was going to work. PS, Mr. Rivera was wearing a tie with the Puerto Rican flag on it. Props!

Rayshawn went first. With all the confidence, he said, "I live with my mother and my grandmother. But we're not poor. My mother is a nurse. My grandmother is too."

If it had been quiet before, it was like someone had hit the mute button now.

Then Ivy spoke. "I have a cousin in law school. And I have another cousin in prison."

Someone else: "We don't all love fried chicken. I'm a vegetarian!"

Everyone laughed at that.

Someone else: "We want a decent education just like everyone else. And we deserve it too."

Mr. Rivera leaned back into the microphone. "Thank you. Thank you. Next question. What is it that you never want to hear again?"

This time my friends launched right in.

"Oh, you're Black, so you must know someone who's a dealer, right?"

"Is your mom a crackhead?"

"Why don't Black people know how to swim?"

"If you get into an Ivy, it'll only be because of affirmative action."

"Is it true what they say about Black guys?"

The whole auditorium erupted at this, kids yelling "Oh shoot" and "He went there!" and "Oh my God!"

"Moving on," Mr. Rivera said, loud. "Last question. How can we be allies and assist you?"

METCO stepped up.

"Please ask questions, don't just make assumptions."

"There's more to us than our hair. And no, you can't touch it."

"Get to know me, not just the color of my skin."

"Maybe come to *my* neighborhood once in a while."

"Teachers, please don't constantly ask if I need a pass to use the computer lab. You know, I do have a MacBook at home."

At that, a few adults shifted in their seats.

"Thank you," Mr. Rivera said, that eyebrow of his raised

high, high, high. "You can all step back. Now, if you identify as Latinx, please step forward."

There were fewer of us. Seven to be exact. Yep, some were mixed. I knew I had to participate and all, and I knew what I wanted to say, but I wasn't sure I'd have the guts to go through with it.

"All right. Same first question. What is it that you want us to know about you in terms of race and culture?" Mr. Rivera asked.

Well, Brianna had no problem speaking up. "You know what," she said, raising a finger. "There's a lot more to me than my accent, and my nails, and my attitude. A whole lot. I love snowboarding. And kids. I want to be a preschool teacher maybe. Or a veterinarian." She paused. "That's all."

"Thanks, Brianna. Who's next?" Mr. Rivera asked.

"I'm an only child. Shocker, right?"

"I don't speak Spanish. I would love to study Japanese in college, actually."

"I love speaking Spanish, but I don't love being asked to help you on your Spanish homework."

"My parents are legal citizens."

At the last comment, I almost choked. The stage became a blur. But . . . I *had* to do this.

"So, I was born here . . . but . . . my parents weren't," I said. "They're from Central America—one from Guatemala, the other from El Salvador. And they aren't criminals or rapists. They moved to the United States for better opportunities— you know, health, education, jobs. And . . ." I shut my eyes tight, and when I opened them again, I blurted out, "And . . . four months ago my father was deported."

I searched the rows of teens and teachers, braced for some dumb-ass comment. Crickets. Then, I swear I heard a couple of sniffles. Maybe it was that teacher in the aisle.

Weird thing was . . . I felt . . . free. Yeah, it would be out there now. Not crammed *in* me. Yeah.

"Thank you," Mr. Rivera said. His eyes looked—wet? Wait, was he *crying*? He blinked hard. "Next: What is it that *you* never want to hear again?"

Genesis raised a finger. "That I need to go back to where I come from. Because I'm from my mother's womb, and that would be really uncomfortable." That brought a few hoots from the crowd.

After an awkward pause, Brianna chimed in with, "Oh, and I am so over people asking me if I eat burritos every night for dinner. I'm Dominican! We don't even like burritos!"

Out came: "That I'm abusing the system. That my family and I are on welfare."

"Go back to Mexico."

"Go back to Boston."

"Thank you," Mr. Rivera said when we were done.

It was done.

Wow.

It had happened . . . and it had been . . . okay?

Oh, wait. Mr. Rivera forgot to ask the third question. I was going to remind him, when out of nowhere a kid in the audience stood up. Steve. Really? And he yelled out, "Hey,

Lili! Aren't you going to ask some white kids to come up onstage? You know, white lives matter too!"

We all looked at each other wide-eyed, then at Mr. Rivera.

Steve pressed it. "I mean, you're all about racial equality or whatever. So why don't you have some of us come up there too? You *did* say you were going to do that."

"Yeah, and what about Asians?" another kid called out. I looked at the crowd to see who it was.

"And Native Americans?" someone else added.

"And Muslims?"

Mr. Rivera tapped the microphone. "All right, settle down. Settle down."

"You're right!" I called back. Mr. Rivera turned to me in surprise.

I mean, technically Steve *was* right. They were all right. And if Steve had been patient, he would have realized that was where we were headed next. "Let's start with *you*, Steve."

To *my* surprise, Steve made his way down the aisle and walked up onto the stage.

"Anyone else want to join him?" I asked, breathing hard. Mr. Rivera called to me, but I ignored him. I couldn't help but glance at Dustin, who was literally shrinking in his seat.

A few more white kids actually did join Steve onstage, about ten.

"Same questions for you, then." Mr. Rivera was tugging on his tie, hard. "What is it that you want us to know about you in terms of race and culture?"

A girl stepped forward before Steve had even opened his mouth. "Well, I guess I want others to know that white people can't be lumped into one big group the same way that people of color can't be, or, like, shouldn't be."

Another girl spoke up. "I am white . . . but I can dance."

Steve then announced, "I am white and proud, and don't think others should feel bad about being white. You can't control what color you are, so what's the big deal?"

Mr. Rivera's eyes literally bugged.

"I know what's he's saying," Matt, from my math class, said. "Like, we're not slave owners or whatever. So why should we be blamed for like, all of history or whatever?"

Some students in the audience actually clapped.

"Next question," Mr. Rivera said instead. "What is it that you never want to hear again?"

"Oh! I got one!" Steve practically yelled. Apparently it was now the Steve Show. "You're a white boy. You can't play ball. Um . . . yes, I can." He raised his arms in the air as if to hit a three-pointer. Oh, give me a freakin' break. Brianna was rolling her eyes.

I could feel a shift in the crowd.

"Others?" Mr. Rivera asked.

Another girl onstage raised her hand. "We're not all rich."

Then another guy added, "And some of us actually want to learn about, you know, other cultures, but it's not always easy to like, just ask someone, 'Hey, tell me about your culture.'" A few people laughed, but it was a laugh of like, support. Agreement. And yeah, I could see his point.

Then Mr. Rivera called out, "Okay, okay. And the final question. How can we be allies and assist you?"

One kid was totally ready for this one. He said, "Well, like Steve said earlier, it's not our fault we're Caucasian. So why do we have to stand back and let . . . other kids . . . get scholarships and full rides to college when our parents and families have worked wicked hard to get us here too? How is that fair?"

This provoked an actual cheer. I looked around uneasily. This was . . . not going the way I'd imagined.

Mr. Rivera pressed him further. "Yes, but how can we be allies then, and assist you?"

"Well," Steve said. "There could be scholarships for white kids too."

Brianna and Rayshawn yelled simultaneously, "There are!"

That's when someone in the audience yelled out, "White lives matter! White lives matter!" And someone jumped in with "Build the wall! Build the wall!" Then—no way, but yeah—others joined in, and it became a chant. "White lives matter! Build the wall!"

Teachers were pointing at students, telling them to quiet down. When they didn't, the teachers began telling them they were getting detention. But it seemed to only make everyone more amped.

And then, a pencil flew past my head, just missing my eye. I was too shocked to move. A pen followed it, clattering onto the stage, then another pencil, an eraser, and then other objects I couldn't make out because now I *was* moving, covering my head and ducking behind the podium, almost bumping into Rayshawn, who was doing the same thing. Students were bolting up from their seats, crowding the aisles. The teachers and administrators were shouting "Stay seated" and "Stop that right now or else." No one was listening. Next thing I knew, people were being spit on. Insults were flying faster than the pencils and crumpled papers. Someone actually chucked a text-book at the stage!

Now the METCO kids were shouting back. More text-books came flying. One hit Rayshawn on the side of his head, and he went wild, jumping off the stage. I peeked out from behind the podium. The whole student body was just going cray-cray. Kids shouting, "Black lives matter!" and "White lives matter! and "All lives matter!" They were throwing punches, dodging punches, screaming, crying. The auditorium was total chaos. The teachers, shouting and threatening, were being totally ignored.

And Mr. Rivera looked like he was about to have an aneurysm.

Finally, the principal's voice boomed over the PA system. He ordered us to report to our homerooms. Immediately. And immediately everyone paused—students *and* teachers. Then, like we'd all been trained, everyone, reluctantly, started filing out of the auditorium. The principal told us to remain in our homerooms until the final bell. Then he canceled all after-school sports and clubs. I already knew that a bunch of resident students would tell their parents that the METCO kids had started all of this, which would be a lie. Still, if our presentation was supposed to have turned down the dial on racism at Westburg, I would say it was an epic fail. Like, 100 percent.

Numb. That's how I felt. The weather turned lousy, gray, sleeting, matching the entire day. On the way home I watched as the suburbs morphed into the packed concrete and the traffic of the city. My city. As we approached Forest Hills, I watched another pocket of Boston trickle by—even the snowbanks looked different here. In Westburg they looked clean and were piled up in neat little mountains, whereas here they looked like blobs of concrete midpour. A scrawny-looking older man scurried into the intersection at a stoplight to beg for change. His tattered cardboard sign read: HAVEN'T EATEN FOR TWO DAYS. GOD BLESS YOU. A Black driver (female) argued with a white biker (male) about who was in the wrong lane. Finally the biker gave the lady the finger and rode away.

At my stop, instead of walking home, I shivered all the way to the park. It was empty except for one lone dude on a skateboard. An empty Fritos bag skittered past my feet. I didn't feel like going home, even though, while it had stopped sleeting, the cold was beginning to creep into my bones in that way that takes forever to get rid of. Still, I sat down on a bench all tagged with graffiti and pulled out my purple notebook. Come to think of it, Dad's the one who'd bought me the notebook, at Walgreens. It hadn't even been on sale.

Where *was* he? At this exact moment. Thinking about me? My brothers? Mom? What if . . . What if he never saw us again? I thought about how he might never see these streets again. How who we are on paper apparently matters just as much as—no, who am I kidding? *more* than—who we are in person. And, as much as the presentation was a bomb with a capital B, we *did* it. We did it because we *know* we matter. So there was that, right? We *did* something. We tried.

And all of a sudden I was crying and writing, and my parents were *always* trying and would never give up, and I was crying and writing even when a couple more dudes on skateboards showed up. They started bumping their boards down the concrete steps, doing tricks and flips. The temperature seemed to drop minute by minute. My hands tingled with cold—I couldn't write anymore. The dudes lasted awhile, but eventually even they left. The bench across from me was tagged up big-time, but for once I actually started reading it. *Boston Strong* and *Mas Poesía, Menos Policía.* Cool play on words, that last one. More poetry, less police. I liked it. It was like its own line of poetry, about poetry. Dad would have pointed that out—he always noticed things like that. Deep down I knew what he would say about the situation at school, as messed up as it was. He'd say, *Try to make it better. Try harder.*

* * * *

Back at home, I couldn't focus on my homework, so I started final-final touches for Sylvia's Salon, which I'd put aside for a minute. I got kind of obsessed cutting little paper flowers and gluing them onto toothpicks, then sticking them into pots I'd made from shampoo caps. I wanted to finish the flowerpots before Mom came home with the boys. I should have been prepping dinner. But I couldn't help it. I *had* to finish. And I did. Yes! Then my phone buzzed. Jade, asking me to come over.

"Dang, girl. This is dope," I said, gazing around her bedroom.

The mural she had started weeks before was now complete. It *was*. She had painted an underwater scene, but it was also a city. Like, fish were swimming around skyscrapers, and seaweed spiraled around bus stop signs. How did her brain work like that?

"Thanks, Liliana."

"No. Really. This is . . ."

Jade sat on her bed and hugged a pillow, a big grin on her face. Yeah, my girl had skills. "Anyway, what's good with you?"

"Nothing. It's just that this is so great. You are so talented, you know? But, well, things at school have gone to shit."

"How?"

"Well, remember that assembly we went to the library for? We had it, today, and it started off okay, but then went south like, real quick. People throwing books and saying racist shit like 'Build the wall' and shit. It was bad."

Jade gaped at me. "For real?"

"It was just so freaking frustrating. And I think the whole school is in trouble. I just wish there was something else I could do, you know?"

Jade didn't respond, just stared at her mural, the strangest look in her eyes.

"I know that look," I said. "What are you thinking?"

"Hold up. Gimme a second. What you just said. Liliana, I have an idea."

"Yeah?"

"Well, so, you should actually build one."

Okay, Jade had lost it. "Uh, wanna run that by me one more time?"

"Just hear me out. . . ."

I did. And before I knew it, my mom was blowing up my phone asking where I was and if I had eaten. I begged her to let me stay at Jade's until nine. She agreed. We spent the next couple of hours planning out the details. I guess when you're at the bottom of the ocean, the only way to go is up.

33

In the morning I almost missed the bus. It was trash day and I forgot to bring the bins out last night, so I had to lug them out. My fingers ached from the cold; I think I dropped my gloves in the park. Ugh.

At school, the principal had taken away privileges like the frozen yogurt station in the cafeteria, and he stopped allowing hall passes. Oh, and he canceled the winter pep rally. But then he retracted the cancellation; apparently a parent stormed in and said it was "unacceptable" to cancel a positive school spirit event. But then he retracted *that* and said we'd reschedule it for early January.

Teachers were on edge, students barely made eye contact with one another, and the principal made an announcement that anyone caught "misbehaving" would be immediately suspended. Oh, and the administrators visited classrooms like every five seconds. I was washing my hands between classes when the vice principal came in and said, "Just checking." Um . . . just checking what? Besides, it was a girls' bathroom and he was not a girl. Whatever. Truth—every time I passed a white kid in a hall, I looked away. And I avoided

Steve and Dustin like poison ivy. But at the same time, I was jazzed up—kind of thrumming. I'd been that way since I'd left Jade's last night.

In study hall I asked Mrs. Davila if I could have a strip of blue bulletin board paper, long enough to cover the entire length of the wall by the cafeteria—like eight regular bulletin boards long.

"What's it for?" she asked. She was unpacking a box of acrylic paints, sorting tubes by color.

I gave her my most angelic smile. "Can you just trust me on this one?"

She gave me an appraising look, like, *How much trouble is a girl who makes miniatures going to cause*, then nodded. "Yeah, I can. Here. Let me help you."

On my way out I realized I'd forgotten a few key items. "Oh, can I also borrow some black markers? Oh, and some string and tape? And colored pencils?" I smiled the hundred-watt smile again. "Thank you *so* much!"

Next, I sent a group text to Genesis and Brianna and Holly, asking them to meet me after third period by the sneaker. The thrum dialed up when I saw them. "Guys! Listen. Okay, I have this idea. We're going to flip this whole idea of a *wall* on its head. Like, let's make an *actual* wall. We can have three sections, you know, with the three questions from the assembly thingy, and we can leave markers out and stuff, and this way everyone, or anyone who wants to, can participate. But I need your help." I paused for a breath. They were all staring at me.

But I was on a mission, folks.

"So—who's in?" I asked.

Holly actually teared up. "Me!"

I looked from Genesis to Brianna. Genesis said, "Man, I thought *I* talked fast! Yes, girl. I'm in."

"Bri?" I asked.

"Hand me that tape!"

We met again at lunch. Holly and Genesis held the stream of paper, while Brianna and I taped it up then secured it down with more tape on the corners. I think it was the first time the three of them had actually hung out together all at once. Kinda crazy, given that they'd been in the same schools since like first grade. With the colored pencils, we drew in outlines of bricks around the edges so it would look like an actual wall. Holly came up with the idea of using different colors for the bricks. Done with that, we stepped back to take a look. Bri had added some shading to give it a more three-dimensional look. So we all did the same. Genesis took it up a notch with multicolor shading. Cool! Then I divided the wall into three sections. Across the top of each I wrote one of the following questions:

> *What is it that you want us to know about you?*
> *What is it that you never want to hear again?*
> *What can we do here at Westburg to help?*

Bri announced that we had, yikes, only five minutes before the bell. We quickly tied string to the markers and taped them to the wall, the first bell ringing just as we finished. Holly reached for a marker.

"We're good, Holly. Let's go!" I said. Standing there when everyone flooded past on the way to their next class was not part of the plan.

"Hello," Holly said with her signature sass. "I might have something to write, you know."

"Oh. Right!" So I left her to it, starting down the hall with Genesis and Brianna.

But then Brianna stopped short. "Wait," she said. "I have something to add too."

"Fine. But hurry up!"

Brianna paused in front of the first question, then snatched up the marker and began scrawling. When she was done, she brushed at the corners of her eyes.

"What's wrong?" I asked her.

"Nada," Brianna said. "Vámonos."

I glanced at what she had written.

I'm a girl and I like girls.

I looked at Holly and Genesis, then back at Brianna.

Genesis broke the ice. "Girl, tell us something we don't know."

And we all cracked up, even Brianna.

Then Genesis had her phone out, snapping pictures—close-ups of what had been written on the wall, then a panoramic of the wall itself. Two minutes later they were up on Instagram.

*   *   *   *

So I gotta admit, I was worried. What if no one took the wall seriously? What if they only wrote a bunch of racist crud and then it was in permanent marker? Or what if no one wrote anything at all? Which, as I thought about it, was just as bad. What if the principal flipped out over our making the wall in the first place?

I was going crazy, so after geometry, I took the long route to my next class and intentionally passed the wall. A cluster of girls stood in front of it, each with a marker in hand. A tall guy hovered behind them, as if in line for movie tickets or something. I inched closer, and my heart gave a little leap: The wall was already filling up! I started to read the bricks, bracing myself. I mean, there were going to be a few nasty ones, obvs. Right?

Right. There was one that read *WTF. I am the victim of reverse-racism*, and another said, *I don't see color, honestly, so I don't know what the big deal is about race.* I scanned the wall for more obnoxious comments. But—that was it.

Calmer now, I slowed down, took it *all* in.

<u>*What is it that you want us to know about you?*</u>

I am half Colombian but no one knows that.

> Just because I'm white doesn't mean I am a white supremacist.

I'm too embarrassed to share.

JENNIFER DE LEON

I wish Black kids were more ... approachable.
Sometimes I just don't know what to say to them.

My parents forbid me to date Black guys.

My dad is a recovering alcoholic.

My dad isn't my "real" dad.

I don't know what to do to help.
What can I do? Like, just _me_?

I am Jewish and sometimes that's hard
in this town that has like, 10 Jews.

Some people had even put up Post-its. Maybe they
hadn't wanted anyone to see what they were writing? But,
still, props.

I am Chinese and I suck at math...

I am gay.

I am gay too.

I wish there were more muslims in this school.

What is it that you never want to hear again?

You're gay.

You'll only get into Harvard because your dad teaches there.

You must be rich.

Where are you from?

If a girl has sex, she's a slut.
I'm not a slut!!!

Bitch.

Loser.

What are you?

Where are you really from?

You must have gotten a perfect score on the SAT.
(I actually had an anxiety attack the night before and never took it.)

Spic

White boy

Can i borrow some money?

And finally,

What can we do here at Westburg to help?

Actually have conversations about race,
like in class and stuff and not just at
random assemblies

Hire more teachers of color.

Maybe have a student-led Diversity Day
conference like with speakers? My old
school had one and it was cool.

Field trips to inner-city Boston

Grow the METCO program.

Add a work-study program?
For <u>all</u> kids who might need it

Definitely bring in guest speakers
(like Beyoncé)!

Okay, so some of these ideas weren't totally realistic, but
still.

* * * *

Eventually Mr. Rivera heard who had put up the wall. (Bet Mrs. Davila had something to do with that.) He congratulated us and said he was going to let the principal know about what we'd done. But we actually asked him not to— we wanted the whole thing to remain anonymous. For the rest of the day, kids continued adding stuff. I could tell that teachers added stuff too, because I doubted teenagers would come up with *Seek out professional development opportunities to raise cultural competency*. It was cool, actually, that everyone was participating. Look, I'm not saying that after this project everything went smoothly and that Westburg became a national model for diversity or whatever, but . . . it was something.

Later, in Creative Writing, when Mrs. Grew wrote in a blue Expo marker on the board, *Write about a neighbor from your childhood,* I just couldn't hold back. I *was* going to write about people from my neighborhood, and I *was* going to share. No joke. Maybe I'd write about Jorge, the forty-year-old dude who lived with his mom in B-3 in my apartment building. Or maybe I'd write about Señora Luz, who gave every kid on the street school supplies in September. Markers and everything. *Crayola* markers, not the cheap kind from the Dollar Store. (Those markers ran out after coloring like two pictures.) Anyway, maybe I'd write about my dentist on Centre Street, and share his stories about working in the Dominican Republic, how one time he had to rip a loose tooth from a baby who'd been born with a full set of teeth, or the time a notorious army general came to see him about a throbbing, stinking rotten tooth, and the dentist pulled it without anesthesia. I was getting amped just thinking about all the possibilities.

So I wrote. And I wrote and wrote and wrote. When Mrs. Grew asked for volunteers to share, I raised my hand high. First hand up, thank you very much. Participation! Even Rayshawn stared. And stop the presses, Mrs. Grew *called* on me. So I read. I read about the people in my Boston neighborhood, and how no, not all of them were drug addicts or in a gang. In fact, most of them weren't. In fact, only one was a drug addict, and she was mad funny. I mean, sometimes we teased her because she'd wear snow boots in the summer and sandals in the winter. So after I shared, my classmates clapped and Mrs. Grew wrote something down on her clipboard.

After class I pulled out my rewrite of the trip essay and handed it to Mrs. Grew. It'd been in my bag for a minute, and I kept putting off giving it to her because I didn't want her to tell me it was too late to change the grade. But that day, right then, I didn't care. Mrs. Grew's face—one-third shock, one-third pleased, and one-third curious—was lit. Then Paula came up to me to say she really liked what I'd read. And Jeremy D. tapped me on the back—a little too hard, but I let that slide. On the bus ride home I was so psyched that I took a picture of what I'd written and posted it on Instagram. And no lie, by the time I got to Jamaica Plain, I had seventy-three notifications, including twelve reposts! My first thought:

Dad would be proud. My second thought: *Rayshawn is one of those who "liked" me!* Truth—okay, maybe my first and second thoughts were in a different order. MAY-be. Still, I couldn't stop refreshing the page. So much so that, boom— my phone went dead. And yeah, you know that the minute I got home, I was going to charge my phone and check the page again.

Walking up to our building, I saw neon Christmas lights blinking on and off in the apartment window above ours—someone must have just put them up. I also noticed that the trash bins had already been returned to their spot in the side yard. No way my brothers would have done this. Their chores amounted to putting their clean clothes away or stripping the sheets off their beds.

I swore I could hear Mom upstairs, all loud. Wait—was she . . . laughing? She must have been on the phone. Come to think of it, I hadn't heard her laugh in a minute. In fact . . . not since . . . Dad!

I ran up the stairs two at a time and flung the door open. Mom immediately popped up of the couch. Her makeup was smeared; she looked like a raccoon. And I could now hear my brothers laughing and talking over each other in their room. *What* was up?

"Liliana . . ." My mother started.

Then I heard my name a second time, a second voice. "Liliana."

Dad?

Dad!

It was Dad!

I spun around, and there he was—Dad!—stepping in front of the sheet that separated the living room from the boys' room. I swear, I almost fainted. I know people say that all the time, like "I almost fainted," but I really almost did. Like my blood had been replaced by air.

My brothers burst out behind him. And he, Dad, MY DAD, was next to me and pulling me into his arms. "Liliana, mija," he said, in that voice that had lived inside me for four months. And I didn't let go until I knew it was real, he was real, that it wasn't a dream. But—how? How was he here?

Finally I stepped back to look at him. He'd lost weight. He was darker, too, and his eyes looked older than the rest of him somehow. His hair was cut short, but in no particular style, and that along with his sunken cheeks made him look sad, sadder. But—Dad. DAD!

"You . . . ," he said, catching the cry in his throat. "You . . . you look so grown-up. Una señorita."

"Ew," Benjamin wailed. And we all cracked up.

I swung round to my mother. "Why didn't you text me? Dad! How long have you been home?"

"Mija, I *did* call you! The moment he got home. That was"—she looked at her watch—"forty-five minutes ago."

"What?" I checked my phone. Still dead. Of course. "But—oh my God—Dad! How are you here? I mean, how'd you get here? Did Tía Laura and Tío R. give you the money? Well, of course they did. That's how you got here. Hey, are you hungry? Benjamin and Christopher are mad good at cooking now. Me too! Well, sorta. But how do you feel? Are you tired? What happened?" I couldn't shut up. I couldn't even let my dad answer a single question. It was like I had to get them all out in case he disappeared again in the next three seconds.

"Whoa, Liliana, chillax," Benjamin said.

"Okay, yeah, I'm kind of hyped! But yeah, Dad—so, tell us everything."

So Dad sat down on the couch, and we all glommed onto him. Mom had her hand on his shoulder, Christopher clasped one arm, me the other. I couldn't stop petting Dad's hand like it was a kitten. And Benjamin sat on the rug, staring up at Dad like he was famous.

"Go. Tell us. Everything. Don't leave out one single part," I begged.

Dad grinned, his teeth so white against his brown skin. "First things first, mija. Tell *me* everything. How's this fancy new school of yours?"

"I'll tell you, but you first! Go."

Benjamin poked me. "Dang, Liliana. You're all bossy. He just got home. Give him a second."

I resisted the urge to tell him to shut up.

"You sound so grown-up, mijo," Dad said. Benjamin gave himself a pat on the shoulder. What a dweeb.

"Dad . . . please!" I cried out. "At least give us the short version. Oh! Do you want some coffee? I can make you some coffee! Oh, and the twins—wait till you see what *they* can make. So, would you like a coffee? Then later you can tell us the whole story."

Dad was laughing. "Mija, you sound like you've had *too* much coffee. I'm good."

"Daaaaad! Can you give us the short version at least?"

"Vaya, vaya." He looked at Mom. She gave the slightest of nods, but it was enough.

He started by telling us how much he'd missed us, how much he'd thought of us every single minute. "Believe me, you are the reason I am here. You and God."

He gazed from one of us to the other, his eyes glistening. "The crossing now, mijos, it's very dangerous. More than ever. You have to believe me. I tried four times.

"The desert," Dad went on, even though no one had said anything about a desert, "is dry, mijos. It makes you remember that we are just bodies, bones and flesh, thirsty for water. Any kind of water." His eyes drifted, as if watching a scene we couldn't see, wouldn't want to see. He cleared his throat. "You really want to hear all this?"

"Yes!"

Mom made the sign of a cross on her chest.

Dad continued, "In the end, I was lucky. One time, a few weeks earlier, I was nearly seen, right by the border! But there were lots of tumbleweeds in the area and I hid behind one as big as a car, grabbing on as hard as I could. If I let go, I'd have been caught!"

"A tumbleweed? A *tumbleweed* saved you?" That was INSANE.

Dad nodded. "Big as a car!" Of course, I needed more.

"So then what happened? Wait—how'd you get to Boston? And where did you stay while you were waiting to cross? How did you—"

"Liliana!" my brothers yelled in unison.

But my dad only laughed. "Some things haven't changed." Then he grew serious.

"Well . . ." He let out a long breath. "I'm home now. That's what's important. Sylvia, would you please get me a glass of water?" It was as if just thinking about his journey was making him thirsty.

"Claro." Mom hopped up with more energy than I'd seen in months.

"At the border, did you have to literally climb over a wall?" Now it was Christopher firing off all the questions.

Dad rubbed his hands together. "Vaya. So I was part of a large group of people crossing. Our coyote arranged it all. First, our group met in Tijuana, where we rented a small room and stayed one night. The day after that, close to sundown, we started walking. And we walked for hours. Then—" His voice caught.

Mom returned with the water. We all watched him drink like a new parent watches their baby take its first steps, all pressed against him on the couch, the room growing darker with each wintry minute.

"Then—there was a little boy," Dad began again. "He was five years old, I'd find out later. We ran into him in the desert, all alone. He'd stepped on a cactus, and his group had left him behind. Who knows how long he had sat there picking out the thorns. He couldn't walk, and he could barely talk. He was near hysterical. So I had no choice; I picked him up and carried him with us."

"You did?" Christopher crept onto Dad's lap.

"I did, mijo. The coyote told me to leave him, that I was a fool, that he wasn't going to return my money if we got caught. But I had to. And I would do it again."

"Ay, Fernando." Mom began to dab at her eyes with a tissue.

I couldn't believe what I was hearing. Suddenly my calf cramped. I stood up to stretch, but then sat right back down and reached for Dad's hand again. "Then?"

"Then we got picked up by a man in a car. We drove to a checkpoint, you know, where we met more people who were going to cross, about fifteen. From there another man drove us to an empty parking lot."

Christopher's eyes were huge. "Don't worry, mijo," Dad said. "I'm okay. I'm here. I'm home now." Benjamin smushed his face into Mom's leg, and Dad stroked his head.

"In the parking lot a huge semi-truck carrying bananas pulled up. The coyote told us to get in there. He said 'It's going to be cold. It's a refrigerator truck, but there is an area where we're going to put you inside. You get three gallons of water. Your trip will be about three or four hours long. You cannot talk and you cannot make any noise. You cannot do anything that could get us in trouble.' And then he took off."

"Oh my God." I covered my mouth.

"There was a young woman in the group." Dad looked at me. "She was pregnant. And another young father with a young kid. We all looked at each other. . . . Anyway, we got into this very tight place. It was freezing. I wished I had a coat for the woman . . . for the little boy. Three hours became four hours became five, then seven."

"Dios guarde." Mom pulled Benjamin up onto the couch next to her.

"What about the little boy?" Benjamin asked.

"He sat beside me. He told me it was his birthday the next day. He just kept whispering that over and over. 'Mañana cumplo seis. Mañana cumplo seis.' But there was no way to know what time of day it was. So, in the middle of the night— what I *thought* was around midnight—I held him close and told him, 'Happy birthday, happy birthday. You're six.' I wanted to make sure that at least he heard it from someone."

Christopher pressed even closer to Dad, which hardly seemed possible. "What happened to him? Where is he now? The little boy?"

"When we finally got out of the truck, we were across. In America. Thank God. Another coyote was waiting, and we were separated into different cars going different routes at different times, so it wouldn't be obvious we were together, you know? We were all exhausted. The pregnant woman— she took that little boy and said she would watch over him. Tell everyone he was her son."

Christopher looked stricken. "So you just let him go with her?"

"It was all I could do, mijo . . ." Dad's voice trailed off, and his chin twitched. But I understood. What was he *supposed* to have done? Bring the boy back with him? He'd look more suspicious than she would.

"Then?" I prompted.

"Once I crossed, I took a bus to Houston. There I got in touch with an old buddy from when I drove big rigs. He let me ride with him all the way to Boston. He was going to New York"—now Dad blinked hard—"but he drove eight hours out of his way to make sure I got here."

"Why?" I clearly couldn't get the story out of him fast enough.

"Because he's a nice guy," Dad said.

Benjamin's face suddenly grew stern, almost angry. "Could you get deported again?" My body tensed. I wanted to know the same thing.

Mom gasped, but Dad didn't flinch. "Yes, I could," he said, tracing his thumb along Benjamin's face. "I'm not going to lie. I'm still undocumented. That means I don't have legal papers to be in this country right now."

The boys nodded.

Dad raised his chin defiantly. "I'm going to do everything humanly possible to get my papers in order so we don't have to be afraid anymore."

"What about ICE?" Benjamin asked.

I gaped at him. I didn't even know he knew that word.

"That's enough for today," Mom said abruptly. She let go of Dad's hand and turned on another lamp. But Dad stayed put, then suddenly dropped his head into his hands. His shoulders started to shake.

Benjamin clutched Dad's arm. "Dad, Dad! Are you okay?"

It was a few moments before Dad lifted his head again, brushed away the wet. "Yes," he murmured. "I'm just . . . I'm just so happy to be back."

"We're ordering pizza tonight," Mom announced, smoothing her blouse. "Liliana, get the coupon on the fridge."

"Okay. One more minute." I pleaded with my eyes.

"No, Liliana. That's enough. Your father is tired."

Dad stood up. "Pizza sounds great. And your mother is right. I want to hear about you!"

"Fine. Dad! You know what I wanna do? I want us all to go to Castle Island. Let's go tomorrow!" I said.

"Hold on, there," Mom interrupted. "It's the middle of winter!"

I turned on the last lamp in the living room. That's when I saw my brothers' beaming faces.

"And . . . I want us all to see a WWE show, like WWE SmackDown, or Chaotic Wrestling!"

I don't think I'd ever seen Christopher and Benjamin so still. For real, they looked like mannequins.

"De verdad, Liliana?" Dad asked. "Those tickets are really expensive."

"Not the live show! We can get it on pay-per-view. That's way more practical."

"Well, I guess some things really *have* changed since I've been gone." And he pulled me into his arms again.

Dad was *home*. And Mom—raccoon eyes and all—finally looked at peace. Like, truth, I could switch up all the spices and she wouldn't say boo. And that made me think of something *else*. I ran to my room and returned with a cardboard building.

"Oh, Liliana . . . ," Dad said. "That's beautiful."

"Thanks," I said, grinning. "But, it's not for you."

"Oh—"

 Now we all laughed.

"It's for you, Mom." I placed it in her hands. Sylvia's Salon. Mom took in the hot-pink cursive letters, the images of hair rollers and blow-dryers in the tiny windows, the aluminum foil that Christopher had suggested I use for the satellite dish on the rooftop. Her face crumpled. She stood up and hugged me tight, her chin trembling against my neck. Then she squeezed even tighter.

All the next morning I was still buzzing about Dad. Every few seconds I had to remind myself that it was true. He was *home*. I'd gone to bed mad late, buzzing. Got to school, buzzing. He was home!!! I dug my math book out of my locker, then slammed it shut to see Dustin standing there. I literally jumped.

"Oh my God, you scared me!"

"Sorry." He looked down at his Converse. Dustin. What a wimp. I willed myself to stay chill.

"For scaring me?" I could smell his smell—shampoo and ChapStick and boy. Damn it. I was *not* prepared for this sensory slide into my memory.

Then he surprised me. "For everything, Lili."

We stood there for a long time, and he finally looked up at me, looked like he had more to say. I waited.

"I turned him in," Dustin finally said.

I blinked and blinked, trying to process. "Steve?" I said at last.

"Steve. For making the memes."

"Seriously?"

"Look, you have to believe me when I tell you that I did NOT tell Steve about your . . . father's situation. I didn't. I never told *anyone*. Not a single—"

I cut him off. "I believe you." And I actually truly did.

"You do?"

"Yeah."

Dustin let out a breath. "I don't think he made *all* the racist memes in history, but he did make"—he looked down at his sneakers again and mumbled—"certain ones." He looked back up. "His family's all messed up. His dad didn't get some huge promotion at work and keeps telling Steve it's because he's white—and all this other stuff."

I rolled my eyes.

"I know. I know. No excuse. But so, yeah, I turned him in. And I guess he got suspended."

"Whoa—"

"Yeah, his parents are super pissed. Apparently his father went ballistic; he said this wouldn't look good at all on his Harvard application. I mean, that's an understatement. Anyway, Steve basically hates me now."

"I bet."

We both went quiet. "So I guess I'll see you around, then," Dustin said.

"Yeah, I guess."

"Yeah?" He sounded hopeful. I swear he leaned forward a smidge.

"Yeah."

I couldn't resist checking out the wall again before my next class. But when I rounded the corner—I stopped in my tracks. A couple of administrators . . . they were taking the wall down! And . . . Mr. Rivera was helping them! Hot tears instantly pricked at my eyes. Why were they taking it down?

"Excuse me? Um . . . what are you doing?" I tried to sound firm and still student-y.

"Oh, hi, Lili. I'm actually glad to see you—" Mr. Rivera began.

But I interrupted him. "Are you going to throw that away? Mr. Rivera, are they? This isn't right. You know, a lot of students—" And that's when I noticed he was standing beside a girl I'd never seen before. Latina?

Mr. Rivera cut me off. "That's why I'm glad to see you. I have great news! A reporter from the local paper wants to write a story on this . . . wall. And she plans to bring in a photographer. So we're just bringing it to the main office for a couple of hours, where there's better light."

I blinked. "Really?"

"Yes. And then we'll probably put part of it behind

Plexiglas. It's now a part of our school history." He smirked. "Kudos to you."

I didn't know what to say.

I couldn't wait to tell Dad.

And now I could.

At home.

Today.

"Liliana? You all right?"

Then, I didn't care if it was appropriate or whatever, but I rushed over and gave Mr. Rivera a big bear hug. Just as I turned to leave, Mr. Rivera said, "Oh, and Liliana, meet Yasmina. She's a new METCO student."

She had short brown curly hair. Her eyes were . . . green? She blinked like crazy behind dark-rimmed glasses. And she wore a faux leather jacket—it was cute! But the peep-toe heels were a little much. Why was she dressing like she was on a movie set of a high school rom-com? *Whoa. Back up, Liliana,* I checked myself. *Don't be so judgmental.* Ha. I thought of Dorito Girl that first day on the bleachers. I thought of Holly and the gum on her shoe. So I reached out my hand. "I'm Liliana," I said, with a big smile.

On the first Saturday after Christmas, I heard three knocks and a loud "Yo, Liliana!" from Jade's window.

"Hold on!" I hollered back. It had snowed last night, and it was mad windy. I needed a coat. And my water bottle— and yeah, I had the Guatemalan cover on it, the one Tía Laura and Tío R. had given me. But I *needed* my notebook. *Needed.* The purple one. The one with the story that I wanted to workshop. I couldn't find it. It was already ten to nine, and the workshop started at nine. It would take fifteen minutes to walk over there, less if we ran. But still. Miss Amber had said that if we were late, she wouldn't let us in.

"Hold up, J!" I bellowed again, slamming through drawers.

A minute later Jade was at my bedroom door, wearing new purple kicks.

"Girl, help me," I said. "I can't find my notebook."

"You know what time it is, right? I'm *not* going over there just to have Miss Amber close the door in my face. I mean, what'd I wake up so early for, then?" I had convinced Jade to take this writing class with me in exchange for me attending a few art workshops at the Urbano Project with her.

Where was that stupid notebook? I dug a hand between the mattress and the wall. Boom! There it was. "Let's go." I grabbed my coat and we raced for the front door.

On my way past the kitchen I smelled mint. I stopped short. Mom stood at the stove, stirring. "Mom, are you making pho?"

She stopped stirring and grinned all crazy like—happy crazy! Mom was making pho! Mom was making pho!

"Mom . . ." I couldn't help it. My eyes watered.

"Give me a kiss good-bye," she said.

"I'm on my way to the writing center. I gotta go!"

"A kiss," she repeated.

A kiss. Then, "Bye!"

In the hall I ran right into Dad. He was holding a news-paper.

"Whoa!" he said. "Where are you flying off to?"

"The writing center! Mom knows!" I hugged him until Jade hollered "Come on, girl!" from the front door.

"Bye!"

"Be careful, mija." There was so much in his voice.

"I will."

Then I heard Dad again. "Liliana?"

"Yeah?"

"Maybe next weekend, we can all go somewhere. It says here"—he waved the newspaper in the air—"there's free admission at the science museum."

"Sounds great, Dad." It did. It really did.

As Jade and I pounded down the stairway, I inhaled the

stale weed smell, but also the smell of Doña Rosario's insane cooking (mmm . . . sancocho?), and I practically floated out the front door. It slammed behind me, and I swore if it was made of glass, it would have broken, but they didn't put glass doors in apartment buildings like ours—the landlord was too cheap. Don't get it twisted. I wouldn't trade living there for anywhere else. Not now anyway. There was so much going on all the time; I'd never run out of things to write about or build. I'm hip.

I broke into a run. We had like a negative minute to get there. Jade was yelling and laughing a few feet behind me. That little Spanish dude—correction, Dominican dude; he wasn't from Spain, hello—with the mustache in front of Lorenzo's Liquor was whistling at us. I know what I must have looked like, like some crazy teenage girl with flushed cheeks running with her coat unzipped in fifteen-degree weather. Thing is, now more than ever, writing was like oxygen to me. Ha. Got you. I would never write that; that's a cliché. At 826 I was learning all about those things—clichés, tropes, narrative distance, and adding FAT (feelings, actions, thoughts) to dialogue. Stuff like that.

We dashed across the street, not even waiting for the light to blink, and raced for the door. We buzzed, and Vicky (she was fifteen but acted like she was twenty-one) opened the door enough for us to see her wag a sanctimonious (vocab word) finger and say, "Naughty-naughty. You're late."

Whatever. We pushed past her.

Inside the center, framed close-up photos of kids' faces

greeted us. So many stories inside them. Inside us. Inside this space, where we workshopped our stories and had open mic sessions. Where stickers and neon flyers covered the podium: WE ARE A NATION OF IMMIGRANTS. NO DEPORTATION. NO WALL.

My stomach rumbled. I hadn't had breakfast. Someone had set up bagels and cream cheese and empanadas on paper plates in the back. The bagels were piled high, but the empanadas, they were almost gone. Someone needed to make more next time. Wait. Maybe *I* could? I could ask my brothers for help. And Dad would try the first one, and say something like, *You really did this?* And it wouldn't sound like a question at all.

ACKNOWLEDGMENTS

The day my book sold, my dad sent me an emoji of a watermelon and said, "This is great news, the fruit of your labor is here." But this is the truth: Nothing good in my life would be possible without my parents, without *their* labor. My mother and father, Dora and Luis De Leon—who celebrate fifty years in the United States this year!—motivate me to work hard every single day. Mom, you've been my number one champion from day one. And Dad, in your quiet and reserved way, you're tied for number one. To my sisters, Karen and Caroline De Leon—thank you for everything, and I love you.

I would not have completed this book without the encouragement and support and feedback of so many people—too many to name, but I will try!

To Faye Bender—my fierce and kind and wicked-smart agent—thank you for orchestrating that magical week when the book went to auction. Your faith and enthusiasm mean the world, and I am grateful to you beyond measure. To my A+ editor, Caitlyn Dlouhy—you inspired me to roll up my sleeves. You held the flashlight while I did the digging, and when I didn't know how to dig anymore, you took out two flashlights. You're amazing. I'm honored to work with you. And to Elena Garnu for the gorgeous cover art, Justin Chanda, Clare McGlade, Milena Giunco, Alex Borbolla, and the entire team at Simon & Schuster/Atheneum. You are fire.

For their writing and cheerleading superpowers—my beloved writing group, the Chunky Monkeys. Christopher Castellani, Chip Cheek, Calvin Hennick, Sonya Larson, Celeste Ng, Alex Marzano-Lesnevich, Whitney Scharer, Adam Stumacher (more later!), Grace Talusan, and Becky Tuch: You fill the well, and I am so lucky you all agreed to meet up at Sonya's apartment for that first meeting. So many years and pages later, I'm bound to you for life.

For Eve Bridburg and the GrubStreet Creative Writing Center, I give you a bone-crushing hug. Can't imagine my life without Grub. To my OG Fab Five Writing Group—Kris Evans, Jeremy Lakaszcyck, Lily Rabinoff-Goldman, Barbara Neely, and the UMASS Boston MFA program. Thank you to the editors and magazines who supported my work, especially *Kweli* and *Ploughshares* and *Briar Cliff Review*. And a very special thanks to Julia Alvarez, Sandra Cisneros, and all the greats who came before—and all the Wise Latinas. I am because we are.

I would also like to thank the Voices of Our Nation Arts Foundation (VONA), the Macondo Writers' Workshop, The Bread Loaf Writers' Conference, Virginia Center for the Creative Arts, Hedgebrook, Vermont Studio Center, and Richard Blanco—for letting Adam and me write in your Maine cabin—the timing could not have been better. Gracias.

The Boston Book Festival and One City, One Story—Sarah Howard Parker, you're the best. My writing professors and teachers and guides: Askold Melnyczuk, Miguel Lopez, Herb Kohl, Jennifer Haigh, ZZ Packer, Jenna Blum, Holly Thompson, Chris Abani, Reyna Grande, and especially Junot Díaz—I have at least four marble notebooks full of wisdom from you at VONA and I go back to these lessons more than you know. Laura Pegram, for starting *Kweli*! And also for that magical phone call while I sat in the parking lot at the Milton Public Library.

To Tayari Jones—for *that* phone call when you took the time to help me realize my time, my worth. Thank you. I will never, ever forget it.

It is entirely possible that this book might never have existed without the incredible support of the Associates of the Boston Public Library's Writer-in-Residence Fellowship. Or my former student and friend, Josie Figueroa, who emailed me the info about the WIR.

That year at the Boston Public Library, in my Harry Potter–esque office, I got to w-r-i-t-e . . . what a gift! Thank you to the anonymous donor who changed my life.

To We Need Diverse Books and the Walter grant committee—that grant kept me going in so many ways, and kept Liliana Cruz going too. To the City of Boston Artists in Residence program, Karen Goodfellow, and my fellow Boston AIRS—let's get together on a rooftop and clink glasses soon. To the New England Foundation for the Arts (NEFA).

For reading early drafts—Katie Bayerl, Niki Marion, Hasadri Freeman, Karen Boss, Stéphanie Abou, Lexi Wangler, Rob Laubacher, Hillary Casavant, and of course, Jenna Blum, and to everyone in her workshops for your smart and generous feedback. Alonso Nichols, for my author photo! Sonja Burrows, for my website, and for so much more. Francisco Stork—thank you for your important and beautiful work, and for introducing me to Faye! METCO students and Young Adult Writing Program (YAWP) teens and those I met in the Boston Public Library Teen Room—and teachers and counselors I met with—thank you for your help with questions. Especially JJ for your tips with slang. Lit, bomb, I'm hip . . . lol.

For their friendship over the many years—Hannah Levine Vereker, Patricia Sánchez-Connally, Katie Seamans, Abby Greco, Aylin Talgar Pietz, Glen Harnish, Jamie Arterton, Emily Schreiber-Kreiner, Yeshi Gaskin, Wanda Montañez, Norma Rey-Alicia, Ru Freeman, Charles Rice-Gonzalez, Amanda Smallwood, Yalitza Ferreras, Tim Host, Carla Laracuente, Desmond Hall, Val Wang, Eson Kim, Willy Barreno, Tasneem Zehra Husain, and to Justin Torres and Frances Cowhig, and all my fellow waiters at Bread Loaf. To Anne Flood Levine—for taking me to places like Vermont and Nantucket, and D.C.—thank you. To Leroy Gaines, Kristen Miranda, Jerica Coffey—for letting me crash at your apartments in San Francisco while I took writing workshops at VONA. Carissa and Carra Joyce-Dominguez, for those times in elementary school when we shared our own novels over the phone and dressed up for New Year's Eve, and all of SMOC programming for giving me a childhood full of play. A big thanks to Judy Levine, for taking me seriously when I was sixteen and told her I wanted to spend a summer in Zimbabwe. You made it happen! To my mentors when I was young, especially Margo Deane (rest in peace, dear friend), Argentina Arias, and Esta Montano.

To my sixth-grade teacher, Mrs. J. Shapiro, who came to my reading at Harvard Bookstore all those years later, I'm glad I got to say goodbye. Thank you for believing in me. Big thanks to Carolyn Chapman, for lifting me up again and again. Aime Galindo and all my students at Arbuckle Elementary School in San Jose, CA, when I was part of Teach For America.

For all my students and former colleagues, especially at the Boston Teachers Union School. You inspire me. To my students and colleagues at Framingham State University— thank you for being so supportive! For teachers and librarians, the ones on the frontlines, the ones putting books in kids' hands—I thank you. For all the young people reading this—we need you. Continue to walk in your power. To all the kids out there waiting for an undocumented family member or parent who has been deported, to come home again—I see you. Hold on.

To my grande familia! Too many to name here, but I have to give a shout out to my cousin Mynor Flores (I forgive you for writing on my chalkboard in permanent marker) and my nephew Julian Flores—your future is so bright.

I am grateful to God, for so much, especially for putting Adam on my path. This book would not have happened without you, Adam, my husband and partner in life, in parenting, writing, teaching, and more. All roads led to you and I am breathless to think how lucky I was, I am, we are. And finally, for my boys, Mateo and Rubén—everything is for you now.